SUSANNE O'LEARY was born in Stockholm in 1946. After graduating from a French lycée in 1966, she married an Irish diplomat and has since travelled the world. She is a qualified fitness instructor, and has published two health and fitness books, *Look Great, Feel Great for Life* (Gill & Macmillan, 1999) and *The Life in Your Years* (Gill & Macmillan, 2000). Her highly successful debut novel *Diplomatic Incidents* was published by *beeline* in 2002.

European Affairs

Susanne O'Leary

beeline

First published in 2003 by Beeline
an imprint of Blackstaff Press Limited
Wildflower Way, Apollo Road
Belfast BT12 6TA, Northern Ireland

Susanne O'Leary has asserted her right under the
Copyright, Designs and Patents Act 1988
to be identified as the author of this work.

Typeset by Techniset Typesetters, Newton-le-Willows, Merseyside

Printed in Great Britain by Cox & Wyman

A CIP catalogue record for this book
is available from the British Library

ISBN 0-85640-742-9

www.blackstaffpress.com

Till Mamma och Pappa

CHAPTER 1

The snow fell softly outside the tall windows. It settled on the manicured lawns of the big garden, on the branches of the cherry trees, on the Greek statue in front of the swimming pool and the roof of the small greenhouse where geraniums slept their winter sleep.

Eva looked up from her laptop and stared into the white world outside. Good, she thought. Snow. Brussels looks much better like this. All covered in a carpet of pure white. She hated litter and dirt, mess and confusion. It was a pity the EU had to have its headquarters in such a chaotic city, when there were so many lovely, clean and orderly cities in Germany.

She looked down at her work. She had nearly finished. She didn't normally bring work home, but Guido had asked her, his lovely eyes pleading, his hand on her bottom. 'Please, *Cara*,' he had said, 'just for me. You're the best linguist in the European Commission. I need this to be perfect.' She had reluctantly agreed. And he was right. She *was* the best linguist in the Commission. And Guido was the best-looking man, even if he was a Commissioner.

It was becoming chilly. She rose and started to poke the dying embers in the period fireplace. She glanced at her image in the gilt mirror over the mantelpiece. Her short blonde hair gleamed, neat and perfect, her face was flawless and the navy wool suit looked as if it had been made for her (it had). Was that a wrinkle beside her nose? She leaned closer and peered at it. No, just a shadow. Her face was as smooth as ever, thanks to a huge array of expensive creams and weekly visits to her beauty salon, where, in the hands of a very skilled beautician, she was cleansed, massaged and toned in an attempt to make her look not a day over thirty.

Eva looked at the Cartier watch on her wrist. Half-past four. Perfect. Time for a drink. She had taken to drinking vodka, starting at about this time in the afternoon, drinking steadily until bedtime. It was the perfect drink. Very few calories, no smell and it helped her through the evening. She never got drunk, just had enough to blur the edges; to help her forget all her problems and feel confident and cheerful.

Her eyes strayed to the family portrait in the silver frame on the mantelpiece. It had been taken last Christmas and they all smiled into the camera, looking like a perfectly happy family. Dan looks good there, she thought, that dark, wild Irish hair and tall, athletic frame. If only those girls weren't so hopeless. If they were *my* daughters ... But of course that was impossible. And *her* daughters would have done something with their lives. They would have chosen proper careers, instead of flitting from job to job like those two. Hopeless, she thought, no ambition, no drive and no style at all. Just my luck to get stepdaughters like that. Eva didn't know which one of them was worse. Louise, blonde, busty and vague, or Maria, dark and thin, intense, hostile and complicated. She had tried her best with them, she really had.

Eva was on her second very stiff Bloody Mary when the door opened and Dan came in.

'Hello, darling.' He smiled as he walked to the drinks trolley to make his usual gin and tonic. 'Why are you sitting there in the dark?'

'Oh, hello,' she replied. 'I didn't notice it was getting so late.' She switched on the lamp by the fireplace.

'What are you drinking?' he asked. 'Tomato juice? Would you like something a bit stronger?'

'No, thanks. We have to go to that dinner at Val Duchesse, remember. Must be on my best behaviour.'

'Oh, yes. I nearly forgot. The farewell for Helmut.'

'That's right. Big night for him,' Eva said, wondering what she had done with her little hip flask, the one that slipped so neatly into her evening bag.

'He must be happy to be going back to Germany,' Dan remarked. 'He has worked so hard all these years.'

'More fool him,' Eva replied. 'Some people just don't know how to delegate.'

'It's not as easy as you think. Helmut had so many responsibilities in his position. The ambassadors have to do a lot of extra work.'

'Thank God you're not one of them,' Eva sighed.

Dan looked fondly at her as he sipped his drink. She

hadn't changed much since the early days, despite the fact that she had had a brilliant career, brought up two stepdaughters (she had found an excellent boarding school in the west of Ireland) and helped him rise like a rocket in the ranks of the Commission at the same time. The girls were grown up now, living their own lives. She must miss them, he thought, she'll be so pleased to have them here.

'Won't it be nice to have everyone here soon?' he asked.

'Everyone?' Eva asked, a note of panic in her voice.

'Yes. Don't you remember? Louise called you. Both of the girls are coming over.'

'When?'

'The week after next.'

'Oh, great,' Eva muttered.

'I thought you'd be pleased.' Dan looked at her, slightly puzzled.

'Yes, of course. I was just a little surprised.' That's all I need, she thought. My darling stepdaughters. Louise will be traipsing around in her dressing gown all day, and Maria will argue with me and tell me I'm exploiting the servants.

'And there's great news. Louise is engaged.'

'What? I don't believe you.'

'It's true. She's met the man of her dreams, she told me.'

'Again.'

'This time it's for keeps. He wants to get married straight away. But I think she wants to wait. They have only just met, and Louise doesn't want to rush into marriage, she said.'

'I can imagine,' Eva remarked. 'I can't see Louise turning into a wife in a hurry. She's far too independent. And she hasn't a clue how to run a house.'

'Well, she'll learn.'

'I wonder what he's like. Not one of those grotty students, I hope.'

'Not at all. He has his own company. But you'll meet him soon. He'll be coming over with the girls.'

'That should be interesting.' Something suddenly occurred to Eva. 'But we'll be giving that dinner for the Irish Commissioner when they're here, had you forgotten?'

'Oh, yes, I had actually. Will that be a problem? The girls and Louise's young man could be at the dinner, couldn't they?'

Eva sighed. 'Why don't you pay attention when I tell you what's going on? That dinner is very important for me, you know that.'

'I know, darling. I'm sorry.' Dan shrugged and smiled apologetically. He looked so sweet, Eva couldn't help but smile back.

'Never mind, sweetheart, it's not a big deal. And it might be a good thing to have them at the dinner. They'll liven things up a bit. And I'll get Mildred to tidy up the guest room if Louise's boyfriend is coming to stay.'

'No need,' Dan said. 'He's staying in a hotel. Oh, and Maria will be here for a week. She's still tired after the accident. Needs a bit of a rest.'

'Of course. But I won't have time to nurse her. She'll have to look after herself.'

'I'll keep an eye on her,' Dan promised. 'I think

she's very low actually. She seemed a little depressed when I spoke to her.'

'I'm not surprised. It must have been awful. Poor Maria. But she was lucky. It could have been a lot worse.'

'I know. I don't even want to think about it.' Dan shook his head and looked away.

'Oh, darling,' Eva soothed. 'It's all right. Maria's fine.'

'I know.' He cleared his throat. 'Sorry.'

'And I would help if she'd only let me, you know that.'

'I know. It's not your fault.'

Eva looked at Dan with a little smile. 'I was just thinking that those daughters of yours never *do* anything. And now Louise has found true love.'

'I was as surprised as you,' Dan agreed. 'I never thought Louise would want to tie herself down like that.'

'I wonder how it happened?' Eva mused.

'Will you marry me?' he had asked.

Louise turned in the bed and smiled sleepily. 'It's OK,' she murmured, and lifted her hand to smooth his thick hair back from his eyes. 'I'm on the pill.'

'What?' His eyes were confused. 'Did you hear what I said?'

'You asked if I was worried,' she replied.

'No, I asked if you'd marry me.'

Louise stared at him, suddenly wide awake. She couldn't believe it. Men had asked her to do a lot of things in bed, but never that. Married, she thought, I don't want to be married. She knew that she would be one day, just as she knew that she would have varicose veins and go through the menopause, but that was a thousand years away. She had seen married women at the supermarket, dressed in tracksuits, shouting at their children. They didn't seem very happy and she certainly didn't want to join them. She suddenly shivered. This was not the kind of thing she liked to think about. She wanted love and fun, with no strings, promises or obligations.

'So?' he insisted.

'You're joking, aren't you?' she pleaded. 'Please say you are. We barely know each other.'

'No. I'm not joking.' He wrapped his arms around her and held her close, his eyes serious. 'I want to get married,' he said. 'I'm ready. And I really want to have children. Don't you?'

'Well, yes, but not this instant, actually.' She was beginning to feel a little frightened. Was there something wrong with him? Maybe it had been a mistake to go home with someone she had just met in a pub? Maria had always warned her to be careful. Could she be right? 'I think I want to be really sure before I have children,' Louise mumbled.

'Why wait?' he demanded. 'I'm the perfect age. I'm making real money and I have found the ideal woman. Don't you feel there's something special between us?'

'Oh, yes, I do,' she agreed. 'But . . .'

'But what?'

She cleared her throat. 'Well, I . . .' she started.

'There's nothing to worry about,' he insisted.

'You'll never have to work again. I make enough money for two. Or three or four.'

'Oh,' was all she managed to say. But I want to work, she whimpered in her mind, I love working.

But he was not going to give up. 'I knew I wanted you the moment I saw you,' he insisted. 'The very first second.'

'I know,' she agreed. 'Isn't it strange? I felt the same.'

It was true. She had been getting a drink from the bar and someone had said hello behind her. She had turned around, looked into his sexy, sleepy eyes and fallen in love. Just like that, without small talk or chat-up lines or flirting. Instant attraction. And to think she had nearly stayed at home that night. But then Maria told her she was going away until Sunday and Louise had not wanted to stay alone in the big, empty apartment, and decided to join her friends at their local.

'Then you bought me a drink,' she continued, 'and later ...'

'You seduced me.'

'Me?' she protested. 'It was *you* who forced *me* to go to bed.'

'But you asked to see my flat. Then you refused to leave and started to take off my clothes. I'm not used to that kind of thing. I'm just an innocent country boy.'

'A very sexy country boy.'

'You're not so bad yourself. What was it you said your name was?'

'Have we not been introduced?'

'Not formally, no. I only know your first name.'

'Oh, God.' She giggled. 'I don't believe this.' She took his hand from her thigh and shook it. 'Louise Connolly's the name. Nice to meet you.'

'Paul Ryan,' he replied. 'Charmed, I'm sure. So how about it?' he insisted. 'Now that we've been introduced.'

'Oh, Paul, you're crazy. We can't get married just like that.'

'Why not? It's the best way. Don't you want to be with me always?'

'Oh, please,' she sighed, 'slow down. I do want to be with you. Just give me a chance to catch my breath.'

'All right. But how about getting engaged?' he suggested. 'Just for now.'

Engaged, Louise pondered. That sounded all right. Kind of romantic. And she'd have a lovely ring. A diamond, she thought, that would be nice. Or maybe a sapphire with smaller diamonds around it. Or a beautiful antique ring. Maria would be violently ill with envy and Eva would be seriously annoyed. But no, it would be dangerous to agree. They would be committed and she would be stuck.

'I don't think so,' she said. 'I'm sorry but . . .'

'Will you at least think about it?'

God, he was persistent. She knew if she said no, she might lose him, and saying yes was out of the question. What was it her grandmother used to say when she didn't want to commit herself? Oh, yes, she remembered now.

'We'll see,' she said.

'Good,' Paul replied, sounding as if the matter was decided.

'I had better go,' Louise muttered, and started to get out of bed.

But Paul held her back. 'Why don't you stay the rest of the day?' he suggested. 'The weekend is nearly over. Or are your parents waiting for you?'

'No, I live with my sister. We share a flat in Sandymount.'

'And she's waiting?'

'No, actually, she's not.' Louise looked back at him. His lovely eyes were pleading. Oh, God, he's gorgeous, she thought, and settled back into bed. 'You're right. She's out. Said she'd be gone till Sunday. I will stay, but only if you give me breakfast in bed.'

'Absolutely,' he promised. 'And lunch too.'

He put his arms around her and they lay back against the pillows.

'So your sister's gone down the country?'

'She didn't say. Maybe she's at a protest rally or something.'

'Really? What about?'

Louise put her head on his shoulder. 'It could be anything. Animal rights, the environment, travellers' rights, Afghanistan. You name it, she's there. She travels all over the country.'

'And is she for or against them?' Paul asked.

'For or against what?'

'Afghanistan, animals.'

'For ...' She stopped, confused. 'I mean against ... Oh, stop it!' She hit him on the arm. 'You know what I mean.'

'She sounds like a very serious girl.'

'She's serious all right. I bet she's discussing a lost cause right now. She's probably arguing with some politician about housing for the poor.'

But Maria wasn't arguing with anyone. She was in hospital, trying to remember who she was.

'Miss Connolly?' a voice called. 'Maria? Can you hear me?'

The woman in the bed stirred. 'Forgive me, Father, for I have sinned,' she muttered. 'It is six years since my last confession. I'm having an affair ... with my dentist.'

'Don't worry about that now,' the nurse soothed.

'But you don't understand ...'

'She's still groggy,' the doctor said. 'Let me try.' He leaned over the patient and took her hand. 'Try to wake up,' he urged. 'Please, Maria.'

'I didn't mean it,' Maria said, and opened her eyes. She peered at the doctor in his white coat. 'Are you room service?'

'No. I'm a doctor.'

'Oh?' Maria muttered, and tried to look around the cubicle. 'What happened to the hotel?' She put a hand to her head. 'Jesus,' she muttered. 'This is one hell of a hangover. What did I drink?'

'You didn't drink anything. You've been in an accident.'

'My head hurts. And my face. My nose ...'

'You've broken your nose,' the doctor told her. 'I had to set it.'

'And I can't see very well.'

'Your eyes are badly swollen,' the nurse said. 'But that should ease in a day or two.'

'Oh, God,' Maria moaned. 'I don't understand. What happened? I can't remember ...'

'You crashed your car into a tree outside the Random Inn in County Wicklow,' the doctor replied. 'Must have hit an icy patch. The roads are very bad tonight. You were brought in by ambulance a while ago. You were lucky. You're not seriously injured, except for the broken nose, two black eyes and a deep gash on your forehead. We had to put in a few stitches. You chipped a tooth as well, but that can be dealt with later. And there's the concussion.'

'I don't ...' she mumbled. Her head was throbbing and her face felt as if she had bashed it into a brick wall. Her eyes didn't seem to want to open. They kept calling her Maria, but she wasn't even sure that it was her name. 'I don't remember anything,' she whispered.

'You are suffering from concussion,' the nurse said. 'It will all come back to you in time. Just try to relax. We'll give you something for the pain.'

Maria felt a sharp prick in her arm. 'That name,' she said. 'Maria. Is that my name?'

'That's what it says on your driving licence,' the doctor replied. 'Maria Josephine Connolly.'

'Mmmm,' Maria mumbled.

'Look,' the nurse urged, and held something in front of her. 'That's you.'

Maria squinted at the photo of a young woman with dark, wavy, shoulder-length hair, blue eyes and strong features. The face was vaguely familiar.

'What about your family?' the doctor asked.

'Could we get in touch with them?'

'Brussels,' Maria muttered. What? she thought. Why did I say that? But it's true. They *are* in Brussels. At least Daddy is. Mum is ... Where is she? Why can't I remember? And Louise ... where was Louise? And *who* was she? 'I live in a flat,' she said. 'With my sister.'

'And where's that?' the nurse asked.

'It's in ... in ... can't remember.' The pain was slowly easing and Maria felt sleepy. 'Lovely duplex apartment,' she muttered. 'Two reception, three bedrooms. One en suite. Stunning sea views. Belongs to my parents. Haven't a clue where ...'

'Don't worry about it,' the nurse soothed. 'Try to sleep. We'll bring you up to the ward now. I'm sure you'll feel better in the morning. We'll try to contact your sister.'

Maria let her head sink into the pillow. She closed her eyes and tried to sleep, but so many thoughts were twirling around in her head, so many questions wanted to cram into her mind. She tried to remember what had happened the night before. The hotel, she thought. I was meeting someone. But who? What happened there? It just wouldn't come back to her. She drifted into sleep.

'So, are you going to sue?' Louise asked as she munched on a chocolate from a box on Maria's bedside locker on Monday evening.

Maria was feeling a little better. The headache was now just a dull throbbing and her face was less sore. And most of her memory had come back. She knew it was the end of February, she could remember her family – her father, her dead mother, her sister, Louise, and her stepmother – everything except the circumstances of the accident.

She hadn't been brave enough to look in a mirror, but Louise had cheerfully confirmed her suspicions by telling her she looked a fright. 'You would get a part in a horror movie looking like that,' she had joked.

'Sue who?' Maria asked.

'The guy who did this, of course,' Louise explained.

'What guy? I smashed into a tree. You can't sue a tree. And it was probably my fault anyway, so if trees could sue, it would sue me.'

'Oh,' Louise said, and helped herself to another chocolate. 'I thought you were at a protest rally and someone attacked you. That's where you told me you were going.'

'Didn't they tell you what had happened?'

'Not really. There was a message on the answering machine at the flat when I came back this afternoon that you were in hospital, that's all. So where were you going?'

'I can't remember a thing,' Maria sighed.

'That's weird,' Louise said, munching. 'But maybe it will all come back. All I know is that you looked too tarted up for a protest meeting when you left on Saturday night.'

'Saturday night?'

'Yes, don't you remember? Don't wait up, you said, looking like you were going to meet someone special. That was about six o'clock.'

'Oh, yes,' Maria muttered as she racked her brain. 'I remember getting dressed up. And then I left. And then ... nothing.' She sighed. 'Nothing at all.'

'You're in denial,' Louise stated. 'Something happened and your brain won't let you remember. It must have been something really awful. Maybe you were drugged and raped?'

'Oh, shut up,' Maria snapped. 'Of course I wasn't raped. Why do you always have to be so morbid?'

'Just trying to help,' Louise muttered. 'To jog your memory.'

'I'll jog yours, if you're not careful,' Maria said grimly.

'Calm down,' Louise ordered. 'Try to relax.' She looked around her. 'You were lucky to get a private room.'

'I think it used to be a broom cupboard,' Maria remarked. 'Until they realised they could squeeze a bed into it.'

'I know what you mean. Oh, by the way, the AA left a message to ring them back. I didn't know you had a drinking problem.'

'What?'

'The AA,' Louise explained. 'You know, "My name's Maria and I'm an alcoholic". The AA.'

'You twit,' Maria sighed. 'That must have been the Automobile Association. As in "My name's Maria and I am a driver". They must have called about the car.'

'Ooooh,' Louise said. 'Right. Of course.' She reached out for another chocolate, but Maria snatched the box away.

'Sorry. They're delicious. Who brought them?'

'Gráinne. She came in this morning.'

'That was nice of her. My boss would never visit me if I were in hospital. She'd just complain that she had to answer the phone herself, the cold bitch.'

'You should stay away from chocolates in any case,' Maria stated. 'You put on weight very easily. Did you bring any of my things?'

'Yes, sorry.' Louise lifted a big bag onto the bed. 'I brought you a nightie. One of mine, because yours are so boring. You never know, you might meet a good-looking doctor while you're here –' she produced a black flimsy nightgown from the bag – 'and some underwear, your toiletries and make-up. But I can see that make-up would not make you look much better,' she added. 'When are they taking the plaster off your nose?'

'Next week. But they said that I can go home in a few days, as soon as they are happy that there isn't any serious damage to my brain from the crash.'

'Why didn't you ask them to make your nose a bit smaller while they were at it?' Louise wondered. 'You missed a great opportunity to have a cheap nose job.'

'There's nothing wrong with my nose,' Maria snapped.

'If I was in hospital, I would ask them to wire my jaws shut for a few days,' Louise continued, 'then I could lose some weight at the same time.'

'I wish someone would,' Maria said, under her breath.

'Anyway,' Louise chattered on, 'I brought you some other things that will make you feel a lot better.'

She delved into the bag again. 'Here! Aromatherapy candles and massage oil and –'

'Who's going to massage me?' Maria snorted.

'Well, I thought maybe one of the nurses ...'

Maria laughed. 'If I can catch one I'll ask her.'

'Anyway,' Louise continued, 'I also brought you a book on meditation. I know you think it's a load of rubbish, but now might be the time to try it. You have all the time in the world here, and I promise it's a great help. It makes you relax and think positively.'

'Yeah, right.'

'It would really help you,' Louise insisted. 'You're so negative. It's not your fault, of course,' she soothed, 'it's because of your sign.'

'Sign?'

'In the zodiac, I mean. Sagittarius is such a difficult sign to cope with. Especially when you're the victim of this kind of disaster.' She held the book out to Maria. 'But this book will help. You just choose a mantra and away you go. Well, not literally of course at the moment.'

'Please,' Maria pleaded, 'shut up for a minute. Leave me alone. I was coping very well until you arrived.'

'I was just trying to help.'

'Go away.'

'I will in a minute. But I just *have* to tell you what happened to me!' Louise exclaimed.

'Let me guess,' Maria mumbled, feeling suddenly very tired. 'You were abducted by aliens and spent the weekend on Mars.'

'Well, nearly. I met this guy, this ... this man. Oh,

Maria he's so wonderful. He even asked me to marry him.'

'What?' Maria demanded, suddenly wide awake. 'He asked you to what?'

'Marry him.'

'I don't believe this. Men will say anything to get a girl into bed these days.'

'But that was afterwards,' Louise protested. 'He asked me after we ...'

'You mean you went to bed with him? Just like that?'

'Yes. And then he –'

'You barely know the guy and you've already been to bed with him and he's talking about getting married. Was he on something?'

'Of course not.'

'He wasn't smoking anything?'

'No. Stop it.'

'He didn't go to the loo and come out wiping his nose?'

'You mean someone has to be on drugs to want to marry me?' Louise asked, disappointed in Maria's reaction. 'Don't worry,' she continued. 'I have no intention of getting married.'

Maria looked at her younger sister's glowing face and felt a curious stab of envy. 'That's sensible at least.' She sighed.

'I might get engaged though,' Louise said. 'Just for fun.'

'You're too young.'

'I'm twenty-four.'

'Exactly. Far too young.'

But Louise just sighed happily. 'Oh, Maria, he's perfect.'

'Aren't they all?'

'This one's different,' Louise argued, without noticing the bitter tone in Maria's voice. 'He's not like other men.' She smiled to herself as she thought of the morning before.

'Who is this wonderful creature, then?' Maria demanded. 'What do you know about him?'

'Well, his name's Paul Ryan and he's in waste disposal.'

'Sounds really glamorous.'

'There's a lot of money in it apparently. And, judging by his flat, it's true. And he's written a book about recycling. It's called *Don't Waste Your Rubbish*.'

'How clever. How old is he?' Maria demanded.

'He's, eh ...' Louise paused. She had never asked him. It didn't seem important. 'I don't know. About your age. Maybe a bit older.'

'You really know nothing about him,' Maria stated. 'He could be a convicted criminal for all we know.'

'Don't be silly. He's from County Mayo.'

'He *must* be all right then. What sort of background does he come from? What does his father do?'

'Not a lot.'

'Don't tell me he's unemployed.'

'No. He's dead.'

'Oh. Sorry.'

'Yeah. Anyway,' Louise sighed happily, 'that's it. I'm in love.'

'Again.'

Louise rose. 'Got to go. I'm meeting Paul later. I'll be back to see you tomorrow.'

'Oh, Louise,' Maria said. 'Could you call Daddy and tell him what happened? Try not to worry him though.'

'I already called them,' Louise replied. 'Daddy was in Luxembourg for a meeting, so I only got Eva.'

'I'm sure she was wildly concerned.'

'She was cool and collected as usual,' Louise replied. 'She said she hoped you were not too badly hurt.'

'How kind!'

'And she said she'd inform Daddy.'

'Probably next week,' Maria muttered.

'I'll try his office later,' Louise offered. 'They'll be able to get in touch with him.'

'Great. I'd love to talk to him. It would really cheer me up.'

'We're going over there the week after next, remember. You should stay a bit longer. Just to rest up.'

'I will. Eva won't be too pleased to have me as a house guest, but I don't care.'

'Eva will be too busy with her work to worry about you. And Daddy would love to have you.'

'And we can spend some time together,' Maria said. 'I haven't had a good chat with Daddy for ages.'

'I'll tell him to call you in any case,' Louise said.

'OK, thanks.'

'I've asked Paul to come as well. To Brussels.'

'You what! Are you sure that's a good idea? I mean, it's a bit early to introduce him to the family, isn't it?'

'But if he wants to marry me, he'll have to meet them.'

'Eva will give him a bit of a fright.'

'I know,' Louise smiled. 'That's what I thought. It might slow him down a bit. I mean, imagine Eva as a mother-in-law? He'll not be in such a hurry to set a date.' She rose. 'Got to go. Bye, darling.' Louise kissed Maria on the cheek. 'I hope you feel a lot better soon. Just try to be positive.'

'Thank you,' Maria replied. 'I'll do my best. And you be careful. With ... with, what did you say his name was?'

'Paul.'

'Right. Paul. Don't let him push you into anything.'

'Of course not.'

The ring was lovely. A large square-cut aquamarine surrounded by small diamonds, it gleamed seductively on its blue velvet cushion in the jeweller's window.

'It's looks very old,' Paul said. 'At least a hundred years, if not more.'

'It's so beautiful.' Louise sighed, looking at it longingly. 'But no, I couldn't. I don't want to get engaged just yet.'

'Why don't you just try it on?' Paul suggested. 'Then, when we do decide to get engaged, we'll know it fits.' He took her by the arm and, before she knew what had happened, they were in the shop and the ring was on her finger.

'It's a very good choice,' the shop assistant declared. 'This ring is Victorian and in very good condition.'

'Did you hear that?' Paul asked.

Louise looked down on the ring again. The diamonds glittered as if they could speak. 'Say yes,' they whispered. 'You can always give us back.'

She sighed.

'We'll take it,' Paul said to the girl.

CHAPTER 2

Making love to Eva, Dan thought, was like travelling in a very expensive sports car, a Ferrari or a Maserati, with soft leather upholstery. And she always let him drive. There were five gears: lust, arousal, sensuality, ecstasy and, finally, nirvana. She never uttered a sound, but her breathing became faster and her face softened. Her cheeks glowed, her eyes sparkled and she looked even more beautiful.

When they met, he had admired her beauty but never dared hope she would be such an enthusiastic lover. Her fervour had surprised him at first, as her cool, perfect exterior suggested frigidity rather than sensuality. But in the bedroom she became a very different woman. Her smouldering sexuality came as a shock, but, as the years wore on, he delighted in it, realising he was a very lucky man. And now, he thought, at least that part of our marriage is perfect.

'Darling,' he breathed as their bodies parted, 'you're amazing.'

'And you're wonderful,' she whispered, and ran her hand down his chest. 'What time is it?'

'Nearly seven o'clock.'

'Time to get up, then.' But she didn't move. She put her head on his shoulder.

'I hate Monday mornings.'

'But this one has started rather well,' Dan smiled.

'Not bad,' Eva agreed, 'not bad at all. Is it raining?'

'I think so. Do you want me to check?'

'No need. It always rains in Brussels,' she sighed. 'Five more minutes. Then I'll have to face the day.'

Dan settled back against the pillows. He didn't want her to get up either. He didn't want her to change into that other Eva: cool, efficient and un-emotional. Then she was no longer his, but a career woman with nothing on her mind but her work. He knew he came a very poor second to her career, but at these moments he liked to pretend that he was first on her list of priorities.

She got out of bed and stretched luxuriously. 'Time to get ready. I have a very busy day ahead. What about you?'

'Not too bad.' Dan smiled as he admired her slim, toned body.

She had been so clever, the way she had managed his career, he thought. She knew he was not the kind of man who wanted to live only for his work; to spend long hours in the office and never have any time off. Through discreet but ingenious networking, and some very good luck, she had managed to get him ap-pointed director-general in charge of statistics, which was perfect. A fancy title and lots of money. The fact that it involved more golf than statistics was some-thing they never mentioned. She was the one with ambition and drive, the one who fought for her job and her career. It seemed perfect, at least Eva thought so; they were both doing what suited them.

But there was great tension between Eva and the girls, especially Maria. Dan wished they would get on a bit better, that they would have been able to resolve their differences now that the girls were grown up. But it didn't look as if they would ever be close.

Dan sat up in the bed and swung his legs over the side. 'I'll get up too. I want to read the papers, and if Maria is up we can have breakfast together.'

He knew it would take Eva at least an hour to shower, wash and dry her hair and put on her make-up. She had her own bathroom and it was her sanctuary. He had no idea what she did there, only that it took up a lot of time and the beauty products cost a lot of money, but the result was always stunning. She would emerge from her ablutions polished and perfect, ready to tackle whatever came her way.

He sighed happily as her bottom disappeared into the bathroom. But suddenly she was back. Still naked, she stood in the doorway.

'I just have to say this,' she started. 'Don't get me wrong, but ...'

'Yes, darling?'

'Maria.' Eva folded her arms across her spectacular breasts.

'What about her?'

'I know she's been in an accident ...'

'But?'

'Well, she's a spoiled little bitch who thinks the world owes her a living. It's time she stopped feeling sorry for herself and grew up. She's nearly thirty years old. You have to stop treating her like a baby. There. I've said it.'

Dan stared at Eva. 'That was a little severe. Just now, Maria needs support.'

'She needs a kick in the *Arsch*.' Eva turned on her heel and went back into the bathroom.

Dan looked at the door that had just banged shut. Eva's use of strong language, for someone so well bred, had always puzzled him.

Feeling very satisfied, Eva stepped into the shower and turned on the taps. I'm glad I said it at last, she thought. It's time Dan faced the truth about his daughter.

The hot water of the shower bit into her skin. She lifted her face, closed her eyes and tried not to think about last Friday and the dinner.

It had started so well.

The drawing room looked lovely. The soft light from the lamps, the fire flickering in the grate and the smell of the pink roses in the large vase on the mantelpiece made the large room warm and inviting. The muted colours of the Persian rugs on the oak floors were beautiful against the thick cream curtains, the sage-green and soft yellow of the sofas and chairs. The antique rosewood coffee table and side tables gleamed, polished to perfection. Eva knew the dining-room table looked fabulous. She had done the flowers earlier. Dan was getting dressed upstairs and then he would do the place settings. The girls, who had arrived the night before, would be down in a minute. Everything was ready.

She looked into the mirror to check her hair and make-up. Yes. She looked good. Very good. The black strapless evening gown was so simple and classy. Black was the only colour to wear with a diamond necklace.

She touched the stones. They felt cold against her fingers. Bring me luck tonight, she thought, and opened the drawer in the small Victorian escritoire beside the drinks trolley. She took out the hip flask, unscrewed the top and took a large slug. She lifted the flask and saluted herself in the mirror. Cheers, darling, she said. Have a great evening. She took another quick slug and put the flask back in the drawer.

'Madame?' Fernando, the Filipino servant had just slipped into the room.

'Yes?' Eva snapped. Why did he have to sneak around like that? she thought. He was always sliding around the house in his sandals, it was positively scary.

'What do you want me to do about the drinks?'

'Drinks?'

'The drinks for the guests, madame. Before the dinner.'

'But I told you only an hour ago. We're having champagne. I thought I told you to chill it this morning.'

'Oh, yes, madame,' Fernando beamed. 'And I did. I put six bottles in the freezer.' His face fell. 'But now I can't open them. They're ...'

'Frozen!' Eva shrieked. 'You *verdammte Schwachkopf*!'

'Yes, madame,' Fernando agreed, his face expressionless.

'What are we going to do?'

'I don't know, madame.'

'What's going on?' Dan stuck his head through the door. He was naked except for a pink towel that he clutched around his waist. 'Why are you shouting?'

'Why aren't you dressed?' Eva demanded. 'The guests are arriving in a few minutes. I thought you were doing the place settings.'

'I fell asleep in the bath. Sorry.'

'I don't believe this,' Eva moaned. 'The champagne is frozen and you're standing here naked and ...' There was a sound of wheels on the gravel outside. 'And here's the Commissioner now.'

'How do you know it's him?'

'Because it would be so typical. Get away from the window, you fool. Go and get dressed.'

'Right.' Dan clutched his towel tighter. 'There's a crate of champagne in the garage. Won't be chilled, but near enough.'

'Yes, OK.' Eva shooed him away. 'Go. Get dressed. Fernando?'

'Yes?'

'Do you think you could *possibly* manage to find those bottles and open them?'

'Now, madame?'

'No, next time there's a new moon. Of course now. Go on. Do it.'

She sighed, exasperated, as he left. He was such a klutz. But she couldn't fire him. He had a wife and five children in the Philippines who depended on his salary to survive. He was, however, quite useful most of the time, and the only servant she had ever had who put up with her moods and sudden temper tantrums without as much as a flicker of an eyelid. She often felt a little guilty at the way she treated him, but you had to shout from time to time to get him going.

'The waiters are here,' Louise announced as she came into the room. 'They want you to come and tell them what to do.'

'Thank God. I thought it was the Commissioner. What *are* you wearing?'

'A dress.'

'I can see that. But isn't it a bit tight? And short? And low-cut?'

'I think it's lovely.' Louise admired her reflection in the mirror. The silk shimmered silvery in the light of the fire, clinging to her generous curves, and the straps seemed nearly too thin to take the weight of her bosom. Her blonde hair curled around her glowing face and her extraordinary grey eyes sparkled. 'Paul will love it,' she stated. 'I hope he'll make it on time. He was supposed to be on the midday Ryanair flight, but he didn't call me to say he had arrived.'

The doorbell rang.

'Shit,' Eva muttered. She took a white cashmere throw from the arm of one of the sofas and draped it around Louise.

'What? But ...' Louise protested. 'I'm not going around wearing a blanket all evening.'

'Just say it's a pashmina.'

'Hello?' A tall, dark, very handsome man peered in.

'Paul!' Louise exclaimed. 'You made it!'

'Hi, sweetheart. Am I too early?'

'Not at all,' Louise gushed, rushing up to him and grabbing his hand. 'Come in. Eva, this is Paul, and Paul, this is Eva, my stepmother. Paul's my boyfriend and —'

'I know.' Eva smiled and adjusted the cashmere throw that had slipped off Louise's shoulders. 'Calm down, Louise.' She held out her hand. 'Hello, Paul. Nice to meet you.'

'Hello, Eva.' Paul's voice was deep and his smile wide and charming. He was, Eva thought, a very good-looking man. Lovely eyes — bedroom eyes, her mother would have said. I wouldn't mind him in my bedroom, she thought, startled at her own reaction.

'Thank you for inviting me,' he said.

'I'm so glad you could come. Dan will be here in a minute, and Maria too. So you'll meet the whole family.'

'I'm looking forward to that,' Paul replied.

The doorbell rang again. Fernando came in with a tray of glasses of champagne. 'Open the door,' Eva snapped.

'But the drinks . . .'

'Let Mildred do the drinks. You go and open the front door.' Eva took the tray and pushed him towards the hall.

'All right, madame.'

'What about the place settings?'

'That's all done, madame.'

'Good.' Dan must at least have managed to do that, Eva thought. She held the tray in front of Paul. 'Would you like a glass of champagne?'

'Oh, lovely. Thank you.' He took two glasses from the tray and handed one to Louise. 'What about yourself?' he enquired.

'No, I don't think I should. I drink very little, just a glass of wine now and then. I have to be on my toes most of the time, if you see what I mean.'

'Very pretty toes,' Paul said to Louise, as Eva moved away to greet the first guests.

Maria was in her room getting ready. She knew she should have been downstairs at least half an hour ago, and she could hear the guests chatting and laughing in the drawing room below. But she had delayed her arrival. She didn't feel like going to a party. Especially one of Eva's parties.

She had come in earlier, swishing about in her black evening gown, admiring herself in the mirror, touching things and chatting nervously.

'I hope you will behave yourself tonight. It's a very important evening for me. The Irish Commissioner is coming and . . .'

Maria looked up from her book. 'OK. Don't get your knickers in a twist. Why is the Irish Commissioner so important to you anyway? I thought your boss was Italian.'

'Because he's very close to the President of the European Commission.'

'He is?'

'That's right. And you could show a bit more interest,' Eva complained.

'I don't have to.'

'You're in one of your moods again.'

'I'm just a bit tired actually. I have been in an accident, you know.'

'You look almost fully recovered,' Eva remarked. 'Which is good, because I have invited someone for you. A man I think you'll like.'

'Oh, God. Not again.' Eva was always introducing her to 'suitable' men.

'You have to learn not to be so picky,' Eva remarked.

'Who is it this time, a sixty-year-old businessman from Argentina?'

'No. It's someone young and good-looking. Mark White. He's an English journalist. The *Financial Times*. And he's got great connections, because he's related to the Foreign Secretary and his cousin is a lord. I think you would be perfect together.'

'I suppose you have planned the wedding in your head already.'

'Why are you so negative? God knows, you haven't managed your relationships very well in the past. One disaster after another. You should be grateful for any help you can get.'

'I prefer to choose my own men, thank you,' Maria snapped.

'Where did that get you? Nowhere.' Eva picked up a framed photograph. 'Nice shot of Louise here. Where was that taken?'

'Kerry, last year,' Maria muttered.

'Thank God she's set up anyway,' Eva said, replacing the frame. She sat down carefully on the edge of the bed. 'What are you reading?'

'Nothing you'd like,' Maria said, and closed her

book. 'Why are you prowling around my room? Shouldn't you be downstairs polishing the bread rolls or something?'

'I just came in to tell you about Mark. And to make sure you know it's black tie tonight. Wear your blue dress. The one I gave you last Christmas.'

'Fine.'

'And do try to smile occasionally.' Eva sighed. 'I don't know why you always look so sour. Louise is much more cheerful. At least she always makes an effort.'

'If you leave me alone, I'll be the life and soul of the party, I promise.'

'You don't have to do much. Just try to look nice, do your hair and put on that dress. And please, be polite to Mark.' Eva opened the door and glided out.

An hour later, Maria was struggling with her thick dark hair, putting it up in a knot on top of her head, with just a few ringlets curling around her face. The intense colour of the dress suited her blue eyes and fair complexion. She didn't look too bad, she decided, even if there were still faint marks under her eyes from the accident and her nose had a small scar across the bridge. Her mother's pearls, a little powder, blusher and mascara, and she was ready. Lipstick? She didn't normally, and she only had that dark red, bought in London last year in a mad fit to try to be fashionable. But why not? She took it out of her make-up bag, carefully applied the red colour to her wide mouth and stood back. Mmm. Not bad.

The drawing room was full of people, chatting, laughing and drinking champagne. Maria stood just inside the door, trying to decide whom to talk to. Louise was over by the window, smiling up at a tall, thin man with dark red hair and glasses. Must be Paul, Maria thought. Not the 'babe' she described, but love is blind, I suppose.

Then she saw him: dark, handsome and very tall, standing alone near the fireplace, studying an antique print of Dublin. Eva hit the jackpot this time, Maria thought, and moved forward. I'll tell her everything is forgiven.

'Mark?'

The man turned around, and she noticed he was even more gorgeous close up.

'Sorry?'

'Hi.' Maria held out her hand. 'I'm Maria.' She smiled mischievously. 'I knew who you must be, as you are the only man here below the age of forty, except for my sister's new boyfriend over there. He's some kind of yob from the west of Ireland. Haven't met him yet, but he's supposed to be really clever. Heaved himself up from a working-class background by starting his own company. Waste, if you don't mind. He collects rubbish and has made a fortune out of it.' Maria knew she was babbling, but couldn't stop herself. 'So now he's nearly a millionaire –' she laughed – 'and lives in one of the poshest parts of Dublin. Weird, don't you think? But that's modern Ireland for you. Class is dead.' She stopped for just a second to breathe. 'Louise is madly in love,' she prattled on, 'but that's not really unusual. She's been in love about a thousand times, which isn't so strange, considering her looks. She told me he wants to marry her, but I doubt she'll agree. She's the good-time girl of the century. Must have been through half the male population of Dublin by now.' Maria looked up at him and smiled into his lazy brown eyes. 'But enough about her,' she went on. 'What about you? How are you enjoying Brussels and the Euro-stocracy? I invented that word,' she said proudly. 'Quite witty, even if I say so myself.' She laughed softly and looked at him seductively. At least she hoped it was. She had never tried this kind of come-on before. But it always worked for Louise. She wet her lips. That was supposed to be sexy, she had read somewhere.

The man looked slightly stunned and there was a strange expression in his eyes. 'I'm really having fun,' he said. 'The last few minutes have been especially interesting.'

'Paul?' Louise had joined them. 'I was going to introduce you to Maria, but I see you've already met.'

Maria froze. She felt the blood drain from her face. Her mouth stopped pouting and her hips were no longer swivelling. 'What?' she stammered. She looked up at the dark man. '*You're* Paul?' she whispered.

'That's right,' he said, draping an arm across Louise's shoulder. 'Paul Ryan, otherwise known as the yob from the west.'

'Oh, Jesus,' she muttered. 'Shit. You must think I'm a complete idiot.'

'I thought it might have been the accident,' he suggested. 'That bump on the head.'

'What are you talking about?' Louise asked, her eyes going from Paul to Maria. 'Have you met before or something?'

'No,' Paul laughed. 'We haven't. How could I possibly forget if we had?'

'Anyway,' Louise interrupted, 'Mark was looking forward to meeting you. He's that nice, tall, red-headed man over there. Look, he's coming over.'

Mark White was not much better-looking close up. 'Hello, there,' he said, pushing his glasses up on his nose.

'Nice to meet you, Mark,' Maria replied, feeling disappointment settle on her like a damp flannel.

'Louise was telling me about you,' Mark said. 'We were talking about your job. Marketing and publicity. Must be interesting.'

'It's great.' Maria tried to smile.

'You must be so good at it,' Paul interjected. 'I mean, marketing books must demand a special talent: intuition, judgement and, well, personal charm, I suppose.'

'Excuse me,' Maria muttered and moved away. I'll just go, she thought, I'll go upstairs and pack a bag and leave. Go to the airport and just wait there for the next flight back to Dublin.

'There you are.' Eva's voice made Maria jump. 'Enjoying the party?'

'God, yes. It's magic.'

'Have you met Mark yet?'

'That too.'

'Isn't he really nice?'

'Fantastic.'

'I knew you'd like him.'

'You were right. We're perfect for each other.'

'Are you trying to make fun of me?'

But before Maria had a chance to reply, someone came in through the door.

'The Commissioner,' Eva murmured, 'at last. Now we can go in to dinner.'

Eva ushered Sean Dogherty, the Irish Commissioner, into the dining room, where a long mahogany table set with Waterford crystal, exquisite china and antique silver awaited them. The light from many candles in huge candelabras flickered and there was a delicious smell of food. She felt a great sense of relief mixed with satisfaction as she surveyed the room.

The guests studied the table plan set up on the antique mahogany sideboard and then looked for their places around the table. Eva showed the Commissioner his seat.

'Everything looks lovely, my dear,' he assured her.

'She's such a perfectionist,' Dan smiled from the other side of the table.

'And such a beauty too,' the Danish ambassador, a tall man in his mid-fifties, chipped in from the bottom of the long table, where he was pulling out a chair for Maria. 'This is such a treat. What a good idea to mix up the guests like this.'

Eva froze. 'What?' she demanded. She stared in dismay at the guests, who were now either sitting down or in the process of pulling out chairs. 'Oh, God.'

The table plan, so carefully worked out the night before, seemed to have gone completely wrong. Nobody was sitting where they should be. The Danish ambassador was chatting to Maria, Dan was beside Mark White, and Louise, who seemed to have lost her improvised wrap, was smiling up at the Commissioner. What a disaster. What would the Commissioner think?

Eva felt sheer panic rise in her throat. '*Alles is falsch*!' she called out.

'Sorry, what was that?' the Commissioner asked, tearing his eyes away from Louise.

'It's all wrong,' Eva exclaimed. 'Everyone is sitting in the wrong place. You have to get up.'

'Oh, but I'm very happy here,' the Commissioner declared.

'*You're* in the right place,' Eva replied. 'It's Louise who's wrong. Get up!'

'But . . .' Louise protested.

'I'm sorry,' Eva announced to the guests, who were now staring at her in confusion. 'You'll all have to get up and move. Dan?'

'Yes, darling?'

'Where's the sketch we did last night?'

'I don't know. Let's see.' He felt his pockets. 'Oh. Here it is. I forgot to give it to Fernando. He must have improvised a little.'

'That's putting it mildly,' Eva remarked. 'Now, if you'll all stand up, we'll sort it out in just a moment.'

Eva took the piece of paper from Dan and proceeded to sort out the table. The guests, with much joshing and laughter, found their correct places. When everything was finally all right, she signalled to Fernando that he could start serving and sank down on her chair.

'I'm sorry about the confusion, Commissioner,' she

murmured, smiling into his eyes.

'No problem, dear girl,' he soothed, patting her hand. 'These things happen. Not your fault. But please call me Sean. You can't go on calling me Commissioner all the time.'

'Of course not . . . eh . . . Sean.'

'I'm so sorry my wife couldn't come. But she's not here very often. She works in Dublin, you see.'

Eva tried to look concerned. 'What a pity,' she said.

'She's a secondary school teacher. A very difficult and time-consuming job.'

'But I thought teachers in Ireland were either on holiday or on strike. Surely she could manage a visit to Brussels now and then?'

'Not really. She's also doing a university course.'

'I see.'

'Lovely girl, your daughter,' he continued.

'Stepdaughter.' Eva flicked the napkin into her lap.

'Is that right? And the other girl as well? The tall, dark one with the lovely legs?'

'Maria? Yes. They're my husband's children from his first marriage.'

'Really? I didn't know he'd been married before.' Sean helped himself to a large dollop of hollandaise sauce.

'His first wife died twenty years ago. When the girls were very small.'

'Oh. How very sad. How did she die?'

'She caught the mumps. Developed complications. Bizarre, don't you think? At the time of modern medicine, I mean.' Eva had always thought it a very silly way to die. So careless, somehow.

'Yes,' the Commissioner agreed, 'but tragic all the same.'

'Of course.'

'You don't have any children of your own?'

'No.'

Sean Dogherty took a big slug of wine and didn't notice the expression in Eva's eyes. 'But you brought up those two girls?' he asked, wiping his mouth. 'That must have been hard for a young woman such as yourself.'

'It wasn't easy,' Eva sighed.

'But you did a wonderful job. They're marvellous girls. Really marvellous,' he declared, and glanced down the table to where Louise was putting a large piece of salmon into her mouth.

'Yes, I suppose,' Eva said. 'But never mind them.' She put a hand on his arm and smiled. 'Sean, there's something I want to discuss with you.'

'Yes, my dear?' Sean Dogherty smiled back. 'What can I do for you?'

Eva sighed with relief. At last. She had his attention and she was sure he would be able to help her. The stress of the last few weeks rolled away and she felt suddenly more hopeful.

She leaned closer to the Commissioner and lowered her voice. 'Well, it's like this . . .'

CHAPTER 3

M aria looked down at the salmon on her plate. Unlike Louise, she didn't feel the least bit hungry. The piece of pink flesh and the blob of yellow hollandaise looked unappetisingly rich. She put down her fork and picked up her wine glass. Across the table, Paul was talking softly to Louise. God, what a fool I made of myself, Maria thought, what an utter stupid bloody eejit he must think I am. But why didn't he speak up? Why did he let me go on and on like that? Bastard. She drained her glass.

'You like the wine?' Mark asked. He was sitting on Maria's right and had tried to make conversation for the past few minutes.

'Yes, it's lovely.' She turned to the young man on her left. 'What do you do?' she asked. 'And please don't tell me you work in the Commission.'

'*Nein,*' he replied. 'That is what my wife does. I am from the embassy. The German embassy.'

'Well, that's not too bad,' Maria said.

The young man looked relieved. 'And what do you do, *Fräulein?*'

'I work in publishing.'

'Ah, books. I see.'

The conversation stalled.

Mark turned to Louise and Paul. 'Well, how did you two meet?'

'In a pub in Dublin,' Louise replied. 'Paul was celebrating the launch of his book and –'

'Brochure, really,' Paul interrupted. 'About recycling,' he added.

'Anyway,' Louise continued, 'we just sort of looked at each other and, you know ...'

'We can imagine,' muttered Maria.

Louise sighed. 'So, that was it, and here we are.'

'In Brussels.' Paul smiled. 'Amazing, isn't it? And I've met your whole family already.'

'Your mother's very beautiful,' Mark said.

'Stepmother,' Louise corrected.

'The Dobermann pinscher,' Maria added.

There was an embarrassed silence. Mark, Paul and Louise stared at Maria.

'I beg your pardon?' Mark asked, with a worried glance at the top of the table, where Eva was smiling and putting her hand on the Commissioner's arm.

'Surely that's a little strong,' Paul remarked.

'Maria doesn't get on with her,' Louise said. 'I don't think she's so bad. When she's in a good mood.'

'Which only happens once every two years,' Maria continued. She knew she was overdoing it, but she didn't care. The wine made her feel reckless and all her pent-up feelings towards Eva bubbled to the surface. She lowered her voice. 'But poor Eva has a lot to cope with. She had a tough childhood. And then that catastrophe.'

'What catastrophe?' Mark demanded, looking a little apprehensive.

'Well,' Maria began, 'I'll tell you the whole story. You'll love this. Poor Eva grew up with the terrible sadness of her family having to leave their *Schloss* –'

'That means castle in German,' Louise whispered to Paul.

'Right –' Maria nodded – 'their fairytale castle in Saxony –'

'That's in the east of Germany,' Louise murmured in Paul's ear.

'– which the communists had grabbed after the Second World War,' Maria continued. 'Eva's father's family, who are called Mebius –'

'Pronounced May-be-us,' Louise interjected.

'Stop interrupting,' Maria ordered.

'I just wanted to make it easier to understand.'

'OK. But keep quiet while I tell the rest. Anyway,' Maria went on, 'the family had to run away from the communists at the end of the war. They went to live in West Germany, where Eva's father married a Swedish girl. They had two children, Eva and Dieter, who grew up with the pain of knowing that they should really be living in a huge castle. It was hard. But the family had managed to put money away in Swiss bank accounts, so they had a little bit to survive on. For many years the Mebius family had to struggle on in their luxury villa in Munich, where they coped with their awful loss. They bravely lived on caviar and champagne and sent their children to expensive schools, only to keep up their very high standards, you understand. Poor little Eva had never been to the castle. She had only seen the pictures that her heartbroken father showed her. She lived with the family tragedy all her life. Then, a few years ago, the awful thing happened. They got the castle back.' Maria paused expectantly.

'What was awful about that?' Mark enquired.

'It was a wreck,' Louise interjected. 'It had been totally neglected for over fifty years. And the family had to move back there.'

'Why?' Paul asked.

'Family honour,' Maria explained. 'They had to go back to claim the land and restore the Mebius family to its former glory. But fortunately for Eva, she had a brilliant career in Brussels and a husband to look after. And Dieter had his hands full, running a shoe factory in Düsseldorf. They didn't have to join their mother and father in the castle.'

'But the parents had to spend all their money to repair it,' Louise said.

'Must be tough being an aristocrat,' Paul remarked. 'Or should I say Euro-stocrat?' He smiled across the table at Maria. 'I heard that word just recently. Quite witty, don't you think?'

'Hilarious,' Maria replied with a stiff smile.

An hour later the last of the guests were finishing their after-dinner drinks in front of the dying embers of the fire in the library.

'It's time to go,' Paul said. 'I should really get a taxi and get back to the hotel.'

'But it's early,' Mark remarked. 'Only half-past

eleven. How about going for a beer in the Grande Place? It's the oldest part of Brussels,' he told Paul, 'and it looks its best at night, with floodlights on all the old buildings.'

'Sounds great,' Paul agreed. 'How about it, darling? Can you get away?'

Louise looked around the room. 'No problem. Everyone seems to be ready to leave. Daddy is saying goodbye to the Danish ambassador and I think Eva's gone out to the kitchen.'

'Probably beating the servants to death,' Maria suggested.

'No, she said she was getting more coffee,' Louise said. 'I'm going to change. Can't drink beer in this thing. Are you coming with us, Maria?'

'I don't think so. I'm very tired.'

'But we'd love you to come,' Paul said. 'Right, Mark?'

'Right,' Mark mumbled, his eyes following Louise's departing figure as she shimmied across the room. 'What did you say?' he asked, when the door had closed behind her.

'Oh, nothing important,' laughed Paul.

'I'm going to bed,' Maria suddenly announced. And, without saying another word, she turned on her heel and marched out of the room.

'Strange girl,' she could hear Mark say as she left. 'Not at all like her sister.'

'I believe she's had a knock on the head,' Paul replied. 'Some kind of accident. Could have unhinged her a bit.'

'Maybe that's the reason.'

Great, Maria thought, they think I'm a nut. I really know how to turn men on.

She walked slowly up the stairs. She wasn't really tired and she knew she wouldn't be able to sleep. The outing to the Grande Place for beer seemed suddenly quite attractive. Maybe she could change her mind? Give Mark another chance? He seemed quite nice, she thought, even if he wasn't exactly a hunk. It might be fun. And I'll have a chance to talk to Paul and show him I'm not completely mad. I'll just change and tell Louise I'm coming after all.

'I'm so glad you decided to come,' Louise said, as they walked down the stairs together a few minutes later. 'Mark was really disappointed that you just left like that.'

'I bet.'

'No, I could tell. He looked really upset. I think he likes you.'

'Maria changed her mind,' Louise said to Paul, who was waiting in the hall. 'She's coming with us after all.'

'Oh, great,' Paul replied.

The door to the kitchen opened and Eva came out. She looked at them, startled.

'Are you leaving already?'

'We're going to the Grande Place,' Louise replied. 'With Mark.'

'But it's early,' Eva protested. 'I haven't had a chance to talk to Paul at all.' She took him by the elbow. 'This is the moment when I can finally relax. The party is coming to an end. Nothing else to worry about. Won't you join me for a drink?'

'But I think Mark's calling a taxi,' Louise argued.

'It'll take a while for it to arrive. Have a brandy while you wait.' Eva's smile was suddenly warm and charming, full of dimples and beautiful teeth.

'OK,' Paul said. 'Just a small one while we wait for the taxi.'

'But ...' Louise started. Then she gave up. 'Fine,' she muttered, putting her coat on the banister, and she and Maria followed Paul and Eva into the library.

'Where is that taxi?' Louise demanded half an hour later.

'I don't know,' Mark replied, looking worried. 'They said they'd be here soon.'

'That could mean any time in the next two hours.' Eva laughed. 'This house is not easy to find.'

'Give me your mobile, Mark,' Louise said. 'I'm going to call the taxi company.'

'I don't know why she's fussing,' Eva remarked. 'I'm sure the taxi will be here soon. And in the meantime, we're very cosy.'

She was curled up beside Paul on the big, comfortable sofa in front of the fire, entertaining him with stories of her first years in the Commission. She was feeling relaxed and relieved. The dinner had gone quite well, apart from the mishaps, which no one seemed to mind, and she had been able to have a very useful chat with Sean Dogherty. And here she was with this gorgeous man. The evening was taking a turn for the better. She smiled at him, momentarily forgetting that he was Louise's boyfriend.

'I hope I'm not boring you,' she commented.

'Not at all. You've had an amazing career.'

'I've been lucky.'

'I suspect there was a lot of very hard work involved,' he remarked.

'Oh, I don't know.' Eva tried to sound modest.

'And you're the head of a very important cabinet. Justice and Home Affairs. Must be very interesting.'

'I'm the deputy *chef*,' she corrected. 'Very interesting, yes. And a lot more difficult than I thought at first.'

'Why is that?'

'Because the *chef de cabinet* ...'

'The one you're deputy to?'

'That's right. He's never there. He has only been in the office five times since he was appointed four years ago.'

'Why is that?' Paul wondered, looking concerned.

'All kinds of reasons. Sick leave mostly.' Eva sighed. 'It means that I practically run the cabinet single-handedly.'

'But what about the Commissioner?'

'Not much use,' Eva laughed. 'Charming, yes, everyone's darling. But practical? Not at all. I spend a lot of time working around him, if you know what I mean.'

'Must be very difficult, all right,' Paul agreed.

'I'm used to it by now,' Eva smiled. 'But enough about me. I don't know much about you.'

'Me? Oh, there's not much to my life. I had a very ordinary childhood.'

'But you've done very well, according to Louise. Your own company.'

'It's not that amazing really.'

'Tell me about it. Louise said you were in waste management. Is there really that much money in emptying people's bins?'

'Well,' Paul looked at her as if he was trying to figure out whether she was mocking him, 'it's a little more than that. Waste is actually one of the most serious problems these days. If we don't have proper waste management, there is a very real threat to the environment.'

'I know,' Eva nodded. 'We produce an enormous amount of rubbish in the western world. But how do you propose to tackle this?'

'Recycling. That's what I, or my firm, I should say, specialise in.'

'And how did you end up in this field?'

'Well, I have a degree in environmental science. I learned a lot about the effect of waste on the environment while I was at college. But I also have a business degree, so I thought, why not combine the two and ...'

'Save nature and make a lot of money in the process?' Eva enquired with a little smile.

'Well, eh, yes.' Paul looked both annoyed and embarrassed.

'That's absolutely brilliant,' Eva beamed. 'No one could argue with that. And to have done so well at your age is –' She stopped. 'But how old *are* you? Louise didn't say.'

'I'm thirty-six. Not exactly a child.'

'The perfect age for a man,' Eva nodded.

'And the perfect age to start a family, don't you

think?' he replied.

'Oh, I wouldn't know.' She glanced at her watch. 'But it is getting late. What about that taxi, Louise? Any luck?'

'They said it should be here soon.'

'Excuse me, sir.' Fernando, who had just stuck his head round the door, beckoned to Dan. 'Could you come out to the kitchen for a moment?'

'What's the matter?' Dan asked. He excused himself to the remaining guests, the Commissioner and the Danish ambassador. 'I'd better go out and see what he wants.'

'Thanks, darling,' Eva called. 'I just don't have the strength to get up.'

'It's been a lovely evening,' Sean Dogherty said.

'And the dinner was superb,' the ambassador added.

'All thanks to Hannibal,' Eva smiled. 'He does all my dinners.'

'The Portuguese?' the Danish ambassador asked. 'Wonderful caterer. But very difficult to get hold of. You have to book him months in advance.'

'Really?' Eva looked surprised. 'But he came tonight at a moment's notice. Maybe he had a cancellation. He's an awful snob though. He insists on knowing who's been invited. And if the guest list is not up to scratch, he won't do it.'

'I know,' the ambassador laughed. 'And he's such a prima donna. Behaves as if he's royalty.'

'I couldn't manage without him,' Eva confessed. 'Even if he's a pain in the neck.'

Sean Dogherty rose. 'Well, as I said, it's been a

lovely party. But now I really have to be thinking of going.'

'I'm afraid you can't.' Dan had just returned.

'I'm glad you want me to stay, but –'

'No, it's your car,' Dan protested, looking very distressed.

'Don't tell me it's broken down already!' the Commissioner exclaimed. 'Bloody Mercedes!'

'It's been stolen.' Dan put a hand on his arm. 'I'm so sorry.'

'What?' Eva gasped, sitting up. 'Here? From outside the house?'

'But how? My chauffeur? What happened?' The Commissioner's voice became agitated.

'Your chauffeur is all right,' Dan soothed. 'He's in the kitchen having a brandy. He's had an awful shock.'

'What happened?' the Commissioner asked again.

'Well,' Dan explained, 'he said he was standing beside the car, having a cigarette, waiting for you. He heard someone running up the drive, and then this man came up behind him, put a gun to his head and told him to hand over the keys. He had no choice but to do as he was told. Then the man got into the car and drove off. It all happened in a matter of seconds.'

'Fuck,' the Commissioner muttered.

'It's terrible,' Dan said, 'really terrible. I am so sorry, Sean.'

'This happens all the time in Brussels,' the Danish ambassador said. 'In fact it's getting worse. I was at a dinner at the Swiss embassy last week and all the ambassadors' cars were taken in the same way. Very embarrassing for the host, I have to say.'

'You had yours stolen too?' Dan asked.

'No. I don't have a car.'

'What?' Eva exclaimed. 'You don't? How do you manage? How do you get around?'

'On my bike. I cycle everywhere.'

'That must be such fun for your wife,' Eva replied without thinking.

'She's not here much,' the ambassador replied, unabashed. 'She prefers to spend most of her time in Copenhagen.'

What is it with Brussels wives? Eva thought.

Fernando came back into the room. 'The police are here,' he announced.

'Oh, no,' Eva moaned. 'Who called them?'

'I did, madame,' Fernando replied, looking proud.

'God,' Eva sighed. 'Now we'll be up all night with bloody PVs. Thanks a lot Fernando.'

'PVs?' Paul whispered to Louise.

'*Procès-verbal*,' Louise whispered back. 'Statements. The Belgian police love them. The longer the better, and in as many languages as possible. We can kiss our night out goodbye.'

'I just have to say one thing,' Sean Dogherty stated. 'I don't want any of this to get into the papers.'

'But,' Mark protested, 'I'm a journalist.'

'I don't care if you're bloody Shakespeare, I can't have this come out.'

'Why not?' Dan asked, confused. 'It's not as if it's your fault.'

'The Taoiseach wouldn't like it,' Sean Dogherty

said. 'He doesn't like anyone to be associated with crime.'

They had been up until the small hours of the morning, being interviewed by two enormous Belgian policemen who had laboriously spelled out their statements on the wads of forms they had brought with them. Everyone was questioned in detail about their backgrounds and movements during the evening, until Eva was ready to confess to being responsible for the crime, if only to be able to go to bed. She knew she had behaved like a raving lunatic, screeching at the police about crime in Brussels and giving poor Fernando a hard time, but she had been so upset.

'This is all your fault,' she snarled at Fernando.

'I'm sorry, madame,' he replied, looking wounded.

'Now, darling,' Dan soothed. 'I don't think that's quite fair.'

'What about your guests?' one of the policemen asked. 'Could you make up a list of who was here?'

'No.' Eva shook her head. 'That won't be necessary. I know all of them very well. There's not the slightest possibility that any of them could have had anything to do with this.'

'But we need to know who was here,' the policeman argued.

'No, you don't.' Eva was getting impatient. She was exhausted and stressed and dying for a drink. Why can't they all just go away? she thought. Why do we have to go through all this? 'Look,' she said. 'This really isn't necessary. You just have to trust my judgement. I have a lot of connections in the legal department of the Commission. Jean-Claude Bonhomme –'

'You know *him*?' The taller of the two policemen looked at her with respect.

'We're very close,' Eva replied. (The only time she had met him was at the European Christmas bazaar, when she had sold him a German beer mug, but what better way to start a close friendship?)

'What about your servants?' the other policeman piped up.

'Mildred is the most honest woman in Brussels,' Dan stated. 'She has been with us for years. So has Fernando.'

'Even if he is an *espèce de petit con*,' Eva filled in.

'How do you spell that?' the policeman asked, his pen poised over one of the forms.

'Don't you speak French?' Eva enquired.

'Not very well, no.'

'But you're Belgian.'

'We're Flemish,' he corrected.

'But how do you manage when you have to deal with French-speaking Belgians who don't speak a word of Flemish?'

'We speak English,' the big policeman said.

'And if they don't speak ...'

'We arrest them.' He laughed uproariously at his own joke.

'Very funny.' Eva smiled ironically.

'Never mind that,' the Commissioner interjected. 'How am I going to get my car back?'

'That's not very likely,' the smaller policeman said. 'It's probably halfway to Chechnya by now.'

'What do you mean?' Dan demanded.

'Well, you see,' the taller of the policemen explained, 'these cars are stolen to order. There are so many people in Brussels with big, expensive cars – ambassadors, Commissioners and so on. The easiest way to steal them is when there's a chauffeur waiting to pick up his boss. They can just put a gun to his head, ask for the keys and that's it. Then they drive to Eastern Europe and sell them there on the black market.'

'Pretty clever, when you think about it,' Dan remarked.

'But why did it have to happen tonight?' Eva sighed.

'They must have known the Commissioner would be here.'

'But how?'

'We don't know. They seem to have a very efficient network.'

'Why didn't they take my wife's Saab, then?' Dan wondered. 'Or my BMW? They're both parked in the garage.'

'They have to get the keys in order to sell the car. And they want a quick getaway. Hot-wiring cars or breaking into houses is too slow and demands too much effort. And this part of town is very convenient for the motorway. They can be at the border in an hour.'

'Let's get back to the PV,' the other policeman suggested. 'There are a lot more questions left.'

'What do you mean "more questions"?' Eva demanded. 'We have told you everything. What do you want, our dental records?'

After another tedious hour, the policemen wound up their investigation. The Commissioner and his driver departed in the taxi which had finally arrived, while Mark and Paul borrowed Fernando's old Fiat to take them into the city. The Danish ambassador cycled slowly home.

A window banged. Maria sighed and got out of bed to close it. The rain was pouring down outside and, with a little shudder, she got back into bed. The weekend was over, Louise and Paul had gone back to Dublin, and Monday morning loomed ahead.

A smell of toast and coffee wafted up the stairs. It must be later than I thought, Maria said to herself as she looked at the small carriage clock on her bedside table. Eight o'clock. She got out of bed and put on her dressing gown. She was suddenly very hungry, looking forward to a cup of *café au lait*, orange juice and fresh croissants.

Downstairs in the small, cosy breakfast room off the kitchen, she found her father, dressed in suit and tie, reading the *International Herald Tribune*.

He looked up as she came in. 'Hello, sweetheart,' he said. 'You're up early.'

'I couldn't sleep.' Maria yawned and sat down. She poured hot, black coffee into a big cup and added warm milk. 'This smells divine.' She reached out for a croissant from the bread basket. 'There's nothing like a French breakfast. Even in Brussels. It's so decadent somehow.'

'Make it really sinful and have some apricot jam.'

'Lovely.' Maria smiled and put a big blob on her croissant.

'How are you feeling?' her father asked, putting down his newspaper. 'You look a lot better now than when you arrived.'

'I'm feeling very well actually.' Maria bit into her croissant. 'The weekend was really restful.'

'Apart from the dinner on Friday night,' Dan remarked. 'I hope it wasn't too tiring for you. We didn't get any sleep at all that night. At least the Commissioner became resigned to the loss of his car.'

'I know. It was really terrible. But apart from that, the party wasn't too bad.'

'I liked Paul,' Dan said. 'He seems very nice.'

'I suppose he's OK.'

'Not your type?'

She was silent for a moment. Drops of rain pattered against the window and there was a sound of a Hoover upstairs. 'I found him a bit smarmy,' she explained. 'I don't trust him.'

'Smarmy? Maybe he was nervous. Meeting a girl's family for the first time can be really scary. I was just as unsure of myself when I was young.'

'Hard to imagine,' Maria remarked. 'You're so smooth and sophisticated.'

'That's just old age,' he smiled.

Maria looked at his dear, sweet face, and suddenly her eyes filled with tears and her face crumpled. 'Oh, Daddy,' she whispered.

'Sweetheart, what's the matter?' Dan put his arm round her and looked at her with concern.

'Oh, I don't know.' She sighed. 'If only . . .'

'You still miss her, don't you?'

'Yes ... No ... I don't know. I don't really remember her. But I miss having a mother, if you know what I mean. A bit childish, I know, but ...'

'I don't think you ever grow out of wanting your mother,' Dan said. 'I still wish I could talk to mine.'

'Do you? Really?'

'Of course. But you do have Eva.'

'Oh, yes, we do.'

'She is very fond of both of you,' Dan said in a soft voice. 'And she's so disappointed that you never gave her a chance.'

'But we —'

'No, darling, let me speak.' Dan looked stern. 'Eva tried hard to be a mother to you. But she was so young when we married and didn't know anything about children. She didn't realise she shouldn't have tried to replace your mother, or that if she had been a little more patient, you would have accepted her. So she gave up and built a wall around herself. Maybe to avoid being hurt, I don't know. But it was very disappointing for her.'

'I suppose,' Maria mumbled, remembering herself as a sullen fourteen-year-old. It couldn't have been easy for Eva, she suddenly thought.

'But tell me, darling,' Dan continued, 'are you happy in the flat in Dublin? If you're not, you could come here. Find a job and live with us.'

'Oh, no, Daddy,' Maria protested. 'I love the flat.'

'Good. Eva worked hard to make it nice for you, you know.'

'She did?'

'She was very concerned about making it cosy,' he said, spreading butter on a bit of croissant. 'She worried about it for months. "Would the girls like green or white tiles in the bathrooms?" she would ask. "Do you think Maria likes the Laura Ashley look in her bedroom? And where am I going to find nice lamps for the living room?"'

'Really?' Maria looked at her father, feeling a little guilty. Maybe Eva was not as bad as they thought? Maybe she had been upset about their coldness to her.

'Oh, yes. That flat was the only thing on her mind for nearly a year. She said she thought it was important for you and Louise to have a real home at last. Even though she thought boarding school was the best solution for you, she knew it hadn't been easy.'

'But she went away to school herself.'

'Yes, but she hated it. She was very lonely.'

'I had no idea,' Maria mumbled.

'You know,' Dan stated, 'it would be nice if you gave her half a chance. She's not as bad as you seem to think.'

'Well,' Maria said, 'it's just that . . .' She stopped. 'I always thought she was cold-hearted.'

'She's not cold-hearted,' Dan protested. 'She's warm, beautiful, intelligent and . . . sexy. I'm a man, you know, not just your father. And Eva —'

'I don't want you to be a man!' Maria moaned. 'I just want you to be my father.'

'Don't be childish, darling,' Dan pleaded. 'If you could only . . .'

But the sound of high heels on the marble floor of the hall interrupted his words.

'Good morning,' Eva said as she entered the room. She looked relaxed and happy and her skin glowed. She was dressed in a grey woollen trouser suit, white cashmere polo neck and high-heeled boots. She hung a camel's-hair coat on the back of a chair.

'Coffee, darling?' Dan asked, and rose to kiss her cheek.

'Yes, please,' Eva replied, heaping muesli into a bowl.

'What have you planned for today?' Dan handed her a cup of steaming black coffee. 'You said something about a meeting.'

'That's right,' Eva replied. 'I'm going to that meeting in the afternoon with the Commissioner, so I'll take the opportunity to have a look around the shops in the morning. I haven't had a chance to go to the sales and now it's nearly too late.'

'Why don't you go too, Maria?' Dan suggested. 'Eva knows all the best shops.'

'Well, I . . .' Eva protested, with a hint of panic in her voice. The happy glow was suddenly gone, and she looked stressed and annoyed. 'She wouldn't like the shops I go to.'

'Of course she would,' Dan insisted. 'And a day in Paris is just what she needs before going back to Dublin.'

'Paris?' Maria asked. 'You're going to shop in Paris?'

'Of course,' Eva replied. 'You don't think I buy my clothes here, do you?' She made it sound as if Brussels was a small village in Croatia. 'It's only an hour and a half by train. I'll do the shops in the morning, a quick lunch, then my meeting and maybe a few more shops. I'll be back in time for dinner. But I'm taking the half-past nine train and Maria isn't even dressed yet. She'll never make it. Maybe another time?'

'Don't be silly,' Dan protested. 'There's a train every hour. If you take the one that leaves at half-past ten, you'll be in Paris at twelve o'clock. You'll have all afternoon.'

'And what's she going to do while I'm at my meeting?' Eva's voice had hardened.

'Maria knows Paris very well,' Dan argued. 'We used to go together quite often when she was a teenager and she was here for holidays, remember? Go on, both of you. It'll be fun.'

'I can't really afford it,' Maria protested. 'I'm quite broke at the moment.'

'It is very expensive,' Eva agreed. 'Not at all your thing.'

'No problem,' Dan said, and took out his cheque-book. 'Let me treat you to something new. You've been looking a little glum. Shopping will cheer you up. I'll write you a cheque and you'll just lodge it into your account when you go back to Dublin. Spend the same amount with your credit card.'

Maria looked at Eva. Her face was blank, but the fingers that held her teacup trembled slightly. 'Thanks, Daddy.' Maria smiled. 'I'd love to. And who better to take me shopping in Paris than the most glamorous woman in Brussels?'

'That's my girl.' Dan smiled and handed her the cheque. 'Have a great day, the two of you. Buy some really pretty clothes.' He kissed them both and left.

'Wow,' Maria said as she looked at the cheque. 'I think I'll enjoy this. Shopping in Paris. Great.'

'Fantastic.' Eva's voice was expressionless.

CHAPTER 4

'A table for one?' the waitress asked.
'*Non, deux*. I'm waiting for someone. She'll arrive any minute.'

'*Très bien, madame*,' the waitress replied, and showed her to a table by the window. 'Do you want to order now or will you wait for your friend?'

'I'll wait.' Maria sat down, put her bags beside her and unbuttoned her coat. Where the hell is Eva? she thought. It had been a very strange day so far, not at all what she had imagined.

'Cranberry juice, that's what you need,' Maria had said as the train neared Paris. 'It's very good for the sort of problem you have.'

'What problem?' Eva had snapped.

'Cystitis. Isn't that what you're suffering from?'

'What are you talking about? I don't have cystitis, or anything else.'

'You've been going to the loo every ten minutes. Looks like a bit of a problem to me. Or maybe you have an upset stomach? Too much muesli?'

'There's nothing wrong with me,' Eva said. 'It's just that I had a couple of phone calls to make. Very personal and confidential.'

'I see. I'm sorry. I just wanted to help.'

'If you could just mind your own business, it would be a great help,' Eva barked.

'OK.' Maria was suddenly contrite. What a pity. They had seemed to be getting on so well and she had discovered a different side to Eva. She had been positively chatty during the journey, even cracking the odd joke. But the urge to tease her had been too strong and, before Maria could stop herself, she was at it again. She'd better try to be nice, or the trip to Paris wouldn't be very pleasant.

'Where's the best place to shop?' she asked in an attempt to humour Eva. 'You're always so beautifully dressed. You must know an awful lot of great shops.'

'Of course I do,' Eva nodded, mollified. 'What do you need?'

'Quite a lot. I haven't done any serious shopping for a while. I could do with a suit for work. I need to look good when I have meetings with television and press people about promotions. Then some nice casual clothes and maybe something for the odd party.'

'OK. When we arrive, we'll have a look around Galeries Lafayette. Then we'll have lunch. And then you can have a look in the *haute couture* shops at the Faubourg St Honoré in the afternoon. Where do you want to eat?'

'I don't know. I haven't been to Paris for years,' Maria replied. 'I wonder if that restaurant Daddy used to bring us to is still there. It had lovely food.'

'Where was that?'

'Somewhere near Porte Maillot. They only serve steak and chips and these fantastic desserts.'

'Oh, God.' Eva made a face. 'You must mean L'Entrecôte. I never touch that kind of food, if you can even call it that. I usually eat Japanese. Sushi. You can eat a lot without putting on an ounce. Very healthy.'

'Raw fish and seaweed?' Maria groaned. 'And that awful horseradish. Yuck.'

'I couldn't possibly cope with a steak,' Eva said. 'I haven't eaten red meat in years. And I can't even think of chips without feeling sick.'

'But we're in Paris,' Maria argued. 'I want to eat something really French. And Daddy said you'd take me to lunch wherever I wanted. He'll be very disappointed if I tell him you forced me to eat rice cakes wrapped in seaweed.'

Eva sighed. 'All right, I'll go with you. I suppose I can just eat a salad.'

'Great!' Maria beamed. 'We'll have a lovely time.' She looked out of the window. 'Look, we're nearly there.'

They gathered up their belongings as the train drew into the platform at the Gare du Nord.

'All right,' Eva said as they arrived at the department store, 'let's shop.'

And they did. Maria had never shopped with such an expert. Eva seemed to know exactly what designers would suit Maria and, before she knew what had happened, she had bought a blue wool suit from

Armani, two pairs of Ralph Lauren trousers, a knitted Chanel blazer, a cream cashmere pullover from Céline and a red silk evening dress from Yves St Laurent's final collection.

'Phew,' Maria sighed. 'That was amazing. I have never spent so much money in such a short time.'

'I think that just about covers what you need for now,' Eva said. 'Except for the accessories. Shoes, belts and bags. You can do those this afternoon. That will complete your wardrobe. You're not bad-looking, you know. If you could only stand up straight and try to smile more, you'd look quite pleasant.'

Maria gritted her teeth.

'Now, I'll just get a few things for myself,' Eva continued.

'This should be interesting.'

'OK. Try to keep up. If we get separated, just go on to the restaurant.'

Half an hour later, in the lingerie department, Maria watched as Eva picked up a bra from the counter and demanded imperiously of the shop assistant, 'Do you have this in a 34C?' When the girl produced a couple of bras of the right size, Eva disappeared into the changing rooms.

Maria looked around at the underwear on display, marvelling at the huge prices for just tiny slivers of silk. But what was keeping Eva? She must have finished trying on the bras by now. Maria went into the changing-room area, but all the cubicles were empty. There was a different girl at the counter who just shrugged when Maria asked if she had seen Eva leave.

There seemed no point trying to find her. Maria left the store and took the metro to the restaurant. It was nearly two o'clock and she knew that most Parisians would have finished eating by now. The restaurant would be quiet.

I wish I didn't have to try so hard, Eva said to herself, as the taxi drew away from the rear entrance of the department store. But it was always like this at the end of the Commissioners' term of office. You had to work like a slave to hang on to your job. She had been very hopeful that she had been able to impress Sean Dogherty and that he in turn would talk about her in a very favourable way to the President. And Sean seemed to have liked the idea that he might himself stay on as Commissioner and even get a better portfolio than his present one. Agriculture would be much better than Culture, both for him and for Ireland, she had suggested, and she could nearly see the wheels turning in his mind. Agriculture, he seemed to think, subsidies and grants. Lots of money for the Irish farmers. All thanks to him. His political future would take a turn for the better.

But then the evening had had such a disastrous end, Sean Dogherty had left in an awful mood and Eva was certain he had forgotten all about putting in a good word to the President for her. Now she had to make extra sure her cabinet performed well and she came out of it smelling like a whole flower bed of roses.

Oh, if only Maria could have stayed at home. She had really complicated the whole day. But it was

Dan's fault, Eva thought angrily, he could never resist an opportunity to spoil her, to buy peace of mind with a present or some money. Daddy's little girl, she thought. I'll always be the villain, the nasty woman who stole her precious father. Poor darling. She'll have to find her own way to the restaurant. I really have to sort out the arrangements for that conference in Guadeloupe before Guido arrives. He'll just complicate everything with silly suggestions. But maybe I can create a distraction for him ... Eva took out her mobile and dialled a number.

Maria sat back in the chair and eased her shoes off her aching feet. A trip to Paris always meant a lot of walking. But what a wonderful city it was, even in late winter. The skies were grey, but the light was soft and the air held a promise of spring. And there was that lovely Paris smell, a mixture of coffee, petrol fumes, French cigarettes and newly baked bread. Magic! She sighed contentedly and looked out the window at the people walking past. A couple came into view, arguing angrily, then they stopped and kissed passionately; followed by a young woman, possibly a model between assignments, stick-thin, stunningly beautiful, dressed in a full-length white mink coat, torn jeans and running shoes, talking into a mobile phone; two young men holding hands; an old woman in a torn coat and slippers; a mother with two little girls in school uniform; and a nun. Maria was so engrossed in the street theatre, she didn't notice the man approach her table.

'Maria?'

She looked up, startled. In front of her was a tall, elegant man dressed with unmistakable Italian chic.

'Yes?'

'You do not know me,' he said in heavily accented English. 'But I am the boss of your stepmother.'

'Eva?'

'*Si*. She call me on the *telefono*. She is, how you say, occupied. Deranged.'

'Deranged? You mean detained?'

'That is it.'

'You're her boss?' Maria asked. 'The Commissioner?'

'Yes. I am Guido Fregene de Popolonia. But, please, call me Guido.'

'But,' Maria stammered, 'what happened to Eva? Is she not coming?'

Guido smiled and pulled out a chair. 'She say have lunch with Maria. And meet me at the train.'

'What? Are you going to be on the same train?'

'No.' Guido laughed, shook his head and started again. 'She said she, I mean, her. Meet her. Eva and you on the train. *Capito*?'

'Oh? Right. Fine,' Maria sighed. Oh, God. Now she'd have to have lunch with this gigolo. But it was better than sitting there alone.

'A beautiful girl like you must not eat alone,' Guido stated. 'Let's order. I like this place. I love beef and *frites*. Very good food.' He waved the waitress over and, in rapid French, told her they were ready to order.

As she enjoyed the succulent meat in herb sauce and the accompanying huge tray of chips, Maria was

beginning to have fun. Guido was flirting unasham-
edly, telling her she was lovely and sexy, that she had
beautiful eyes, wonderful skin and a figure like Venus.
He looked into her eyes, touched her hand and
stroked her cheek. She didn't believe a word he said,
but he was so funny and bright that, for a moment,
she forgot the accident, her loss of memory and even
her anger towards Eva. She felt admired, attractive
and young.

'What about Eva?' she asked. 'Are you and she . . .
Do you . . .'

'No, no!' Guido protested. 'Eva and I work together. That is all. She's a very clever woman. Very
beautiful. But she has a lot of, how you say . . . suitcases? Here.' He touched his head.

'Suitcases? You mean baggage,' Maria guessed.

'That's it. She is not what she seems. There's a secret
there. Very sad.'

'What do you mean?'

'I don't know. But I can feel it. Here.' He touched
his chest.

'What?' Maria said. The idea that Eva was harbouring some sort of sad secret was unbelievable. But
Guido seemed very emotional. He probably loved
drama. She finished her meal in thoughtful silence.

'Dessert?' he asked as she pushed her plate away.

'Yes, please,' she laughed. 'I don't normally, but I
know the desserts here are too good to miss.'

'They are fantastic,' he agreed. 'Let's have two
each.'

'Why not?' Maria smiled. 'But then I really have to
go. I need to get a pair of shoes.'

'Shoes?' he said, looking even happier. 'I'll go with you. I love shoes. Where are you going? What do you like?'

'I don't know. I thought maybe Charles Jourdan. Or Ferragamo.'

'Show me your feet.' Guido suddenly dived under the table and grabbed one of her ankles. 'Lovely,' he said from under the tablecloth. 'Beautiful feet. But not Charles Jourdan. They would be too tight for you. You have a high, how you say, instep.'

'Yes, I know,' Maria said, trying to pull her foot away.

'And a little wide at the top.' His voice was muffled from under the table. 'But your heel is narrow. Bruno Magli.'

'What?'

'Bruno Magli,' Guido said, and crawled out from under the table. 'Their shoes are the perfect fit for your feet.'

'But Ferragamo have lovely shoes.'

'Ferragamo,' he sneered. 'Bah. For the cakes.'

'What?'

'The cakes,' he repeated, and pointed at the chocolate gateaus the waitress had just brought.

'Do you mean tarts?' Maria asked, thinking that she was really getting the hang of Guido's English. 'Shoes for tarts?'

'*Si*. That's it.'

'How come you know so much about shoes?'

'I'm Italian,' Guido beamed.

'There you are,' Eva shouted, as she pushed through

the throng at the station. 'No time to talk. Hurry up, or we'll miss the train.' They ran down the platform with their many bags and parcels and managed to jump onto the train just seconds before it started to move.

'So,' Eva said, sighing, as she sank down on her seat. 'Did you have a lovely lunch with Guido?'

'Yes, I did. It was great fun. But what happened to you?'

'Well . . .' Eva hesitated. 'I got an urgent call on my mobile while I was in the changing room. I had to sort out a problem with those people Guido and I were supposed to meet. And I knew I could handle it better than he could. So, as I couldn't see you when I got out of the cubicle, I sent him to take care of you. By the time he met the others, it was all sorted out. Then I needed to do a few more shops and I knew you'd manage on your own, so I just carried on. Got some shoes. Very nice. Ferragamo.'

'I see.'

'What did you do?' Eva asked.

'Oh, I bought some shoes too. Bruno Magli. Guido came with me. He really knows everything about shoes.' Maria suddenly giggled as she thought about Guido and how he had taken over the chic Bruno Magli shop, ordering the assistant to show her the whole stock. 'I bought three pairs. And I got a discount.'

'Excellent,' Eva beamed. 'Guido is so good at shopping.' She seemed a lot happier than earlier in the day and there was a slight flush on her cheeks.

They chatted on in a surprisingly friendly way as

the train swept through the suburbs of Paris and on through the darkening countryside.

'How did you like Louise's boyfriend?' Eva suddenly asked.

'I didn't,' Maria replied.

'I thought he was rather sweet,' Eva said. 'His family is horribly working-class, of course.'

'Oh, yes, horribly,' Maria agreed, with irony dripping from her voice.

'Well, you called him the yob from the west.'

'I know, but –'

'Which he is, let's face it,' Eva continued unabashed. 'But he has been rather clever to start his own business. He's a great catch. I hope she can hang on to him.'

'I don't think she'll have a problem,' Maria remarked. 'He wants to marry her.'

'Then Louise is a lucky girl.'

'I thought he was an arrogant bastard actually,' Maria said, remembering their conversation. 'He was really rude to me.'

'And you were really polite to him?' Eva enquired.

'I didn't do him any harm. I just can't stand him, that's all.'

'I don't see why. And if he's going to be your brother-in-law, you might have to make an effort to be at least polite to him.'

'Louise doesn't want to get married,' Maria remarked. 'She just wants to have fun.'

'She seems very much in love. And he told me they've bought a ring.'

'Which she refuses to wear,' Maria retorted. 'I don't

think they'll get married any time soon.'

'Well, we'll see.'

'Yeah, right,' Maria said, opening a magazine.

The journey continued in silence for some time.

'Do you think I look old?' Eva asked out of the blue. 'I mean, do I seem old to you?' She stared at Maria, looking at once worried and a little sad.

Maria looked up from an article about single mothers and studied Eva for a moment. 'That depends,' she replied. 'On how old you really are, I mean. You've never told us your age.'

'And I'm not going to tell you now,' Eva snapped. 'I just wanted to know in a general way. Just tell me, do I look old?'

Maria considered the question while she looked at Eva. She appeared so perfect, her face smooth and her figure trim. But there was no vivacity in that flawless face, no laughter in her eyes. She seemed troubled. 'No,' she finally said. 'You don't look old. Just tired and stressed, maybe.'

'I am a little tired at the moment. But that's not a serious problem. I just have to make sure I get a little more sleep and try to cut down on my workload.'

'OK.'

Maria turned her head and stared out of the window. She didn't feel like talking, especially about Eva and her looks. The train sped on, past woods, fields and towns. Maria looked at the lights in the windows and wondered what sorts of lives people had in these small towns. Ordinary lives, she thought, just families living quietly with their own concerns and problems, going to work in the morning and coming home in the evening, sitting down to dinner together. She sighed. Will I ever have a family, she thought, little children to put to bed and kiss goodnight, a husband to love, a home to look after? She leaned her head against the window, her mind far away.

'We'll be home in time for dinner.' Eva's voice woke Maria from her reverie. 'Will you excuse me a moment? I have to make another phone call.'

She grabbed her handbag and headed for the back of the train. Maria stared at her departing figure, wondering who Eva could possibly be calling. It was half-past seven, too late to catch anyone in the office. She jumped as the shrill sound of a mobile phone could be heard and stared in confusion at Eva's phone as it vibrated like an angry bee on the little table in front of her seat.

CHAPTER 5

It was a dark, wet April evening in Dublin. There was a delicious fragrance of herbs and spices in the big kitchen of the flat in Sandymount. Maria was cooking Thai chicken casserole and was looking forward to an evening at home with Louise. They were going to open a bottle of wine and watch a video. Paul was away and Louise had said she was in the mood to see a romantic film.

The radio was playing soft jazz, the flat was warm and cosy, and, despite the depression she had been suffering from since the accident, Maria felt a sense of comfort. They were very busy at the office, partly because of the large number of books that were being published that spring, partly because Downtown Publishers were launching Planet, their new nonfiction imprint. Maria was working long hours with the rest of the marketing team, which helped her forget her own problems. But she was still worried about her loss of memory, and the fact that she could not remember why she had been at that hotel on the evening of the accident.

'You'll soon feel better,' the doctor had promised, when she went for her last check-up. 'And there will be no scars or marks on your face.'

'But what about the amnesia?' Maria asked.

'Nothing has come back yet?'

'It's a total blank.'

'You probably won't ever know what happened. Most accident victims can never remember the actual accident and many have blanks in their memories about the hour or so beforehand. Try not to worry about it.'

'But I feel so down,' Maria said. 'So depressed all the time.'

'I'm sure it's nothing to worry about,' the doctor replied. 'Probably just the shock. I'll give you a prescription for a mild tranquilliser to help you sleep. And come and see me again in about a month if you don't feel any better.'

And she had walked out of the surgery with her prescription and a feeling of hopelessness. Nobody cared. Her father and Eva (who would have just told her to pull herself together) seemed far away in Brussels and Louise was so in love she wouldn't have noticed if Maria had turned into a Romanian gypsy. And she couldn't stop thinking of Eva's strange behaviour during their trip to Paris.

'Made your phone call?' Maria had asked, holding the phone behind her back, when Eva returned to her seat on the train.

'I did. Very important. Work, you know.'

'You managed to contact the person you wanted

to talk to?'

'Yes, thank goodness.'

'That was very clever. Miraculous, in fact.'

'Was it? Why?' Eva looked at Maria in confusion.

'Considering you didn't use your phone, I mean,' Maria said, holding the mobile up. 'How did you manage it? Telepathy? Amazing.'

'I ... never mind,' Eva snapped, and grabbed the mobile out of Maria's hand. 'Just mind your own business. That's all I ask.'

'There was a call while you were away.'

'What? Who?' A look of consternation appeared on Eva's face. 'What did he say? What did he want?'

'It was Daddy. He wanted to know if we'd be home in time for dinner.'

'Oh. Good.' Eva looked relieved.

'What are you up to?' Maria demanded. 'Are you having an affair or something? Because if you are, I'll kill you.'

'Absolutely not,' Eva snapped. 'I wouldn't do that. Not to Dan. And that sort of thing is so tacky. Not my style at all.' She sighed. 'I'm just having some problems at work. You wouldn't believe what's going on at the Commission at the moment.'

'Try me.' Maria looked at Eva with a steady gaze.

'You wouldn't be able to understand. Justice and Home Affairs are very complicated.'

Maria started to protest, but at that moment the train pulled into the station in Brussels and Eva slipped away, making a great show of collecting her bags and getting off the train.

★

The front door in the flat slammed and Louise came into the kitchen, bringing with her a gust of cold air.

'Hi.' She picked up a piece of carrot and put it in her mouth. 'Wait till you hear this.'

'You're very late,' Maria remarked.

'I know, and I'm out again as fast as I can,' Louise replied. 'There's been a change of plan. Guess who's in town?'

'But what about dinner? I'm making Thai chicken. Your favourite. And I got the video you wanted. I thought we'd a have a girls' night in.'

'Well, now we'll have a girls' night out instead.'

'But I . . . The dinner's nearly ready. I can't eat all this on my own.'

'Will you listen to me for a moment,' Louise exclaimed. 'We're going out. I mean you, me, Paul and Mark.'

'Mark? What do you mean?'

'Paul called me in the office half an hour ago. His conference was changed to next week. And Mark's in town for some interview. Paul suggested we all go out to dinner. So get a move on. We have to be at the restaurant in half an hour.'

'Whose idea was this?'

'Well, it was Paul really. He said that you seemed depressed the last time you spoke on the phone.'

'I see,' Maria drawled. 'Paul is behind all this? Just like Eva, he thinks he has to fix me up with Mark? Poor Maria, the ugly sister?'

'Why are you such a drip?' Louise demanded. 'Why can't you come out with us? It's just dinner, not an arranged marriage, for God's sake! And I would love you to come. We haven't seen much of each other lately.'

Maria sighed. Louise was right. She was being difficult. And Louise had not been home even one evening the past week, because of her yoga classes and dates with Paul. Oh, why not? she thought. It's not as if I'm inundated with offers. And she seemed to have lost her taste for protest meetings lately. They seemed suddenly so dreary. Even invitations such as the one to chain herself to the railings of Leinster House in protest at a proposed incinerator somewhere in County Tipperary did not seem as much fun as they used to.

'You're right,' she said. 'I'm being negative. I'll come. But just for dinner. No nightclubs or cosy drinks in Paul's apartment afterwards.'

'I promise.'

Paul and Mark were already at the table when Maria and Louise entered the restaurant.

'Sorry we're late,' Louise said.

'But worth waiting for,' Paul replied, giving her a kiss on the mouth. 'You're beautiful.' He turned to Maria. 'And you look very pretty. Is that a new dress? I've never seen you in red before.'

'I picked it up in Paris actually. Hi, Mark. Nice to see you again.'

'Hi, Maria,' Mark replied, and placed a wet kiss on her cheek.

Oh, God, Maria thought, as she sat down, it's already turning into a night in hell. 'Where's our waitress?' she asked impatiently.

'Here she is,' Mark announced, as a beautiful girl with long blonde plaits approached.

'Good evening,' the waitress said, taking a notepad from her apron. 'You all wanna eat?'

'That's right,' Paul replied, trying not to stare. He prised his eyes away and looked at the menu. 'What can you recommend?'

'It's all good,' the girl declared. 'Very delicious.'

'I'll just have a salad,' Louise said. 'I suddenly don't feel very hungry.'

'What's the beef casserole like?' Maria asked.

'Very delicious,' the girl said again, and smiled. 'With dumplings. You want, yes?'

'Sounds interesting,' Maria replied. 'Why not? I'll have that.'

'OK.' The waitress wrote down the order. 'And your men? What they want?'

'You're not from around here, are you?' Paul asked.

'How you guess?' The girl giggled. 'I not look Irish?'

'Well, no,' Paul replied, 'not exactly. And you speak English with just the hint of an accent.'

'Where *are* you from?' Mark enquired.

'Lithuania,' the girl replied with a big smile. 'But what you eat?'

'I'll have ... I'll have ...' Paul hesitated, looking stressed. 'I can't make up my mind. What about you, Mark?'

'The breast of chicken looks good,' Mark said.

'The breast of the chicken,' the girl repeated, and jotted something on her pad.

'Paul?' Louise urged. 'You haven't ordered.'

'I'll have the chicken too,' Paul replied.

'OK.' The waitress consulted her pad. 'One salad. One dumpling. Two breasts. That is all?'

'Absolutely,' Mark agreed.

'What's the matter with you?' Louise asked later, as she and Maria were touching up their make-up in the ladies' toilet. 'Why are you still so sour? Don't you like Mark?'

'I can't make up my mind,' Maria replied, combing her hair.

'I think he's lovely. What have you got against him, for God's sake?'

'He's a nerd.'

Louise shoved her lipstick into her purse and stared at Maria. 'Who do you think you are?' she demanded. 'Here's a lovely, perfectly nice man who seems to really like you, and all you can do is sneer!'

'No, he seems to really like *you*,' Maria argued.

'I don't know what you mean. At least he's not like one of those guys who only think of one thing.'

'Think? Don't be silly. Men don't think at all.'

Maria put her comb down. Then she suddenly felt guilty as she saw Louise's unhappy face. She was in such a filthy mood tonight. But she knew it wasn't because of Mark, who was perfectly nice, it was Paul. He always made her feel stupid, ever since that first evening when she had behaved like such a twit. He was always teasing her and smiling that superior little smile. It drove her crazy. But it was unfair to take it out on Louise.

'Oh, God,' Maria said. 'I'm sorry. And you're right. I should be making more of an effort. OK. I'll try. Let's go out there and be positive.'

'That's better,' Louise smiled, looking relieved. 'And be nice to Mark. Why don't you ask him about his work? Men love that.'

'Yeah, right.'

'We've ordered dessert,' Mark said, as they returned to their table. 'Chocolate cake. And some really good brandy. Is that all right?'

'Lovely,' Maria sighed. 'I'm a chocoholic. Give me a big slice.'

'Here's the dessert now,' Paul announced, as the waitress appeared with a tray. 'And the brandy. The cake looks lovely.' He took one of the plates and put it in front of Maria. 'Tuck in,' he said. 'It looks good.'

Maria studied the cake. It was dark and moist and smelled invitingly of really good chocolate. The high point of the evening, she thought, and picked up her spoon.

'Is it nice?' Louise, who had refused dessert, asked enviously.

'It's divine,' Maria sighed as she let a spoonful melt in her mouth. 'Mmm. Yes. Positively sinful.' She sipped the brandy and began to feel a little better.

'You're so lucky,' Louise said softly. 'You never put on weight, no matter how much you eat. And I can't even look at a piece of cake without putting on half a stone. I don't know how you do it.'

'It's all that anger,' Paul stated. 'It burns a lot of calories.'

Maria looked up at him. 'What?' she demanded. 'What are you going on about now?'

'Nothing,' he smiled. 'Nothing at all.'

Mark, who did not appear to have noticed the continued hostilities, took a huge mouthful of cake. 'This is one great cake,' he stated. 'Absolutely delicious.'

Maria looked at him. She was beginning to like him a little more. He was nice and quite fun actually. Good company.

'So, how are things in Brussels?' she asked.

'Not too bad. There have been a lot of interesting things going on. All the Commissioners are coming to the end of their period in office, so they're all working hard to be reappointed. But there will be a few changes in the autumn.'

'What about those car thieves?' Louise asked. 'Have they been caught yet?'

'No, they're still operating as before.'

'The Irish Commissioner seemed to think he could keep his own hold-up out of the papers,' Paul remarked. 'But they were full of that story the following Sunday.'

'*Hold-up drama in Brussels,*' Louise quoted. '*Commissioner loses Mercedes.* That's only a few of the headlines. Sean Dogherty must have been so annoyed.'

'Last week thieves nicked the President of the Commission's car outside the French embassy,' Mark said.

'Oh, God!' Maria exclaimed.

'He had to go home on the back of the Danish ambassador's bike.'

'No!' Louise gasped.

'No, he didn't,' Mark laughed. 'He got a taxi.'

'I nearly believed you.' Louise smiled, giving him a tap on the arm.

Mark smiled back at her.

'But maybe it's the Danish ambassador who's behind this,' Maria suggested. 'That might be why he goes everywhere by bike.'

'No,' Mark replied. 'He's a former cycling champion. He won the Tour de France when he was young. He always cycles everywhere.'

Louise had lost interest in the conversation. She was looking at something going on at the other end of the room. 'Look,' she said, as three musicians unpacked their instruments. 'A band. There's going to be dancing.'

'Oh, yes,' Mark said. 'I noticed the dance floor as I came in. Dublin is becoming very continental.'

The band struck up a fast tune as he spoke.

'Oh, fantastic!' Louise exclaimed. 'I love dancing. Why don't we have a go?'

'Right,' Mark said, getting up. He held his hand out to Louise. 'Let's do it.'

And, before Paul had a chance to protest, Louise and Mark were on the dance floor, moving to the music and smiling into each other's eyes.

Paul stared at Maria with a stunned expression. 'What happened?' he asked.

'Very quick off the Mark, isn't he?' Maria said.

Paul looked at her and suddenly laughed. 'How about a truce?' he asked.

'Fine,' she agreed. She didn't feel like fighting any more.

'How about a dance?'

'You want to dance with *me*?'

'Yes,' he replied, getting up. 'How else am I going to keep an eye on those two?'

'I should have known you had ulterior motives,' she replied, but stood up and put her hand in his.

The dance floor was filling up, and Louise and Mark were lost in the throng. Paul put his arm around Maria and started to move to the music. His hand felt warm through the thin silk of her dress.

'Am I holding you too tight?' he asked, smiling down at her, his lips nearly touching her cheek.

'Not at all,' she mumbled.

'I didn't know you were such a good dancer.'

'You didn't ask.'

She had never felt like this when she danced before, so well matched and with such perfect rhythm. She looked up at him and he looked back, his eyes warm and his breath hot on her cheek. They danced without talking, like dancing partners in a ballet choreographed specially for them. Maria wanted it to go on for ever, but then the music suddenly stopped and they stood, looking at each other, slightly breathless, and the spell was broken.

Eva was on the rowing machine. She had done twenty minutes on the treadmill, ten on the Stair-Master and she would row for another twenty. Then she was ready for half an hour's hard workout with free weights. She could lift fifty kilos on a good day and manage another ten on the thigh curl. It was so convenient to have a gym at home. Dan had installed it in the basement as a Christmas present two years earlier and she had thought they might work out together. He was getting a little slack around the middle. But he preferred to walk off the extra calories on the golf course and swim in the pool at the club a couple of times a week. The girls didn't like working out either, even though Louise should really lose at least ten kilos and Maria had a tendency to stoop. But Louise was always going on about yoga, and Maria said she walked to work every day, so she got plenty of exercise, thank you very much. Eva was left to sweat it out on her own.

She enjoyed her workouts. Punishing her body to its limits was very satisfying. As she pushed and pulled, heaved and sweated, she felt her body being toned and every muscle tightened. And when it was over, she usually relaxed in the small sauna next door with a feeling of great satisfaction. But not today.

Eva pulled at the handles on the machine and rowed even faster, as she thought about Dan. He was becoming very difficult and she was beginning to find him more than a little irritating.

The conference on combating illegal drug trafficking in Guadeloupe was one example. She was really looking forward to it. A week's work, a little break in the sun and on her own. So relaxing. And it would be a great opportunity to discuss some issues with the people in the legal department. She had heard that even the head of the department, Jean-Claude Bonhomme, was going to be there. He was the *éminence grise* of the Commission, the kingmaker. What better way to get to know him than sipping rum and

Coke under the palm trees, far away from work and spouses?

'Guadeloupe? But that's fantastic!' Dan had exclaimed. 'What a lovely trip. I've never been there. It's supposed to be beautiful. You know, I think I'll go with you. I'd love a little sunshine right now.'

'Oh,' Eva said, trying not to sound disappointed. 'But won't that be difficult for you to organise at such short notice?'

'Not at all. The office runs very well without me. I don't think they even notice if I'm not there.'

'Great. OK,' she said, her voice flat.

'But won't it be lovely, darling?' he demanded. 'A romantic interlude.'

Romantic, she thought, she didn't feel a bit romantic. He had been so boring lately. Talking about retiring, buying a house in the country in Ireland and growing roses. Writing a book maybe. What was the matter with him? Was he getting old? But he was only fifty-two. In his prime, she would have thought.

And he was always so bloody *nice*. Never arguing or complaining, even when she was being really bitchy. And sex was not the thrill it had been. He was as virile as ever, but had started to joke around in bed, making car noises. It was getting on her nerves.

The next evening, just as Eva was about to leave her office, the phone rang.

'Hello?' she replied without enthusiasm. Who had the bad taste to call at this hour, when everybody had already left?

'Madame Connolly?'

'Yes?'

'This is Antoinette Duvivier from the office of Jean-Claude Bonhomme.'

'Oh?' Eva felt suddenly more alert. 'What can I do for you?'

'Well, I was looking for your Commissioner,' the woman said, 'but he had already left.'

'Yes, that's right. He is leaving for Guadeloupe tonight. He wanted a few days to settle in, he said. Is there anything I can help you with?'

'I have a message from Monsieur Bonhomme for the Commissioner.'

'But won't they be meeting at the conference?'

'I'm afraid not. Monsieur Bonhomme won't be attending the conference.'

'What?' Eva exclaimed. Shit, she thought, what am I going to do now? How am I going to get to him in an informal setting if he won't show up at the conference? 'Why isn't he coming?' she demanded.

'He is not very well. He has had a minor accident and twisted his ankle and . . .'

'I don't understand,' Eva said. 'This is a very important meeting. Couldn't he use crutches?'

'I'm afraid his doctor advised him not to travel.' The woman's voice was a little less friendly.

What a wimp, Eva thought. 'I see,' she said, trying to sound sympathetic. 'So what is he going to do about the conference?'

'He's sending his deputy, a Monsieur Yves Dutronc. Maybe you know him?'

'Never heard of him,' Eva replied in a voice that

suggested she didn't deal with deputies, despite being one herself.

'Well, in any case, Monsieur Bonhomme asked me to call your Commissioner to apologise for his absence and to tell him that Monsieur Dutronc will contact him before the conference starts.'

Eva hung up with a feeling of intense irritation. All her brilliant plans had come to nothing.

The trip was exhausting and she was not able to sleep much during the ten-hour flight. Dan was so happy and enthusiastic, chatting about Guadeloupe and how exciting it would be to see it, insisting on watching the in-flight movie and going on about how delicious the food was.

'Isn't it amazing how they can produce a steak cooked exactly right on a plane?' he gushed, showing her a piece of meat for her to inspect. 'Look, just the way I like it. You have to give it to Air France, they have such class. And the air hostesses, have you noticed how pretty they are? None of those old bags you see on all the other airlines.'

'Yes, I know,' she muttered, putting on her eye mask. 'Lovely.'

'But aren't you going to eat something? You've only picked at your fish.'

'I just want to get some sleep.'

'I'll eat it, then,' he said, taking the piece of sole in white-wine sauce from her plate. 'Pity to waste it.'

Eva sighed and closed her eyes. It had been a mistake to let him come. She should have been firm and told him it was impossible. But she hadn't had the heart to disappoint him. Dan loved to travel.

She twisted around in her seat, but could not relax or stop thinking about work. Dan took her hand.

'Just let it go, darling,' he mumbled in her ear. 'Try to sleep now.'

And, as usual, he managed to calm her. His touch was soothing and his presence so reassuring. She put her head on his shoulder and slept.

The big conference hall in Pointe à Pitre, the capital of Guadeloupe, was packed and it was very hot. Eva scanned the hall, trying to find the people from her cabinet. Guido should already be there, but there was no sign of him. She clutched her briefcase tighter and blew on a lock of hair that was threatening to fall into her eyes. The grey sleeveless linen dress stuck to her back and she felt both hot and tired.

'*Excusez-moi, madame.*' The deep voice startled her. She twirled around and bumped into the man standing behind her, making a bundle of papers he had been carrying fly out of his grip and flutter to the floor.

'*Merde!*' he exclaimed, and, getting down to retrieve them, '*Toutes mes notes pour la conférence.*'

'I'm so sorry,' Eva stammered, getting down on her knees to give him a hand. She hastily bunched the papers together and tried to sort them out.

'Just leave it,' he barked. 'You're making it worse.'

'But I ...'

They looked at each other, still crouching on the floor, surrounded by legs and feet. Eva stared at the man. His features were rough, but his skin deeply tanned, his thick, light-brown hair curly and his hazel eyes surrounded by the longest, blackest lashes she had ever seen on a man. Slowly, they got up from the floor.

He straightened the papers, looked down into her eyes and smiled, revealing white, slightly uneven teeth. '*Pardon*,' he said. 'I'm sorry I snapped. I'm just a little stressed at the moment, and the heat . . .'

'I know. Don't worry. It's all right, really.'

'Maybe we should introduce ourselves.'

'Eva Connolly.' She held out her hand.

'Yves Dutronc. *Enchanté, madame*.' He took her hand and kissed it in the polite French way. 'I'm representing the legal department of the Commission.'

'I know.'

'You do?'

'Yes. Someone from your department called us. They told us Monsieur Bonhomme was indisposed. Some sort of accident. Such bad luck.'

'But lucky for me.' He smiled again, making her knees feel strangely weak. 'I was told I would be working with this German *dame de fer,* but here you are, so young and lovely.'

'Oh, eh, well . . .' Eva didn't quite know what to say.

'And your French is remarkable.'

'Thanks . . . I mean . . .'

'But the conference is about to start. Do you know where you'll be sitting?'

'No,' Eva admitted, feeling foolish. 'I was looking for my Commissioner actually.'

'I saw him earlier at the hotel. He was sitting by the

pool, drinking champagne with a very pretty girl. Didn't seem to have a care in the world.'

'He's very relaxed,' Eva replied. 'Very easy going.'

'But he's such a clever man,' Yves remarked. 'I've seen some of the stuff he's written. Absolutely brilliant.'

'Thank you,' Eva said without thinking. 'I mean, I'll tell him.'

Yves looked at her quizzically, one eyebrow lifted.

'But here he is now.' Eva spotted Guido coming into the hall, smiling and clapping people on the back. 'Guido!' she called, waving to him. 'Over here.'

'Well, have a good day,' Yves said. '*A bientôt, peut-être?*' And he disappeared into the crowd.

'Eva!' Guido exclaimed, pushing through the throng. 'At last. I'm late. *Scusi.* How are you? Was your trip all right?'

'It was very tiring,' she replied, his cheerful face suddenly annoying her. He looked cool and rested, without a care in the world.

'But you look wonderful,' he protested. 'Absolutely glowing.'

'Thank you.' Eva tried to look professional. 'I have the briefs here. Everything's ready. If I could only find our seats . . .'

When Eva returned to her hotel that evening, there was no sign of Dan. He had told her he'd meet her for a drink when she got back. She looked around the bar, full of happy holidaymakers, but he wasn't there. The pool, with its comfortable sunbeds and colourful umbrellas, was deserted. She walked down the path to the beach, where palm fronds swayed in the soft breeze, thinking he might still be lying in a deck-chair reading a book, but he wasn't there either. It was half-past six and she knew the sun would soon disappear in a short, tropical sunset. It would be pitch-black in half an hour. He must have gone up to our bed-room, she thought.

She got into the lift and pressed the button for the fourth floor. It had been an exhausting day. The conference had been long and complicated, with many tedious discussions in different languages. Guido had left early, letting Eva take care of most of the work. It would have been easier if Yves Dutronc had not been sitting opposite, glancing at her from time to time and smiling that cheeky little smile. It had been strangely difficult to concentrate.

Eva opened the door to their suite. It was cool, quiet and . . . empty. 'Dan?' she called. But there was no answer. As she put her briefcase on the floor beside the window, she spotted a piece of paper beside the phone on the small desk.

Darling,

I hope your conference is going well. Something amazing happened to me on the beach. I met an old friend from New York who is here on holiday with his wife. They are hiring a sailing boat and going on a trip to the some of the islands and they asked me to come along. I knew you'd be very busy for the next few days, so I accepted their kind invitation. I'll be back the day after tomorrow.

Love, Dan

She stared at the note. What had come over Dan? It wasn't like him to take off like this. He should have been here, waiting for her and ready to listen to her complaining about her hard day. What a bloody nerve, she thought. He was getting out of hand. Then why did she feel this curious sense of relief? Dan would be out of her hair for a while. She could concentrate on her work and then go to bed early. She could do with a bit of peace. She'd have a bath and then get something sent up from the kitchen. But first, a drink. She opened the minibar and poured herself a glass of champagne. Then she peeled off her dress and walked to the bathroom, leaving a trail of underwear and shoes.

The bathroom was huge and luxurious, with a bath the size of a small swimming pool. She walked across the cool tiles and turned on the taps. The huge marble tub slowly filled with warm water and she poured in some sea-green bath oil she had found on a shelf. This is heaven, Eva thought, as she sipped her champagne and sank into the fragrant water. She closed her eyes. She was nearly asleep when she heard a discreet ring beside her. Her eyes snapped open. She hadn't noticed the small phone on the wall just above the tub. The phone purred again.

'Hello?'

'Madame Connolly?' It was Yves Dutronc's unmistakable, sexy voice.

'*Oui?*'

'I'm so sorry to disturb you, but I have some bad news.'

Bad news? Eva thought. Jean-Claude Bonhomme

has recovered and Yves Dutronc is going back to Brussels?

'What is it?' she asked.

'The interpreters are on strike tomorrow.'

'Oh.' Eva didn't quite know what to say.

'All the meetings have been cancelled.'

'Right. I see.' Eva sat up in the bath.

'That means we have a day off tomorrow, so . . .'

'So?'

'So I was wondering if you and your husband would like to come on a sightseeing trip with me. The Guadeloupe countryside is so beautiful and there are so many things to look at. There's a volcano and a fort and even a museum or two. I thought I'd hire a car, you see. I could pick you both up tomorrow morning and . . .'

'Well,' Eva said, 'that sounds very nice, but . . .'

'But?'

'But my husband isn't here. He was invited on a sailing trip with some American friends and he won't be back until the day after tomorrow.'

'I see.' He paused. Eva could almost see him grinning like the big bad wolf. 'So your husband has gone sailing?'

'That's right. With some friends from New York.'

'And you're all alone?'

'Eh, yes.'

'How sad,' he purred. 'Such a beautiful woman all alone. I wonder what I could do about that?'

Eva smiled to herself, enjoying the sound of his voice. 'I don't know,' she mumbled.

'I suppose it would be improper of me to ask you

to come out with me alone?'

'Very.'

'I see. Nevertheless, Madame Connolly, would you like to accompany me on a sightseeing trip tomorrow?'

Eva hesitated. This flirtatious conversation was making her nervous. It wasn't fair to Dan and, apart from that, she knew the dangers of Commission staff getting involved with one another. But her reply was not at all what she had intended.

'All right,' she heard her voice say, 'that would be lovely.'

CHAPTER 6

Eva slowly opened her eyes and stretched. She leaned her back against the trunk of a coconut palm and surveyed the wide sweep of the beach. The fine white sand was as soft as talcum powder, the air was slightly perfumed by hibiscus and frangipani flowers and the blue-green water was crystal clear. A black frigate bird swooped down from the blue sky and dived into the sea. How strange to be here on this small island, when she had thought she was going to be driving around Guadeloupe, looking at points of interest. But Yves had surprised her.

'Slight change of plan,' he had announced as he picked her up in a taxi outside her hotel early that morning. Looking cool and relaxed, he was dressed in lightweight beige cotton shorts and a faded blue shirt. 'We're going a little further afield. Did you bring your swimsuit?'

'No. I mean, yes,' she replied, kicking herself for not having bought a new one in the hotel shop. All she had was an old navy swimsuit she had hastily stuffed into her suitcase before she left Brussels, thinking she would get very little time for leisure activities. It would have to do. At least her light-green sundress was new and she had washed her hair.

'Where are we going?' Eva asked, when she was sitting in the taxi after having retrieved her swimsuit, thinking she sounded like a child on an outing.

'It's a surprise,' he smiled.

The taxi had brought them to the airport and they had boarded a small private plane which had taken them to the nearby island of St Martin. The flight had been wonderful. Eva looked down at the azure sea, the coral reefs and small islands with great excitement. She spotted several yachts and smaller sailing boats.

'Maybe your husband is down there somewhere,' Yves suggested, but she didn't want to think of Dan.

They didn't speak much during the flight, except when Yves told Eva about St Martin, and how half the island was French and the other half Dutch. 'We're going to take a taxi to Orient Bay,' he said. 'On the French part of the island. It has a lovely beach and an underwater marine reserve with a coral reef that is great for snorkelling. But we'll have lunch first. The restaurant is very good.'

'Lunch first?' she protested. 'But it's not safe to swim right after eating.'

'You're very safety-conscious,' he remarked.

'What's wrong with that?'

'Nothing at all. And you're quite right. Swimming after a big lunch is not really a good idea. But in this case, it's quite all right. We'll just have something light for lunch. And snorkelling doesn't require a huge effort. It's not like deep-sea diving.'

The heat was stifling, but the terrace of the restaurant was reasonably cool. Eva mopped her brow with a napkin and studied the menu. She was rather hungry, but at the same time very hot. The thought of eating something warm was not very enticing.

'I think I'll help you choose,' Yves said, looking at her pink face. 'You need something to cool you down.'

He ordered chilled gazpacho that slipped down her throat, smooth and cool, followed by half a lobster and then a lemon sorbet.

'That was perfect,' she said, feeling much cooler. 'And that white wine was heaven.' She sighed.

'Very good,' he agreed, 'very good indeed.'

'This was a wonderful idea.'

'I always have wonderful ideas. I knew you'd like to just relax today and not bother with sightseeing.'

'You were right.'

He took her hand. 'I'm so glad Jean-Claude decided to take a nosedive down that hill. We wouldn't have met if he had taken the car that day.'

'A nosedive down a hill?' Eva asked incredulously, pulling her hand away.

'Well, we're not supposed to talk about it, but if you promise not to tell anyone . . .'

'I swear.' She laughed. 'What was he doing? Something dangerous?'

'For him, yes. He fell off his bike.'

'What?' she exclaimed. 'Was that all? But why was he cycling? I don't know him very well, but I have never heard that he was into fitness.'

Yves let go of her hand and took a sip of wine. 'Fitness had nothing to do with it. It was all the hold-ups. He was going to a party and was worried his car would be stolen.'

'But why didn't he take a taxi?'

'He had rung for one, but it never arrived. And he was going to a dinner where he was guest of honour, so he didn't want to be late. He got his son's bike out of the garage and just took off. But it was a racing bike and Jean-Claude couldn't figure out how to work the gears. He lost control of the bike and it just flew down this very steep hill. Then he collided with a van and, luckily, landed in the compost heap of a garden at the bottom of the hill.' Yves looked at Eva and shook his head. 'He fractured a rib and twisted his ankle.'

Eva suppressed a giggle. 'How awful.'

'I'm sure he wasn't laughing.' Yves looked at her disapprovingly. 'He was in a lot of pain.'

'I'm sorry,' Eva apologised. 'I didn't mean to make fun.' She fanned her face. 'It's very hot.'

'I know. And it's too soon to go swimming. But I have to make some phone calls. Why don't you have a little rest under the palm trees on the beach and then I'll take you snorkelling.'

'Lovely.' And she had wandered off to the beach and lain down on a sunbed under the gently swaying branches of a coconut palm.

Yves walked down the beach in the midday heat. He spotted Eva in the distance, her hands behind her head, looking dreamily out to sea. What a beautiful woman, he thought, even in that rather dreary swimsuit. Her blonde hair, her golden skin and long, toned limbs gave her an ageless beauty. He remembered taking her hand in the restaurant, how her skin had felt – like silk – and the little blonde hairs on her arms . . .

Eva was even more ambitious then he was, he knew that. She was known to be ruthless and unemotional. But he had seen another side of her today, a side that he was sure nobody in the Commission knew about. They wouldn't know about her sense of humour, her lovely laugh, her warmth or her slight nervousness, which had all added to his attraction to her. She had those qualities he always found hard to resist in a woman: intelligence, sensuality and style.

'What are thinking about?' Yves asked. 'You look worried.'

'Oh, nothing,' Eva replied. 'Just work. And it's very hot, even here under the palm trees.'

'It's time to do some snorkelling. Wait here. I'll go up to the hotel and get flippers and masks.'

When they arrived at the reef, Yves showed Eva how to breathe through the mouthpiece. 'It's very easy,' he said. 'Just wet your mask before you put it on and then put your head below water, float and look.'

Eva did as she was told and entered another world.

As she floated, she saw the coral reef clearly, covered in thousands of fish the colours of the rainbow. Yellow, blue, green and red, big and small, round and long. Schools of small yellow fish, groups of bright blue ones, others with little spikes, pointy fins, bulging eyes or long tentacles. It was the most beautiful sight. Sometimes the fish swam up to investigate, peering at her through the mask or even nibbling at her fingers. She felt she could float there for ever, weightless, lost in this soundless world of colour and light. But Yves tapped her on the shoulder and the spell was broken. She raised her head.

'Time to go,' he said, taking off his mask. 'It's nearly six o'clock.'

Eva couldn't believe it. They had been at the reef for over two hours. It seemed like only five minutes.

Eva would never forget that day. It was as if she'd been in some kind of paradise, where everything was perfect. The feel of the air, the white sand, the salt water too warm to bring relief from the heat but soft on her skin, the endless blue sky and the admiring eyes of Yves Dutronc all had a dreamlike quality. 'Thank you,' she said, sighing, 'thank you for this day.'

'Darling?' Dan pressed his ear to his mobile to hear better. 'Can you hear me?'

Crackle ... 'Yes,' Eva shouted. 'But it's a very bad connection. Where are you?'

'I'm just off St Lucia,' he shouted back. 'In the boat.'

'Oh, yes. Are you having a lovely time?'

'Well ... We're becalmed and ...'

'What's that shouting?'

'Oh, that?' Dan walked further up the deck of the boat. 'It's Pam and Bill, my friends, you know? They're just having a small disagreement.'

The shouting from the cabin below became louder.

Then there was a crash of broken china.

'What was that?' Eva asked.

'Something must have dropped in the galley,' Dan replied. 'But what about you? How's the conference going?'

Eva said something.

'What?' Dan demanded. 'I can't hear you.'

'– problems with – day – off.'

'What? A long day? I'm so sorry, sweetheart. You're working hard and here I am enjoying myself.' He winced as the shouting started again below deck. 'I shouldn't have gone off like that, I know, but when I bumped into Bill, it was such a surprise. I hadn't seen him for twenty years.'

'– of course,' Eva shouted. 'Are – having fun?'

'Yes, great fun,' Dan lied. 'But I think we'll be back a bit sooner than I –'

The connection broke. Dan looked at the phone and shook his head. He had barely been able to hear Eva. She had said something about an off day and problems. Poor thing, it must have been a hard day for her, having to work in this heat. He was looking forward to getting back.

When he had bumped into Bill, an old friend from his time in the UN in New York, Dan had been delighted. They had spent the whole morning chatting about old times. Bill's wife, Pam, a well preserved woman in her late forties, had joined them for lunch and, after rather a large amount of wine, she had suggested he come with them on a little trip in their hired boat. But it had not been the pleasure cruise he had envisaged. His hosts, when not fighting, made love ostentatiously in their cabin. Dan was beginning to feel very uncomfortable.

'Hi.'

Dan looked up as Bill's head popped up over the edge of the cabin door.

'Oh, hi. Is everything all right?'

'Yup,' Bill replied, handing Dan a can of beer. 'Everything's fine. You OK?'

'Great, but I'm afraid I'll have to get back to shore soon.'

'Why? Are you not enjoying the trip?'

'Oh, of course,' Dan reassured him. 'It's wonderful. But I just had a call from my wife. She has some kind of problem at work. She wants me to come back as soon as I can.'

'I'm sorry to hear that. Pam was just saying how much she enjoyed having you along.'

'She did?'

'Yeah, just now. But you're in luck, pal. She wants to go back as well.' Bill drained his beer can. 'The wind's picking up. I think we can have you back to the little woman by tonight, if you don't mind some night sailing.'

'Not at all.'

Eva switched off her phone and looked at Yves.

'Bad news?' he asked.

'No. It was my husband.'

'Oh? Is he enjoying his trip?'

'It didn't sound like it. And there were strange noises. People were shouting. And breaking things.'

'What was going on?'

'I don't know. It was a very bad connection.'

'Disturbance on the line maybe?'

'Could be.' Eva put the mobile into her canvas bag. They were on the terrace of the hotel, packed up and waiting for a taxi to take them to the airport.

'Monsieur Dutronc?' The head waiter of the restaurant called from the bar. 'Phone call for you.'

'Now what?' Yves asked, looking worried.

Eva waited as he took the call. 'Problems?' she asked when he came back.

'Yes.' Yves' face was serious. 'Eva, I know you're going to be upset when I tell you, but you have to believe that this is not my fault.'

'What is it? Tell me.'

'It's the plane.'

The happy look on Eva's face was suddenly replaced by worry.

'What's wrong with it?'

'There is nothing wrong with the plane. It's just that it's gone.'

'What do you mean, gone?'

'We were late and the pilot had a schedule to meet. He had to take off. He had a delivery to make on a neighbouring island and he had to make it or he would lose his job.'

'What?' Eva looked at him, confused. 'What are you talking about? Schedule? Didn't you rent that plane for the day?'

'Of course not. What do you think I am, a millionaire?'

'But . . .'

'The pilot is a friend of mine. The pilots are all

French here, you know. He told me he was making this trip today and asked if I wanted to come along. To spend the day here and go back with him this evening. And we would have made it, if it hadn't been so difficult to get you away from the reef. If we had just come back half an hour sooner . . .'

'So now it's my fault?' Eva snapped, beginning to feel angry.

'No, of course not.' Yves smiled at her reassuringly. 'But this might mean . . .'

'What?'

'That we'll have to stay the night.'

'God, no, I can't do that,' Eva protested. Shit, she thought, I should never have agreed to this mad excursion.

'What's the problem?' Yves' smile was just a touch too cheeky. 'Afraid of ruining your reputation?'

'It's not that,' Eva protested. 'It's just that if we stay here tonight, I'll have to wear the same clothes two days in a row.' Why did I say that? she thought. He'll think I'm such an idiot. 'I mean . . .'

Yves looked at her in disbelief. Then he started to laugh. 'Well, that *is* a very serious problem,' he chuckled.

'It is for me,' Eva said, and stuck out her chin.

They looked at each other for a moment. Then his expression changed and he suddenly grabbed her. 'What about this problem?' Yves kissed her hard on the mouth.

Dan hurried up the stairs. The lift was occupied and he had been too impatient to wait. He wanted to see Eva, to hold her and tell her all about his awful trip. 'They were the couple from hell,' he would tell her, and she would laugh at the awfulness of it all, the embarrassment and the pain. She would find it funny, he knew. They would laugh and joke and then fall into bed. He just couldn't wait to see her. He climbed the last flight with a little smile on his lips.

'Eva?' he called, as he entered the room. 'Darling, where are you?'

But the room was empty.

He turned around as the door of the suite slowly opened. 'Darling,' he exclaimed. 'Where have you been?'

Eva didn't reply. He noticed that she wasn't dressed for work, but was in her light-green sundress and sandals, and her face was flushed. She looked at him as if in a daze. 'What are you doing here?' she asked. 'I thought you wouldn't be back until tomorrow.'

'But I told you I'd be back sooner than that,' he protested. 'I just couldn't stand much more of Pam and Bill. They drove me crazy.'

'Oh.' Eva put her bag on the small sofa. 'Could you get me a drink? I'm so tired.'

'Of course.' He took a bottle of mineral water from the minibar.

'No, I need something stronger than that. Maybe a little brandy?'

'But you never drink . . .' Dan started, then looked at her face. 'All right. Of course.' He handed her the glass. 'What happened to you? Why are you here at this hour? Did the conference run late?'

'No,' she replied. 'There was no conference. I . . . I

went to the beach.'

'No conference? But what happened? Why –'

'Please, don't ask so many questions.' Eva drained her glass. 'I'm going to bed. I have an early start to-morrow.'

Eva couldn't sleep. She stared into the darkness as Dan breathed softly beside her and murmured something in his sleep. Poor Dan, she thought, he must have been so hurt. But she hadn't been able to face him, to look into his kind, concerned eyes and lie. And she was ashamed to admit that Yves' gorgeous smile came into her mind every time she closed her eyes. Her skin tingled when she remembered his touch and his hot kiss.

Eva had gasped when Yves had finally let her go. She was unable to speak and just stood there staring into his eyes. A nervous giggle rose in her throat. What was that I could feel? she almost asked. Did you forget to take the coat hanger out of your trou-sers, or were you just happy to see me?

Yves backed away as if he knew what she was thinking.

'Sorry,' he laughed, 'but you looked so sweet just then, so serious.'

'I am serious. We have to get back to Guadeloupe tonight.'

'I know. I was only joking when I said we'd have to stay the night.'

'Really?' Her eyebrows rose ironically.

'Well, you can't blame a man for trying. OK. I think that the best thing to do is to go to the airport.

It's not that late. There might be a commercial flight back to Guadeloupe.'

He was right. The evening flight to Guadeloupe was taking off an hour later. And there was room for both of them. But Yves hadn't brought his credit cards, so Eva had to pay for both their tickets.

'I must say this is really miserable,' Eva remarked sarcastically. 'First you lure me on a mad trip to this island, and then you nearly get us stranded here for the night. And now you make me pay to get us back. Talk about a dream date.'

'But I paid for lunch,' he protested. 'That's why I have no money left.'

'You mean you only brought enough for lunch? What a cheapskate.'

'My mother taught me to be careful with money.'

'She would be very proud if she could see you now.'

'I'm afraid I can't seat you together,' the ground hostess said. 'I have very few seats left.'

'Perfect,' Eva replied. 'As far apart as possible.' She took her boarding pass and went to find somewhere to sit in the departure lounge while she waited to board.

'Eva?' Yves sat down beside her.

'What?' she demanded.

'Don't be mad.'

'I'm not. I'm just ...' She didn't know what to say to him. She was so confused. Why did she find him so sexy? Probably because he was French. Everything sounded so romantic in French, even a grocery list. If Yves had been German or English or Dutch, he would have been a lot easier to resist. But he was sexy, aggressive, totally amoral and ... French. She had to stop him.

'You have to understand,' she continued, her voice prim. 'From now on, our relationship must be totally professional and nothing else. You know that. And any talk of love or friendship is absolutely –'

'*Verboten?*' he teased, gently pulling a strand of her hair.

Eva turned in the bed as she remembered. I shouldn't have let it happen, she thought. I shouldn't have let him kiss me. But that had been all. Just a kiss. What was the harm in that? a little voice asked. It wasn't the kiss, she told herself sternly, and turned again in the bed, it was the way you felt, the way you nearly stopped breathing and your knees felt like jelly. Dan never grabbed her like that, never bruised her mouth with his kisses. He was gentle and sweet, which was why she had been attracted to him in the first place. She had loved the way he touched her then, his soothing caress. And he was so dependable and strong. He was her anchor.

'Wake up, darling.'

Eva's eyes snapped open. She looked guiltily at Dan, who was standing by the bed with a breakfast tray. 'What?' she murmured. 'Breakfast. How nice.'

'You looked so sweet there, I didn't really want to wake you,' he said. 'You had this lovely smile in your sleep. Were you dreaming something nice?'

'I can't really remember,' she lied, feeling her face going pink.

'There was a phone call for you just now.'

'Oh?' Eva suddenly sat up in the bed, making the breakfast tray tilt at a dangerous angle. 'Who was it?'

'Careful, darling,' Dan said, straightening the tray. 'It was Guido. He said the conference is not restarting until eleven.'

'What time is it now?'

'Half-past nine.'

'Oh, great.' Eva stretched her arms over her head. 'I can relax for a bit, then. Was that all he said?'

'No, he also said that Jean-Claude Bonhomme called from Brussels. He's in a bit of a snot, it seems.'

'What? Jean-Claude Bonhomme? But I thought he was in hospital.'

'He seems to have made a miracle recovery. Guido said he was barking at everyone and snapping at his staff. His deputy seems to be in deep shit about something.'

'His deputy?' Eva felt suddenly dizzy. She knew she sounded like a record that had become stuck in a groove, repeating everything Dan said.

'Yeah, that Jaques Dufrond, or something . . .'

'Yves Dutronc.'

'That's it. Do you know him?'

'Slightly,' Eva replied airily. 'What's he done?'

'He disappeared to another island with some tart and was unavailable all day yesterday. There was no one to take the call. Bonhomme's absolutely furious and is threatening to fire Dufour and –'

'Dutronc,' Eva corrected, her face pale.

'He's in a lot of trouble, whatever his name is,' Dan declared.

'Oh, God, how awful.'

'Well,' Dan said laughing, 'as the French say, *Cherchez la femme*.'

CHAPTER 7

'Goodbye, then, Louise. Talk to you soon.' Eva smiled as she hung up. Everything was suddenly perfect, both on the family front and at work. The summer was looking great.

Ever since her return from the Caribbean, she had been on a high. The flirtation with Yves, her networking at the Commission, keeping Dan happy and staying in touch with the girls resembled some sort of very challenging circus act. She was like a juggler, keeping several balls in the air, trying to keep an eye on them all. She didn't sleep much, worked out a lot to release the tension and drank maybe just a little more than usual. But the excitement made her tingle all over and she needed to have a drink now and then, she told herself, to calm down.

The last days of the conference had been nerve-racking to say the least. Yves looked very worried for a while, but seemed to regain his composure and his big grin by the end of the next day. She had tried not to look at him, but it was very difficult. He was always glancing at her from across the room and sending her little notes.

Ma petite Eve, his first note said, *I am so sorry if you were upset about what happened, but I will never forget it.* The next day, she received two more. But she tore them up without reading them. The last afternoon, when the conference was nearly over, and the more important people were all gathered to say goodbye, Eva found another note on top of her documents. She looked across at Yves and slowly tore it up. He looked a little shocked, but then just shrugged and turned away. There, she thought, that's fixed him. With a small pang of regret, she started to put away her papers.

The trip back had been uneventful. Eva slept most of the way, exhausted by everything that had happened. Then they had a very quiet weekend, catching up and reading the papers. Eva saw Yves at meetings, but they never had an opportunity to talk. He never phoned or tried to contact her, which made her feel both relieved and disappointed.

The warm spring weather in Brussels was wonderful for golf, so Dan spent most of his spare time at the club, leaving Eva to work hard and plan her next career move.

She was also trying to think of a way to get Maria and Mark together in a romantic setting. She still felt they would make the perfect couple, and wouldn't it be very useful to have someone in the family with connections in the media?

There were few parties, as the EU prepared for the many meetings and councils that would mark the end of the season before the holidays in August. Eva and

Dan usually spent a few weeks in Ireland, where they stayed with his brother, who owned a house near the golf club in Lahinch. She wasn't very good at golf, but usually had a go, more to please Dan than herself. She felt he deserved to be indulged, after having been so supportive during the working year in Brussels. At the end of the summer they usually went to Tuscany for two weeks.

But not this year.

Eva was going through her wardrobe one morning in June, to see what she needed to buy for the summer, when she got the phone call that would change her entire summer and the course of so many lives.

'Hello?' she muttered into the phone, as she flipped through the clothes.

'Eva, *Liebling!*'

'*Ja? Wer ist das?*'

'It's me, Dieter, your brother.'

'Oh, Dieter,' Eva sighed. 'Hello.' She wasn't too fond of her brother. He was so *irritating*, somehow. It was irritating that he had no style or class and that he had married a woman who could only be described as common. It was also irritating that he had made a huge amount of money selling shoes. Not designer shoes, but cheap shoes most people wouldn't want to be seen dead in.

'How are you?' Dieter asked.

'Fine, just fine.'

'And Dan and the girls?'

'They're fine too. How are you?'

'I'm very well. And Gretchen is in great shape as usual.'

'I'm so glad.'

'The reason I'm calling is that we're going to America in August.'

'You are?'

'Yes. And Gretchen suggested I call you to ask –'

'Not those dogs,' Eva snapped. 'I'm not looking after those horrible poodles again!'

'Even if they're at the villa?' Dieter's voice was as smooth as silk.

'You mean the one in St Tropez?'

'That's the only villa I own. For the moment,' he added.

'Well, I . . .'

Eva was tempted. But no, she would rather die than do Gretchen a favour. That bitch, she thought, that awful tart who never bothered to invite us even for a weekend. And now they come crawling to me because it suits them. Well, I'm just going to tell them what they can do with their bloody villa.

'OK, then,' she said. 'But only if I can have the house for the whole month and invite whomever I like. And I want the pool looked after. And a maid.'

'Of course.'

'The whole month of August? You're not going to be there?'

'Except for a few days. There's a convention I have to go to. But I'll just stay a few nights and then I'm off again.'

'OK. Fine.' She tried to sound cool, while she was doing cartwheels in her mind. Yes, she thought, a whole month in the south of France. Yes, yes, YES!!!

'Good. I'll tell Gretchen the good news. I'm sure

Louise and Maria will enjoy a holiday in St Tropez.'

'And we'll have a guest,' Eva added.

'Oh?'

'Louise has a boyfriend.'

'Doesn't she always?' Dieter laughed. 'She's had boyfriends since she was ten.'

'No, but this time it's a bit more serious than that. This one wants to marry her.'

'I wish him luck. I always thought she'd be marrying late. What's he like?'

'Lovely. A very nice man and a successful businessman.'

'I like the sound of that. I'm looking forward to meeting him when I come for the convention. And I'll phone you later to make arrangements for the dogs. Talk to you soon. *Auf Wiedersehen, liebe Eva.*'

'*Auf Wie ...*' She stopped. 'Convention? What convention?'

But he had already hung up.

Louise and Maria were discussing men over breakfast.

'Why is everybody so determined to get Mark and me together?' Maria moaned. 'I wish you'd lay off. Mark's a very nice guy, but he really isn't my type.'

'What *is* your type?' Louise asked.

Maria thought for a moment. My type, she thought, what is it? She wasn't really attracted to any particular kind of man. She just seemed to fall in love and then ... disaster, most of the time.

'I don't know,' she said. 'He just has to be sexy, that's all. And fairly good-looking. Tall, with a good sense of humour. Intelligent as well, I suppose. That's it really.'

'That's it really,' Louise mimicked. 'You don't ask for much. Just Mr Perfect.'

'But that's what you've got, isn't it? Don't tell me you're having problems.'

'Well . . .' Louise pouted. 'It's just that he wants me to move in with him.'

'And you don't?'

'No. I don't want to change anything. We're having such a great time together. And I'm free to do my own thing as well. Everything's perfect . . .'

'From your point of view,' Maria cut in.

'Well, yes. And . . .' Louise looked a little ashamed. 'I have to admit that I love it when he chases me.'

'I know what you mean. You always like to make them beg. But is that fair? I mean, he's so serious about you. And he bought you a ring and everything.'

'Yes, but I never said I'd wear it.'

'Speaking of which, you never showed it to me.'

'It's lovely,' Louise said, with a sad look in her eyes, 'but it feels like a ball and chain when I put it on.'

'Come on, get it,' Maria urged. 'I want to see it.'

'Oh, all right, then,' Louise said, and got up from her chair, 'but I know what you're going to say.'

Maria looked at the ring on its bed of dark blue velvet. 'Oooh,' she whispered, 'it's exquisite. I love aquamarines and this one . . .'

'It's antique.'

'It's heaven.'

Louise saw the wistful look in Maria's eyes and sighed. 'I knew you'd love it.'

'Can I try it on?'

'Of course. It will probably fit you. It's a little tight for me. I was going to have it enlarged, but ...'

The ring was on Maria's finger. She held out her hand and admired it. 'Fantastic. You should wear it, you know.'

'I can't,' Louise mumbled, 'I just can't. Maybe later on. When I'm sure.'

'You're so silly,' Maria said, handing the ring back to Louise. 'You don't know how lucky you are. That nice man and he bought you this stunning ring.'

'I hate the bloody thing,' Louise exclaimed, and snapped the box shut. 'It scares me.'

'But then you shouldn't lead him on, if you don't really love him the way he loves you.'

'Maybe not. But I do love him in my own way. I don't want to lose him. But he says he needs me. That's what I find hard to cope with, to be honest.'

'Because he wants you there, cooking and looking after him?'

'Yes, I suppose.'

'Tell him to go back to his mother, then.'

'He can't. She's got a job as a travel agent and has moved to Spain. She's having a great time and has met a man who's twenty years younger than her.'

'Well, good for her.'

'That's what I said. But he didn't seem to agree. He said she's too old to behave like that.'

'But you're never too old to be happy,' Maria argued.

The telephone rang.

'You get it,' Maria ordered. 'I have to go to work.'

'But what if it's Paul?'

'Don't answer it, then.'

Maria gathered up her handbag and her jacket and left.

Louise slowly walked to the phone, willing it to stop ringing. What am I going to say? she thought.

But it wasn't Paul, it was Eva.

'I have some very good news,' she heard her step-mother say. She sounded very happy. Now, that was a change. And her news was even more astonishing. Louise listened in amazement as Eva explained, and started to pack her suitcase for St Tropez in her imagination. How marvellous. She couldn't wait to tell Paul. And Maria. She would be so excited. What a summer they'd have.

'We're all going to the south of France,' Louise sang, coming into the living room a few days later.

'You and Paul?' Maria asked. She had just come home after a long day at the office and was relaxing on the sofa with the evening paper. 'When are you going?'

'August. Wait till you hear this! Eva and Daddy are spending the whole month in Dieter's villa. Can you believe it?'

'What? Dieter and Gretchen have invited Eva to spend the holidays with them? What's happened? Last time I met Gretchen she said she would never let Eva inside the door again. Has she had some sort of breakdown?'

'It's the poodles,' Louise explained. 'Dieter and Gretchen are going to America, and they have no one to look after the dogs. They must have known that the only way to get Eva to babysit their darlings was to let her have the house.'

'With the dogs.'

'Yes. Eva's minding the doggies, but she's getting a month's holiday in that beautiful villa as well. She just couldn't resist.'

'Who could?' Maria put down her cup. 'When did you hear about this?'

'Last Monday. I was dying to tell you, but I haven't seen you all week.'

'Has Eva invited you and Paul?'

'And you. She said to tell you to take your holidays in August.'

'That's some nerve,' Maria protested. 'Does she think I'm just going to come when she snaps her fingers? I might not want to go. I was planning to go to Kerry in August. A girl at the office asked me to go camping with her and two of her friends.'

'Camping,' Louise snorted, 'in Kerry? Give me a break!'

'What's wrong with that? It's beautiful there.'

'And wet and cold. I can't believe you would spend your holiday in a tent on the side of a hill in Kerry rather than going to the south of France.'

'Anything to avoid Eva.'

'You'll change your mind when I show you the photos she sent,' Louise argued. 'It's a gorgeous place overlooking the sea. With a pool and tennis court. And the bedrooms are divine. All with their own bathrooms.'

'And Eva and two huge white poodles.'

'So what? I can put up with that. Ah, come on, Maria, it'll be great,' Louise pleaded. 'Think of the fun we'll have, the men we – I mean you'll meet. The sun, the beach, the food.'

'Mmmm,' Maria said, looking thoughtful. 'You might just have talked me into it.'

'Isn't it strange how the French always manage to get weather like this for their parties?' Eva muttered to Dan as they stood in line at the French embassy with hundreds of other people, waiting to greet the ambassador. 'What is it about the French? It never seems to rain on them.'

'You're right,' Dan agreed into her ear. 'They have everything. The best wines, the best food, the best countryside, the best –'

'God, it's so hot,' Eva interrupted, 'and being squeezed up against everybody in this queue doesn't help.'

'I couldn't agree with you more,' remarked a plump woman ahead of her. 'Why do they have to chat for so long with everyone?'

Eva looked ahead to the top of the long line, where the French ambassador and his wife were shaking hands and talking to each guest. She looked longingly beyond him into the huge shady garden, where cold drinks were being served. She could see the trees swaying in the breeze and yearned for its cool touch. She was wearing a new Italian pink linen suit and knew she looked her very best, but it wouldn't last if she had to stay where she was much longer. She fanned her face with the big invitation card and tried to relax her shoulders. July was always a very stressful month in Brussels and this year it was worse than ever. But the prospect of the month of August in the south of France cheered her up and kept her going.

Everything was working out the way she had planned. Both Louise and Maria had accepted her invitation and, of course, Paul. Eva had tried to invite Mark White, but he had told her he had already accepted an invitation to his cousin's villa nearby. That was almost better, she thought, otherwise Maria might still think she had been set up. I'm not even going to tell her he'll be there.

It would be the perfect holiday, apart from the poodles, of course. She had been so annoyed about having to look after them, until she had the brilliant idea of bringing Fernando for that purpose. He could look after the dogs: walk them morning and evening (very early and very late, far away from the villa), feed them and brush them and put them to bed. They would be kept in the shed at the bottom of the garden and not be seen. Gretchen would never know.

They inched slowly forward. Dan squeezed Eva's waist. 'It's very romantic being so close to you,' he muttered into her hair. 'But I'll be in trouble if this lasts much longer. I might have to pull you into the bushes.'

'Please,' she protested, pulling away. 'Stop. It's too hot.' His hands were clammy on her waist and she was beginning to feel more than a little claustrophobic.

Dan blew on the back of her neck. 'Are you all right?' he asked. 'Maybe you could sneak into the garden? I'll tell the ambassador you were feeling a little dizzy and had to get some air.'

'No, that would be impolite.' Eva hated the idea of behaving incorrectly and she liked showing any sign of weakness even less.

'Don't be silly,' Dan argued. 'Nobody would mind. You can explain to the ambassador later. I'm sure he won't think you're being rude. He's a little strange himself at times.'

'I know, but ...'

'Oh, go on, darling,' Dan urged. 'I can see you're beginning to melt. And I just saw the German Minister for Justice going into the garden. You could try to bump into him and have that informal chat you were talking about.'

Eva looked along the line again. There were more than twenty people ahead of them. It would take nearly half an hour to get to the ambassador. And she knew Dan was right about the minister. It would be the perfect opportunity. 'OK,' she mumbled, 'if you're sure.'

'Absolutely,' Dan assured her. 'Off you go. I'll see you later.'

Eva gratefully left the hall and went around the side of the building. She enjoyed the cool wind under the big trees and was looking forward to an ice-cold drink. Then she saw him. He came toward her, walking slowly with a drink in his hand.

'Eva.'

She stopped, not knowing what to say. 'Yves. Hello,' she finally managed.

'You look lovely, all pink and summery.'

'Well, I ...'

'I haven't seen you for a long time. Not since ...' He stopped. 'Well, you know what I mean.'

'Yes.'

'I hear you're going to the south of France in August,' he said.

'That's right.'

'What a coincidence. So am I.'

'Oh? I didn't know.'

'There's a lot of things you don't know about me.'

'But the south of France is quite a large area, maybe we won't be anywhere near you.'

'I'll be in St Tropez. I have a flat there, right in the middle of town.'

He would, she thought.

'You must come and see it. It has a terrace over-looking the harbour. We could admire the sunset over the mountains together.'

'I don't think that will be possible,' she replied rather stiffly.

'Why not?' His hazel eyes smiled into hers. 'We could have a lot of fun.'

'Not the kind you mean,' Eva said, regaining her composure.

'But it will be so lovely, *mon amour*,' he mumbled, taking her hand, 'so romantic. You and me on the Côte d'Azur ...'

'Thank God that's over,' Dan remarked as he took off his tie later that evening.

'I know,' Eva agreed, hanging her dress in the bed-room cupboard. 'But it wasn't too bad.'

'A bit long though,' Dan remarked.

'I know. But I had to wait to talk to the minister. We had a very interesting chat.'

'So you're pleased, then?'

'I think things are going to work out,' Eva replied. 'But a lot can still happen, of course.'

'Those waiters were a little strange,' Dan remarked. 'What were they, Italian?'

'French, of course,' Eva replied. 'Why did you think they were Italian?'

'The looked like hit men in a gangster movie.'

'No, they didn't. They were very classy.'

'Classy?'

'As in class, elegance.' She sighed. 'You just don't know continental chic when you see it.'

'I thought they looked like thugs.'

'That's the style nowadays,' Eva explained. 'Shaved heads and designer stubble is the height of fashion. But you don't ever seem to notice the latest trends.'

'Call me stick-in-the-mud, but that kind of fashion is not very attractive.'

'Wait till you get to St Tropez,' Eva warned. 'That's where you'll see the ultimate in trendy.'

'I didn't think they wore any clothes there!' Dan laughed.

'That's the beach. In town it's a different story. But I'll have to give you a crash course in how to dress, so you won't embarrass me,' Eva teased.

'But I already know the basics,' Dan protested. 'No socks with sandals.'

'No sandals at all,' Eva corrected, 'if you want to walk around with me, that is.'

'I'll try to remember,' Dan promised. 'I saw you

talking to that Frenchman,' he remarked.

'Which one?' Eva laughed. 'It was the French embassy. The place was full of them.'

'That deputy at the legal department. We met him in Guadeloupe.'

'Oh, *that* Frenchman,' Eva said airily.

'You seemed to be discussing something very important.'

'Were we? I can't really remember.' Eva took off her earrings and put them in her jewellery box.

It had been strange to meet Yves again face to face. She had tried to be cool and distant, but it was difficult when he was so annoyingly attractive.

'. . . ran into the Commissioner.' Dan's voice cut into her daydream.

'Who?' Eva asked, confused. 'Where? Which Commissioner?'

'You really are tired. Sean Dogherty. I ran into him tonight, at the party.'

'Oh, I see,' Eva mumbled.

'And guess what?'

'He's going to St Tropez as well?' Eva said. 'I can't think of a single person who isn't.'

'Not Sean Dogherty. That's what I was trying to tell you. *He* is going to Clonakilty.'

CHAPTER 8

The villa was pink and built in the traditional Provençal style. The midday heat was stifling, but the lofty hall and big airy rooms downstairs were cool, as was the large bedroom with adjoining bathroom to which a cheerful Moroccan girl brought Maria.

The house was called Les Cygales and stood at the end of a long drive in the middle of a beautiful garden, where the crickets, which gave it its name, sang their summer song, big umbrella pines scented the air, gnarled old olive trees shaded the terrace and bougainvillaea bloomed, cascading over the walls. The deep blue water of the huge pool, further down the garden, glittered invitingly. Paul and Louise, who had arrived in Paul's Porsche the night before, were sharing a bedroom at the other end of the house and Dan and Eva were in the master bedroom above the terrace.

'This makes having Eva as a stepmother nearly bearable,' Louise said as she lay down on the sunbed next to Maria.

'I know,' Maria smiled, without opening her eyes.

'I mean, if this becomes a habit,' Louise continued, 'we might even be grateful to Daddy for marrying her.'

'I wouldn't go that far,' Maria grunted. 'Where's Paul?'

'He's on the phone. There was a call from his office. But he'll be down later. He wants to play tennis, but I don't know if I'll be able to in this heat.'

Eva was standing on the terrace, looking out over the garden. She saw Maria by the pool and Dan walking down the garden path to collect the post, dressed in shorts and a big panama hat. Paul and Louise were playing tennis. Fernando was coming up the hill with the poodles on a lead, and Fatima, the Moroccan maid, was hanging out the washing behind the garden shed. Only the *chirp, chirp* of the crickets and the occasional soft *plop* of the tennis balls broke the quiet. Everything seemed so calm and peaceful, as if the whole world was on holiday. Eva felt, for the first time in months, quite content. The week before they left had been hectic. There were several very long meetings which required extensive reports, and then they had spent days packing before closing the house for the month and driving to Provence, where Fernando was already installed with the poodles.

It had taken Eva nearly a week to get the house in order. All of Dieter's so-called 'art' had to be removed and stacked in the basement, to be replaced with framed prints she found in an art shop in St Tropez, and Gretchen's taste in colours and ornaments dealt with. The plastic garden furniture was removed and replaced by teak, the colourful umbrellas taken down and white ones put in their place, and white cotton throws were now covering the sofas and chairs in the living room. Eva finally felt that the house was acceptable. Dan complained that they had spent enough money for two weeks in the Bahamas, but she ignored him. They couldn't live for a month in the middle of kitsch and ersatz, what would people think?

'What are you doing?' Dan was coming around the house with the post.

Eva gave a start. 'Oh,' she said. 'Just daydreaming.'

'Where's Fernando? There's a letter for him.'

'He's just come back from the supermarket. I have to cook tonight, because he is working as a waiter in St Tropez.'

'Why is that?' Dan asked. 'I thought he was busy with the dogs.'

'Not that busy. And I thought I'd let him earn some extra money while we're here. I don't really need him all the time. He's going somewhere really posh tonight, he said.'

'I see.'

'Anything else in the post?'

'Nothing much. A postcard to the poodles from Dieter and Gretchen.'

'Are they having a good time in America?'

'I don't know,' Dan smiled. 'I never read other people's post.'

'How are you going to find out anything if you don't?' Eva asked and grabbed the card. 'Look they're in California.' *Liebe Elvis und Marilyn,* she read. *How are Mummy's darlings?* 'Yuck,' Eva said. 'I can't believe they write to their dogs.' *We're having a lovely time, but we miss you very much. We hope Auntie Eva is looking after you. Big kisses from Mutti and Papa.* 'It's enough to put you off your dinner.'

'What do you think they'd say if they knew Auntie Eva keeps their darlings in the garden shed?' Dan asked.

'What they don't know won't hurt them,' Eva said.

Maria was swimming. Swimming in the blue sea. Swimming, swimming, the water cool and silky on her hot skin. She ducked her head into the waves and took long, strong strokes. Her whole body was working: her legs, shoulders and arms. She lifted her head and inhaled, then exhaled into the water, enjoying the sound. She turned on her back and floated, looking up at the sky. A few small clouds were gliding around up there and a lone seagull sailed idly over her head. She could see the vapour trail of a jet plane higher up and wondered where it was going.

It was late in the afternoon and the worst of the midday heat was beginning to ease. She had spent the morning reading by the pool, then lunched on the terrace with Eva and her father, Louise and Paul. After lunch, it had been too hot to do anything else but snooze in her room, and then she had decided to go for a long swim in the sea. Paul and Louise were in the pool, fooling around, laughing and kissing. Maria silently left by the small back gate that brought her onto the shady path to the beach.

As she floated, she looked at a huge white villa,

built in the Italianate style, quite unlike Les Cygales. It sat on a lawn stretching down to its own private beach. A maid was opening the shutters on the ground floor and a manservant in a white jacket was setting up a drinks table on the terrace. It looked like a set from a movie: *To Catch a Thief* or *High Society*. Maria half expected Grace Kelly to come out dressed in white tulle, wearing a huge hat.

She turned and swam slowly around the headland, back to the public beach.

'Hello.' Maria looked around as she dried her hair.

A small blonde girl was standing on the beach, staring at her.

'Hello,' Maria replied. 'Who are you?'

'My name is Edwina,' the little girl replied. 'I live there.' She pointed up at the villa.

'What are you doing here on the public beach, then?' Maria asked. 'I mean, you have your own beach, don't you?'

'Yes, but there's no one there. And my nanny wanted to be on this beach because she was bored. She said if she didn't speak to someone under the age of forty soon, she'd scream.' The little girl sat down beside Maria. 'What's your name?'

'Maria.'

'How old are you?'

'Twenty-nine,' Maria replied.

'Is that old?'

'Very. How old are you?'

'Six,' Edwina replied. 'Are you married? Have you any children my age? Why don't you wear a bikini?

Do you like swimming?'

'Slow down. That's a lot of questions at once. But I'll try to answer. No, no, swimsuits are better for swimming and I love it. OK?'

'OK. I like you. You're much nicer than my nanny. She's like flypaper, my daddy says. But I don't know what he meant. She doesn't look a bit like flypaper.'

'Where is your nanny?' Maria asked.

'Over there.' Edwina pointed at a well-endowed young girl in a very small bikini surrounded by a group of young men. 'That girl on the pink towel.'

'I see,' Maria mumbled. 'Your daddy's quite observant.'

'He calls me his little tartlet.'

Maria laughed. 'What does he call your mummy?'

'Sweetheart.' Edwina drew breath. 'Do you have a boyfriend?'

'Not at the moment.'

'Edwina!' a voice called. 'We have to go back.' The nanny had shooed her admirers away, gathered up the pink towel and was walking towards them.

'OK.' Edwina made a face. 'I have to go now. They're having a party, so I have to have my supper early.'

'I see,' Maria replied. 'Well, it was very nice to meet you, Edwina.'

'Very nice to meet *you*,' Edwina replied. 'Will you come back tomorrow?'

'Yes, why not?'

'Edwina!' the nanny called, standing at the bottom of the steps leading up to the villa.

'I'm coming.' Edwina smiled at Maria. 'See you tomorrow.'

'This is very interesting,' Dan said from behind *Nice Matin*, at breakfast on the terrace the following morning. 'There's a story here about all the well-paid Eurocrats spending their holidays in St Tropez.'

'Oh, really?' Eva looked up from her shopping list.

'Yes. And there are photos. There's one of Jean-Claude Bonhomme with his wife at the market. And look, Guido. I didn't know he was here.'

'He's staying at the Byblos,' Eva said. 'He told me he would be here for ten days. Then he's going to his castle in Tuscany.'

'Some of your countrymen are here too, it seems.'

'Really? Who?'

'The Minister for Foreign Affairs. And your Commissioner. Gunther something.'

'Oh, yes, Gunther Schmidt. Do you want anything from the supermarket? I'm sending Fernando shopping when he comes back from walking the dogs.'

'No, I don't think I need anything. Where's everybody else?'

'Maria is down by the pool. I don't think the others are up yet.'

'But this is the best part of the day,' Dan remarked. 'It's still cool and that breeze from the sea is so lovely.' He turned the page. 'My God!' he exclaimed. 'Wait till you hear this.'

'Milk, butter,' Eva muttered over her list. 'What?'

'Someone had their car stolen yesterday.'

'So? That must be happening several times a day

around here.'

'No, but it's the way it happened,' Dan said. 'The chauffeur was held up outside a house where there was a party. Exactly like in Brussels. Isn't that weird?'

Eva looked thoughtfully at Dan. 'That *is* rather strange. Who was it?'

Dan consulted his paper. 'The car belonged to a French government minister. It all happened at a villa not far from here. It's called Le Mirage. The French police say they have a lead.'

'That's more than the Belgians managed,' Eva remarked. 'But what I don't understand is why they picked out that particular car. St Tropez is full of luxury cars.'

'But don't you see,' Dan argued. 'These cars that they steal are brand new. That's the whole point. That's what it says here anyway.'

'And Sean Dogherty's car was brand new,' Eva added.

'Exactly. So someone must be able to get the information as soon as the cars are delivered. They probably hack into the computers of the sales rooms.'

'That's very clever.'

'You're telling me. I wonder if they have arrested anyone yet?'

The phone rang in the living room.

'Hello?'

'Madame?' Fernando's voice was shaking slightly.

'Yes. What are you doing? Why aren't you walking the dogs?'

'I was, madame.'

'You were,' Eva repeated, mystified. 'And what are

you doing now?'

'I'm on the telephone, madame.'

'Yes, of course you are,' she snapped. 'But why? Where are you?'

'At the police station in St Tropez,' Fernando whispered.

'What? Please, Fernando, could you explain what you are doing there and what's going on. Take it slowly.'

'I've been arrested.'

CHAPTER 9

The car swept down the road, taking the sharp bends dangerously close to the edge.

'Can't you go faster?' Eva urged.

'No, darling, I can't,' Dan replied, clutching the steering wheel harder. 'This is as fast as I'm allowed to go. You don't want *us* to end up in gaol as well?'

'Oh, God,' Eva moaned, wringing her hands. 'I can't believe they've arrested Fernando. He couldn't possibly have anything to do with the car thefts.'

'He's too honest,' Dan agreed.

'No, he's too stupid. Nobody would be mad enough to involve him in anything illegal.'

'I'm sure it will all turn out to be a mistake.'

'But what if it's not?' Eva demanded. 'What if Fernando is really involved with the gang? Imagine the implications for me.'

'Yes,' Dan agreed, his voice concerned. 'For both of us. It will be very embarrassing. We might even be accused of harbouring a criminal.' He shook his head. 'No. It's unbelievable. You'll see, it'll be all right. We'll be laughing about it tonight.'

'I hope you're right,' Eva sighed. 'But the French police are so scary. They are not going to want to admit to having arrested the wrong man. It would make them look very silly.'

'Maybe we need a lawyer?'

'We might,' Eva agreed. 'But who? We don't know any lawyers around here. But let's just see what's going on first. We're nearly in St Tropez. Do you know where the *gendarmerie* is?'

'Yes. It's not far from here.'

Eva nervously brushed her hair and straightened her dress. She would need to be cool and assertive to deal with this. The French police did not take kindly to hysteria.

'Good morning,' she said, and beamed a friendly smile at the officer on duty, a very elegant young man in an impeccable uniform.

'*Oui, madame?*' He didn't return her smile.

'My name is Eva Connolly. You seem to have my *maître d'hôtel* in custody. Fernando Castor?'

'That's right. We're holding him for . . .'

'I know.' Eva smiled conspiratorially 'You seem to think he's some kind of criminal. But poor Fernando couldn't possibly have done anything wrong. He's a bit . . .' She pointed at her head. 'Not all there, you know.'

'*Débile*, you mean?' the officer asked, not a flicker of emotion in his face.

'Something like that. So I think it might be best for you to release him into our care. My husband and I will deal with him.' Eva looked around for Dan to give her some support, but he was engrossed in the photographs of wanted criminals on the far wall.

'Madame,' the young man continued, 'am I to believe that you have a butler who is some sort of mental case?'

'Well, not really,' Eva replied. 'Just a little ... special, you know.'

'There are an awful lot of criminals on the loose in France,' Dan interrupted, peering at a photograph of a bearded man. 'Look at this one. I wouldn't want to meet him in a dark alley.'

'Stop that and come here,' Eva snapped. 'Could you please explain to the officer that Fernando is totally innocent.'

Dan joined Eva at the desk. 'That's right,' he nodded. 'Fernando is as honest as the day is long.'

'And we can't manage without him,' Eva added. 'So we would really appreciate it if you would release him, and we'll forget all about this.'

'How do you mean, madame?' the officer asked.

'Well,' Eva said, smiling, 'it was only a tiny mistake on your part, and you're doing such a good job in every other area ...'

'Mistake?' A frown crossed the gendarme's handsome, tanned face. 'There was no mistake, I can assure you. He was caught *en flagrant délit*.'

'Red-handed?' Eva gasped. 'I don't believe you. It's not possible!'

Dan put his hand on Eva's arm. 'Calm down, darling. Let's find out exactly what happened.' He looked at the officer. 'Now, monsieur –' Dan peered at the name-plate on the desk – 'Bernard. What was Fernando doing exactly?'

'He was caught breaking the law. On the beach. In front of several witnesses.'

'Oh, no,' Eva moaned. It suddenly seemed very hot in the *gendarmerie*. Beads of perspiration broke out on her forehead and she felt the beginnings of a headache. She leaned closer to the officer. 'Listen, Monsieur Bernard. Fernando is totally harmless. I'm sure it was just the heat. He's not normally sexually active and he has never done anything ...'

'I don't know what you mean, madame. Your butler was caught walking two dogs on the beach. That is against the law here. He'll have to pay a fine or go to prison for three months. Take your pick.'

'Oh,' Eva almost shouted. 'Is that all?'

Dan started to laugh. 'That's ridiculous. I mean, we thought ... Just walking the dogs. Ha, ha.'

Officer Bernard did not join in the laughter. 'It's a serious offence here, you know. Very serious.'

'But I'm sure he didn't realise,' Eva said.

'There are big signs everywhere. Your butler might be a little foolish, but he does not appear to be blind.'

Dan took out his wallet. 'Let's settle this and get out of here. I assume you can just let Fernando go if I pay the fine.'

'Of course. And the dogs.'

'Good. So, how much do I owe you?'

'A thousand euros,' Officer Bernard replied.

'What?' Eva exclaimed. 'That's extortion!'

'It's meant to discourage people from walking their dogs on the beach, madame,' Officer Bernard explained. 'You can imagine what the beaches would look like if everyone did that.'

'Yes, but –'

'Even Brigitte Bardot had to pay,' Officer Bernard interrupted. 'Cheque or cash?'

'I'll write a cheque.' Dan sighed.

Fernando and the two dogs were finally released. On the pavement outside, Eva heaped abuse on poor Fernando for a full ten minutes. She continued the tirade from the front passenger seat as Fernando and the two dogs cowered in the back.

'Calm down now, sweetheart,' Dan soothed, putting the key in the ignition. 'I'm sure Fernando realises that he made a big mistake. He won't do it again. Will you, Fernando?'

'No, sir,' Fernando promised.

'But you were no help either, Dan,' Eva complained. 'All you could do was stare at those stupid posters of wanted criminals.'

'But it was interesting,' Dan argued. 'You never know when you might see someone you recognise. And I had this feeling …'

'Don't be silly,' Eva said. 'Let's forget the whole thing. Just start the car and get us out of here.'

'But I –'

'Oh, shut up,' Eva snapped.

Worried about the right clothes to bring for a holiday on the French Riviera, Maria had followed the advice of a fashion magazine. 'White is the best colour for a holiday wardrobe,' the article had said, 'then you may be sure everything will match and it looks lovely with a tan.' On that basis, she had brought two pairs of white trousers, a white linen dress and a pair of white shorts. Five white T-shirts and a short-sleeved silk blouse completed her summer wardrobe. Only her swimsuit was blue. She had been very pleased with it all, until yesterday, when Paul had called her 'nurse' several times. She realised she needed to do some shopping urgently and, late in the afternoon, had driven into St Tropez and its many boutiques.

She had spent over an hour walking down the narrow streets, marvelling at the small shops selling anything from soap to expensive jewellery. The warm air smelled of pine trees, spices and perfume, and she became absorbed in the dreamy atmosphere. After a lot of searching, she found two T-shirts – one red, one black – and a lovely Provençal-print scarf.

Finally satisfied, she walked down a narrow lane until she reached the harbour, where the yachts were moored side by side in front of Le Senequier, the most fashionable café in all of the south of France. She looked up at the deck of a huge motorboat, where the occupants lounged in deckchairs while uniformed crew members tended to floral arrangements and put out buckets containing magnums of chilled champagne. She wondered why people of such enormous wealth would want to tie these floating palaces just under the noses of the crowds on the quay. But maybe showing off was part of the pleasure of having endless amounts of money?

'Maria!' a voice called out.

She looked around.

'Over here!' She could see a tall figure standing up and waving under the awning of Le Senequier. It was Guido, who was making frantic signs for her to join him at one of the red tables.

'*Buon giorno, cara mia,*' he said, when she finally managed to push her way to his table, and kissed her cheek. 'How nice to see you.'

'And you.' She smiled back at him.

'You look so lovely. *Molto bella.*'

'Thank you. You look pretty good yourself,' she replied, thinking what an understatement it was. Guido looked magnificent, from his blond hair and tanned face to his black shirt, beige trousers and Gucci loafers. In fact, he was the best fashion accessory a woman could wish for.

'You want to drink something? An aperitif?'

'I don't usually drink at this hour,' Maria said. 'And this place is a bit too dear. But why not?'

'I know,' Guido agreed. 'It is very expansive, no? A, how you say, riposte?'

'Rip off,' Maria corrected. 'Yes, that's right. It really is. You could have a full meal in a restaurant for what you'd pay for a couple of drinks here.'

'That's true,' Guido said. 'But you have to add the entertainment to that.' He gestured towards the yachts. 'Where else could you watch the rich and famous like this? It is fascinating, no?'

'Oh, yes, it is,' Maria answered. 'I could sit here and watch for hours.'

Guido gestured to a waiter. 'What would you like?' he asked Maria.

'A Campari–orange, please.'

'And I'll have the same.'

The waiter disappeared. They looked at the yachts again.

'It does seem a little unfair,' Maria remarked. 'Those rich people looking down at the poor, I mean.'

'On the contrary. I think it is the most democratic place on earth.'

'How do you mean?'

'Well, anyone can come here to St Tropez and enjoy the spectacle and walk around the harbour. It doesn't cost anything to acquire a suntan. In fact, I think it's the people on the yachts you should feel sorry for. They don't look as if they are having as much fun as the people on the quay. They are trapped in their wealth and their image.'

'You're very deep all of a sudden,' Maria said, laughing.

'Sex and money,' Guido replied.

'What?'

'That's what it's all about. Some people have it, others want it and most people just like to rub up against it.'

'And those who have it like to show it off? They provide the entertainment for everybody here?'

'*Ecco!*' Guido laughed. 'You have understood perfectly. You're very clever, no?'

'Oh, I don't know,' Maria said, trying to sound modest.

'This town is so strange,' Guido declared, 'so full of contradictions. I have just been to the museum over there at the other side of the harbour.'

'L'Annonciade?'

'That's it. And I have admired the beautiful *collezione* of post-Impressionist art. Lovely.' He kissed his fingers. 'And then you go out here and see all that . . .

how you say, rubbish that they sell on the quay. Isn't that so strange?'

'You're just a snob.' Maria laughed again. 'I think some of the pictures are quite good actually.'

'Very few.'

'But it's fun to go along the quay and look, I think.'

'And looking at the people in this café is fun too,' Guido added. 'Look,' he whispered, 'look at that couple. Do you think she's his mother?'

'Or his aunt?' Maria grinned.

'No.' Guido winked at Maria. 'She is just a *very* good friend, no?'

'Absolutely.' Maria smiled and shook her head. 'You're very naughty,' she said.

'Yes, but I am gay,' Guido replied.

'I beg your pardon?'

'Gay,' he repeated. 'I feel so happy and gay. Yesterday I was sad, but now I'm –'

'Gay?' Maria filled in. 'Listen, Guido, I think I will have to give you a very short lesson in English.' She leaned closer and whispered something into his ear.

He laughed uproariously when she had finished. '*Oh, que stupido!*' he exclaimed. 'I knew there was something strange about that word. I said it to someone at a party a few days ago and this man followed me around all night.' He laughed again and put his arm around her. 'Thank you, Maria. You are a good friend. No, I am not gay like that, I can assure you. I love *la bella donna*, you know. And in any case what would my mamma say?'

Maria giggled. He was such fun to be with, so nice and cheerful. He wasn't at all her type and she couldn't imagine falling in love with him, but it was lovely to just sit here, watch the yachts and the people, and see the late-afternoon sun shimmer in the water and bathe the old buildings in a golden light. She listened intently as Guido told her the ins and outs of St Tropez society.

The music was deafening and the disco hotter than the beach at midday. Hundreds of glistening, sweating bodies gyrated under the whirling lights. It was hypnotic, Louise thought, impossible to stop moving. She smiled at Mark, who was dancing so close to her with an energy that surprised her.

'I didn't know you could move like that,' she shouted.

'Well, now you do,' he shouted back, twirling around and bouncing at the same time.

Louise smiled as she bobbed up and down to the music. Mark put his hands on her hips and together they continued dancing. How on earth did I end up here on the dance floor with Mark? she wondered.

It had all started with a bet.

'Let's go to a disco tonight,' Louise had suggested to Paul and Maria as they were having a glass of rosé on the terrace before dinner. 'We could go to the Byblos. I've heard that it is the most fashionable place in town.'

'Impossible to get into,' Paul argued.

'How do you know?' Louise asked. She looked at Maria for support, but her sister was looking down the hill, admiring the view. 'Maria?' Louise said.

'What do you think?'

'About what?'

'Paul says the Byblos disco is impossible to get into.'

'That's right,' Maria agreed, suddenly more alert. 'The disco is called Les Caves du Roy and just getting past the bouncers there is supposed to be one of the biggest social triumphs in St Tropez.'

'How do you know all this?' Louise asked.

'Guido, Eva's boss,' Maria explained, helping herself to another glass of wine. 'I had a drink with him at Le Senequier today.'

'He must be really wealthy if he can afford to buy you a drink there.' Louise's voice was full of admiration.

'I don't know really. But he's very generous. And he knows everything about St Tropez. He's been coming here for years.'

'He's also rather good-looking. We saw him at the beach yesterday.' Louise peered at Maria. 'Are you having a little holiday romance?'

'I didn't think Maria would go for the ageing-gigolo type,' Paul cut in.

Louise glanced at him, surprised at his tone, but the expression in his eyes was hidden by his sunglasses.

Maria looked at Paul. 'Maybe I am,' she said, with a casual air. 'Guido is a lovely man.'

'If you like them old,' Louise added.

'He's forty-two,' Eva said, coming out from the living room. 'Not exactly an old-age pensioner. Darling, what *are* you wearing?' she continued as Dan came up the steps from the garden.

'I got it at the market this morning,' Dan beamed, pushing out his chest to show off his blue and white fisherman's cotton T-shirt. 'I got this pair of trousers as well. They were very reasonable. And look, I even got a pair of boating shoes just like the yacht people wear. Dirt cheap, just because there's no logo. I was trying to get a pair of espadrilles, but it appears they are out of fashion. What do you think? It's called *le look*, the man at the market said.'

'You look lovely,' Maria said, and hugged him. 'If you weren't my father I'd fall in love with you on the spot.'

Eva sighed. 'It's fine for the garden, I suppose. But I don't want to go out in public with you dressed like that.'

'Why not?' Louise demanded. 'He looks just like those men in that old movie. You know, *And God Created Woman*. I bet you'd even get into the Byblos.'

'A bet!' Maria exclaimed, with the kind of high only three glasses of rosé can give. 'Why don't we go there tonight, all of us, and see who'll get in? Those who don't will have to ... to ...'

'Buy more wine?' Paul said, holding up the empty bottle. 'I think you've had a little too much, my dear Maria.'

'Don't you "dear Maria" me. I'm perfectly sober. Which doesn't mean I'm boring, like some we could mention.'

'It's a great idea actually,' Louise soothed. 'Why don't you and Daddy come too, Eva?'

'I don't see why not,' Dan said. 'Just to prove to you that *le look* is the right way to dress.'

'You mean you'd go to the Byblos dressed like that?' Eva exclaimed.

'Yes.' Dan had a stubborn look in his eyes. 'I bet you a hundred euros I'll get in.'

'OK,' Eva said. 'And I bet you the same that you'll be laughed at and thrown out.'

'You're on,' Dan replied. He looked around at the others. 'Any more bets?'

'I'm for Daddy,' Maria laughed.

'So am I,' Louise joined in. 'Paul?'

'I think I'll stay out of this.'

'Coward,' Maria muttered.

Louise suddenly stood up and peered down the garden. 'There's someone coming up the path,' she exclaimed. 'Mark. It's Mark White! How marvellous.'

Mark walked up the steps to the terrace. 'Hello,' he said. 'I was hoping I'd find you all home.' He proceeded to kiss all the women on the cheek and to shake hands with Dan and Paul.

'But how did you know we were here?' Louise asked, thinking Mark looked very different in casual clothes.

Mark glanced at Eva. 'Oh, I knew so many people from the Commission were spending their holidays here, so I thought ...'

'When did you arrive?' Maria enquired, looking suspiciously at Eva.

'This morning, on the early flight from London. I spent a week with my parents before I came here.'

'Where are you staying?' Dan asked.

'With my cousin. He has a place down there.' Mark made a vague gesture towards the bay.

'We were just about to have dinner,' Eva said. 'Would you like to join us?'

'Thanks, but I just came to say hello. I'm expected for dinner at my cousin's.'

'Will you have a glass of wine before you go?' Dan offered. 'I'm sure we can hold dinner for a few minutes.'

'We're going to try to get into the Les Caves du Roy later,' Louise said, when Mark had sat down. 'Why don't you come with us? We won't get in, but it'll be a bit of a laugh.'

'Why not?' Mark replied. 'Sounds like a good idea.'

'We can go somewhere else when we've been thrown out,' Maria said.

'OK,' Mark replied. He rose. 'I'd better go. Let's meet outside the disco at about half-past eleven. The place doesn't really get going until midnight, but it's a good idea to be there a little earlier. Are you all going?'

'Absolutely,' Dan said. 'I know I might be a little older than the usual crowd, but I'd just like to see the place.'

'He has *le look*,' Louise whispered to Mark.

'I noticed,' he had whispered back. 'See you all later.'

The Byblos was a large terracotta building situated on the slope of a hill near the citadel, the ancient fort overlooking St Tropez. It didn't look at all like a lux-ury hotel from the outside, Louise thought, more like a series of pavilions. But when they walked up the marble steps and in through a kind of arcade to the courtyard, she felt strangely intimidated.

There was a long queue outside the door of the disco. Two tall bouncers with short blond hair stood at the door, surveying the crowd. Now and then, they lifted the barrier to admit someone who had been lucky enough to pass the test, whatever it was. Louise couldn't discern anything that the chosen had in common. Women seemed to have no problem getting in, as long as they were young and gorgeous. But no rule seemed to apply to the men.

'How do they pick out the people they admit?' Louise asked Mark.

They were standing at the back of the line with Paul, Maria, Dan and Eva.

'Well,' he replied, 'as you can see, there is no problem for a pretty young girl. But for men it's more complicated. It could depend on the make of their shoes, what kind of watch they're wearing, gestures or manner of speech.'

'I might as well go back home, then,' Dan said, sighing. 'I'm only wearing an old plastic watch from Dunnes Stores.'

'I'm sure it depends on the thickness of your wallet,' Paul said. 'I've heard a drink costs an arm and a leg here.'

'We'll soon find out,' Eva said. 'Anyway, I don't care. I'd much rather go for a drink in Place des Lices, the town square, and watch a game of *boules*. I love that old game.'

'I don't think they're still playing *boules* at this hour,' Maria argued. 'Anyway, what will we do if we don't all get in?'

'I think the people who get in should go in and have a dance or two,' Dan said. 'And then come out and tell us all what it was like. Why don't we agree to meet at that nice bar in the harbour in about an hour? You know, the one that's called Le Vieux Port?'

'Good idea,' Mark replied. 'And we won't wait. If any of you want to make a night of it, just go ahead.'

'Right,' Paul said. 'OK, darling?'

'Yes.' Louise smiled up at him. 'I'm looking forward to dancing the lambada with you.'

'So am I,' he said, and squeezed her waist.

'The queue is moving,' Eva said. 'We're nearly there.'

They shuffled forward a few inches. Louise was glad she had changed into her red dress with the short flared skirt. She knew she looked really good in it, especially now that she had a tan. And Eva looked sensational in her pink skirt and top and those high heels, nearly like a teenager. But Maria looked the best of all. She had changed into a short white backless linen dress and put up her hair. A colourful scarf was tied around her slim waist and there was a string of blue beads around her neck. Her tan, which was deeper than Louise's, made her eyes look even bluer and there was a band of freckles across the bridge of her nose. But that was not the only reason she looked so good, Louise thought, it was the look in her eyes. Maybe she really was in love with that handsome Italian?

They had arrived at the barrier. 'Hi,' Louise said, and smiled at one of the bouncers.

'Hello, darling,' he drawled, to her astonishment, in a very upper-class British accent. 'Go on in.' He gestured to his colleague to lift the barrier.

'Oh, thank you,' Louise gushed, and smiled at him as he lifted the barrier for her. She waved at the others. 'I got in,' she laughed. 'I'll wait here for you.' She watched as her father confronted the bouncers.

'I suppose you're going to tell me to get lost,' Dan joked, half turning to leave.

'Not at all, old chap,' the bouncer said. 'You're in.' He turned to the other bouncer. 'What do you say?'

'Absolutely,' his colleague agreed.

'But I don't really,' Dan protested. 'I mean, I ... Why?'

'You have *le look*. Very in around here.'

'Bloody hell,' Dan laughed. 'Did you hear that, Eva? You owe me a hundred euros.'

'I can't believe it.'

'You can go in too, darling,' the bouncer said, and gave Eva's bottom a little pat.

'Don't be rude,' she snapped, but she smiled as she sailed in through the door.

One of the bouncers exchanged a brief look with Mark, and he was through as well.

Maria tried to follow.

'Hang on a minute,' the tallest bouncer ordered. 'I didn't say you could go in.'

'Oh, but my friends,' she stammered.

'That's what they all say,' the bouncer grunted. 'But I'm afraid you can't go in.'

'Why not?' Maria pleaded.

'You're not quite right.'

'What do you mean?'

'It's your attitude,' the bouncer said. He turned to his colleague. 'What do you say?'

'Absolutely. And the boyfriend too.'

'What's wrong with my attitude?'

'You haven't got one.'

'What *is* wrong with it?' Maria asked, as she and Paul were having a beer at Le Vieux Port.

'With what?'

'My attitude.'

Paul looked at her thoughtfully. 'I can't see a thing wrong with you,' he said. 'You look lovely tonight.'

'But not lovely enough to get into the disco,' Maria said bleakly. She felt utterly rejected, as if she had somehow been branded unattractive and unwanted.

'There was something a bit fishy about that,' Paul remarked.

'How do you mean?'

He leaned toward her across the table and looked into her eyes. 'Maria, you were one of the most beautiful women there tonight. So there must be some other reason why they didn't let you in.'

'Yeah, right.'

She turned away so he wouldn't see the tears in her eyes and looked out across the harbour and the twinkling lights of the yachts. There was a clucking sound of water slapping against the hulls of the boats moored at the marina and faint music came from a café nearby.

'No,' he insisted. 'It's true. You should have sailed in like Louise and Eva.'

'Daddy and Mark got in.'

'That's also very strange. Your father is not exactly the usual disco swinger and Mark is . . .'

'A nerd?'

'Yes. I really like him, but I have to say that the word "trendy" does not exactly come to mind.'

'He wears Marks & Spencer shirts.'

'And he has a row of biros in his top pocket.'

Maria laughed. 'He has fixed his glasses with a bit of Band-Aid.'

'What about those sandals?' Paul added. 'He looks a bit like an overgrown Boy Scout.'

'He is odd actually,' Maria said. 'Maybe it's because he went to Eton.'

'Probably,' Paul agreed. 'Strange things go on in those public schools.'

'Oh, stop.' Maria laughed. 'You make him sound really sinister. I think he's a lovely guy actually. Always so friendly and chatty.'

'I know.' Paul sat back. 'He is. But getting into the disco . . . I don't know.' He shook his head. 'Do you want another beer?'

'Why not? It's really nice.' Maria looked at the side of the bottle. 'It's Belgian. Six per cent alcohol. Isn't that a bit strong? I've already had three.'

'We're not going to drive anywhere,' Paul argued, 'or operate machinery, so what does it matter?'

'OK. Let's have another, then,' Maria nodded.

'Lovely night,' Paul said as he sipped the beer out of the bottle.

'Mmmm.'

Paul looked at his watch. 'They're not coming, are

they?' he said. 'It's after one o'clock.'

'I suppose they're not, no.'

'They forgot all about us,' Paul stated.

'I bet they're having a great time,' Maria said bitterly.

'We're stuck here on our own.' He sounded suddenly fed up.

'Stuck?' she demanded.

'Well, it's not my fault you have no attitude. If it wasn't for you . . .'

'You'd be in there bopping the night away?'

'Maybe.'

'How terrible for you.'

'Well, it is a bit annoying to see your girlfriend go into a disco with someone else actually.' Paul's voice was hard now, hurt and annoyed. 'You must understand that. I would have preferred to be there, dancing with her, instead of –'

'Sitting here with me?' Maria rose. She felt suddenly furious. 'I am so sorry,' she snapped. 'I won't bore you with my presence any longer.' She walked out of the bar and half ran down the street, her high heels clicking on the pavement.

Paul ran after her.

'Maria, don't be silly. I didn't mean . . . You can't go off like that. It's too far to walk. Let's get a taxi.'

'Fuck off.'

'But Maria . . .'

They both noticed the police car cruising behind them at the same moment. A policeman stuck his head out the window. 'Is this man bothering you, mademoiselle?'

Maria turned and looked at the officer.

'Oh, yes,' she sobbed. 'Yes, he is.'

'And now,' the DJ announced, 'take your partners for *le slow*.'

Eva looked around for Dan, but he had gone back to their table. They had been dancing for about an hour and he had said he needed to sit down.

She felt arms gently enveloping her.

'Darling,' Yves murmured, 'Eva, *mon amour*. I've been looking for you all over St Tropez and here you are.'

Eva didn't know if it was the champagne, hormones or just utter madness, but without thinking she melted into his arms and, body to body, skin to skin, they moved to the music as if they were one. The lights dimmed to near darkness. She could hear heavy breathing all around her. With the sensuous music drumming in her ears, Yves' hands roaming over her body and his lips on hers, she totally lost herself in the sensations. She ran her hands over his chest, then inside his shirt until she was gripping his bare back. What am I doing? she asked herself. This has to stop.

The slow music played on for a long time until Eva thought she was going to faint and then, suddenly, there was a change of rhythm. Latin American music exploded through the room and the lights were suddenly brighter. Yves and Eva flew apart. They stared at each other as if in shock.

'Oh, my God,' Eva panted, her hand on her heart. 'What was I thinking? What were we doing?'

'I don't know –' Yves laughed – 'but I liked it. My lovely Eva, we have to get away from here, right now.'

'Oh, no,' she stammered, 'my husband.'

'He seems very happy,' Yves remarked, looking across the room, where Dan was dancing the rumba with a fit-looking dark-haired girl in a yellow dress.

'This is completely mad,' Eva protested, as Yves grabbed her again. 'Please. Let me go. I have to get some air.'

'Of course, *chérie*, I'll go with you.' And, with a firm grip on her elbow, he propelled her through the throng towards the door.

'Hi, darling,' Dan shouted as they passed him, 'this is Mercedes from Spain. She asked me to dance, would you believe it?'

'How nice,' Eva shouted back.

'Great music, don't you think?' Dan said.

'Lovely,' she shouted again. 'I'm going to sit down.'

'I'll be with you in a minute,' Dan promised, twirling the girl around. 'If Mercedes will let me go.'

'Where's Louise?'

'I don't know,' Dan yelled. 'Over there somewhere.' He gestured vaguely.

Eva wrenched free from Yves' grip. 'Take your hands off me,' she ordered.

He backed away, smiled and disappeared into the throng. Eva continued to push through to her table, until she spotted Mark and Louise. They were dancing very close, looking into each other's eyes, then the music suddenly stopped. Eva stared in horror as Mark bent down and kissed Louise on the mouth.

CHAPTER 10

Eva tried to wake up. Her head was splitting and her whole body ached. She had a terrible taste in her mouth and an awful feeling of nausea. Oh, God, she thought, what did I drink? Or, more to the point, what didn't I drink? What is making me feel this awful? Was it the vodka in the afternoon? Or the rosé? Or maybe the champagne Dan insisted on ordering to celebrate gaining entry to the disco? The cognac at the bistro on the way home didn't help either. She had never had such a hangover. Getting tipsy on vodka was one thing. This was more like bingeing.

Dan stirred. 'Please, nurse,' he muttered. 'Alka-Seltzer.'

'You get it,' Eva mumbled. 'I don't seem to be able to move.'

'OK.' Dan turned and went back to sleep, snoring loudly.

Moaning softly, Eva slowly got out of bed and walked to the small table by the window, where she poured herself a glass of water from the jug. There was a packet of Alka-Seltzer in the bathroom, she remembered. Very carefully, holding on to the walls, she was able to get across the room and into the bathroom. She found the box and, after having staggered back into the bedroom, plopped two tablets into the water and managed to drink the whole thing down. She got back into bed and closed her eyes. What a night, she thought. What happened? She could vaguely remember dancing with Dan, and then on her own and with everybody, until … Oh, God, she thought, what was I doing?

Much later that morning, Eva wandered slowly out onto the terrace. The heat was already intense and the glare of the sun was hurting her eyes despite her sunglasses. She was feeling a little better and thought she might even be able to manage a light breakfast. Dan had also recovered somewhat and was having coffee under the shade of the umbrella.

'Where is everybody?' Eva asked.

'I don't know,' he replied. 'I haven't seen anybody yet and it's nearly lunch time. Coffee?'

'No, just orange juice.'

'Morning,' Louise mumbled, shading her eyes as she shuffled onto the terrace. She put on a pair of huge sunglasses and sank onto a lounge chair.

'Morning, darling,' Dan said. 'How are you feeling?'

'I don't want to talk about it.'

'And what did you get up to last night, young lady?' Eva demanded.

'Get up to?'

'I saw you,' Eva said sternly.

Louise turned and looked at Eva over her sunglasses. 'And I saw you.'

'Oh.'

'Where's Paul?' Dan asked.

'I don't know,' Louise replied.

'Madame,' Fatima, who had arrived with fresh coffee, interrupted. 'Mademoiselle Maria is not in her room.'

'What do you mean?' Eva demanded.

'Well, I usually bring her a cup of tea at around nine o'clock. But this morning, her room was empty. And her bed has not been slept in.'

'Telephone, madame.' Fernando stuck his head out of the living room's French windows.'

'For me? Who is it?'

'The police, madame.'

'Again? What have you been up to now?'

'Nothing, madame,' Fernando replied, looking wounded.

'What do they want, then?'

'I don't know, madame.'

'I don't believe this,' Eva groaned as she went to take the call.

Eva had a horrible feeling of déjà vu as she drove along the winding road towards St Tropez and the police station. Dan had not wanted to come with her this time, saying he felt a little tired. 'We have your daughter in custody,' Officer Bernard had said. 'And a young man.' What had Maria and Paul done last night to get them both arrested? It had been such a mad evening, she thought, was there something in the wine they had drunk? Or was it Mark? He was a strange young man, not at all the promising young journalist he had seemed in Brussels, such a suitable match for Maria. Here, in St Tropez, he was suddenly devious and cheeky, even moving in on Louise. Eva was deep in thought all the way into St Tropez.

'Madame Connolly,' Officer Bernard said. 'We meet again.'

'Yes,' Eva snapped. 'I know. But I don't know why I'm here this time.'

'It's your daughter, madame.' Bernard consulted a piece of paper. 'A Mademoiselle Maria Connolly.'

'That's my stepdaughter,' Eva corrected.

'Not your daughter, then?'

'Well, in a way. I didn't actually give birth to her, but –'

'Right,' Bernard interrupted, in a voice that indicated he was not interested in Eva's family history. 'And Mr Paul Ryan,' he added. 'Your house guest, I believe?'

'He's my stepdaughter's fiancé.'

'Yes.' Bernard looked through his papers. 'That's them.'

'Would you mind telling me why they are here?'

'They broke the law, madame.'

'Oh, God,' Eva mumbled, slowly closing her eyes as if in pain. 'Were they ... drunk?'

'Drunk? Not exactly, madame. Mademoiselle Connolly, your stepdaughter, and Monsieur Ryan, her fiancé, were –'

'No, he's not *her* fiancé,' Eva interrupted.

'What? But you just said –'

'He's my *other* stepdaughter's fiancé,' Eva explained.

'Your other ... what?'

'I have another stepdaughter,' Eva snapped, 'called Louise. Paul Ryan is *her* fiancé, not Maria's.'

Bernard looked down at his piece of paper. 'But it's all here in the report.'

Eva sighed. 'Monsieur Bernard, could we please get to the point. I haven't got all day. What were they doing? Maria and Paul, I mean.'

'They were wasting police time,' Bernard snapped.

'Doing what?'

'Well –' Bernard consulted his piece of paper – 'according to ...'

'Give me that.' Eva snatched the paper away from him and peered at it. 'It says here that Maria accused Paul of...'

'Harassment,' Bernard filled in. 'That's right. So we put handcuffs on him and threw him into the squad car. But Mademoiselle Connolly then asked us to release him. She said she was only joking.'

'So?'

'And when we wouldn't let him go, she hit me with her handbag.' He touched the back of his head. 'It was very painful. So we arrested her as well.' Bernard looked sternly at Eva. 'Wasting police time is serious enough, but attacking a police officer is even worse. But I'm not going to press charges for that.' He smiled conspiratorially. 'Women in love, eh?'

'In love? But *she's* not...' Eva stopped. 'Never mind. How can I have them released? Do I need a lawyer?'

'No, just five hundred euros will do.'

'What? That's a bit steep.'

'That's the fine. Or they could stay on here for three more weeks,' he suggested.

'No, it's all right.' Eva dug in her handbag. 'I'll pay. Listen,' she said, while she wrote the cheque, 'don't you have more important things to do than arrest people for these kinds of petty crimes?'

'How do you mean?'

'I mean, what about the car gang? Why don't you spend a little more time trying to find them, instead of annoying people like this? I heard there was another hold-up the other night. The head of Europol this time. Must have been very embarrassing for you.'

Officer Bernard looked suddenly very annoyed. His handsome tanned face was now red and his lovely brown eyes flashed. 'We have everything under control,' he snapped. 'But we do have to keep the peace as well. The citizens of St Tropez have to be protected, you know.'

'From what?' Eva handed him the cheque.

'From people like you. Sign here.'

The evening sun had nearly disappeared behind the hills, its last rays bathing the terrace in a rosy glow. The soft breeze felt like silk and there was a delicious smell of spices and herbs as Fatima served dinner. Eva sipped the cool wine and looked down the hill across the flat calm of the sea, feeling nearly like her old self again.

The drive back home from the *gendarmerie* had been icily quiet. And when they got back, Maria had run up to her room and slammed the door. Paul had gone upstairs to join Louise. He had looked very angry and Eva didn't blame him. Louise had been a silly little fool. Eva had heard raised voices and then absolute silence. The villa had been eerily quiet the rest of the afternoon, all the shutters closed against the baking heat.

'Are you feeling better now, darling?' Louise asked Paul as he joined the others on the terrace.

'I'm fine,' he replied, pouring himself a glass of water.

'That cell can't have been very comfortable,' Dan remarked. 'Were you and Maria in the same one?'

'No,' Paul said, 'we were in separate cells.' He looked at Dan. 'I don't really want to talk about it, if you don't mind.'

'Of course not,' Eva soothed. 'I understand.'

'Where is Maria?' Dan asked.

'I don't know,' Eva said. 'She went out earlier.'

'A hot date?' Louise suggested, glancing at Paul.

'I hope she's having a good time,' Dan said.

It's funny, Maria thought, as she swam back to the beach after a long swim, how everybody has settled into a holiday mode. The days were nearly always spent the same way. Breakfast on the terrace – *café au lait*, orange juice and croissants – with Dan reading the paper, telling them what was going on in the real world, and Eva planning the day. Then the rest of the morning by the pool, swimming and reading, Paul and Louise playing tennis. Then lunch, before everyone retired to their rooms to sleep. Everything seemed to stop for a few hours, while the sky turned nearly white with heat and the sound of the crickets intensified until it became almost deafening.

The evenings were usually spent with Paul and Louise, and sometimes Mark or Guido, having a drink in St Tropez, looking into shops, staring at the yachts and meeting friends. Then dinner either at home or at one of the small restaurants nearby.

In the afternoon, Maria usually woke up before everyone else and walked quietly out of the house, down the little path covered in pine needles, to the beach. She loved these few hours here by herself, swimming, sunbathing and watching other people.

Eva, however, was not always around. She seemed to have her own agenda. Maria didn't know what Eva did in the afternoon, but didn't really care. She was having too good a time.

After her swim, Maria waded out of the sea onto the hot sand, squeezing water from her hair. She sank down on her towel and dried the salt water off her shoulders. She picked up a big bottle of suntan lotion and started to apply it to her arms. You have to be careful, she thought, the sun is really hot right now. When she was satisfied that every inch of her body was covered, she lay down and closed her eyes, enjoying the feel of hot sunshine on her skin.

'Excuse me?'

'Yes?' she murmured, shading her eyes.

'We haven't actually met, but . . .'

Maria sat up and looked at the young girl standing over her. 'Yes?' she said again, vaguely recognising the tall, busty brunette. She had a big mouth full of perfect teeth that gleamed against her dark tan.

'I'm Saskia, Edwina's . . . eh . . . nanny, and I was wondering,' she continued, 'if you could keep an eye on Edwina for a little while?'

'Well, I don't know. Will she mind? Where is she?'

'Over there, collecting shells.' Saskia pointed in the direction of the water's edge, where Edwina, dressed in a red swimsuit, was putting something into a small bucket.

'But why? I mean . . .' Maria looked at her, confused.

'I have to go and meet someone. And there's no one at home. And I know Edwina really likes you.'

'But we've only met once,' Maria protested. 'Do you really think it's wise to ask a complete stranger to mind her?'

'But you're not a stranger,' Saskia protested. 'Your name is Maria and you live in a villa on the hill. Edwina told me. And I've been invited to . . .' Her voice tailed off.

Maria studied the 'nanny'. She was dressed in the smallest bikini Maria had ever seen, not exactly what you'd wear for afternoon tea.

'Well, all right, then,' Maria agreed. 'Just for half an hour.'

'Oh, great!' the nanny exclaimed. 'I'll be back soon, I promise.'

She ran off towards a small rubber dinghy, where a young man was waiting. She called to Edwina, almost as an afterthought as she passed her, 'Maria said she'd mind you for a little while.'

The young man helped her into the dinghy and

started the outboard motor. They disappeared in a wave of foaming water around the headland before Maria had time even to draw breath.

'Look.' Edwina was standing beside her, holding out her bucket. 'I found a little fish.' Her blonde hair was hanging in a plait down her brown back and her eyes were exactly the same colour as the sky.

Maria looked into the bucket, where a small fish was indeed swimming around in about an inch of water. 'What are you going to do with it?' Maria asked.

'I'm going to let him go. Just like in the song. Do you know it? It goes like this: "One, two, three, four, five," ' she sang.

' "Once I caught a fish alive," ' Maria continued.

' "Six, seven, eight, nine, ten." '

' "Then I let him go again." '

' "Why did you let him go?" ' Edwina sang with a big smile.

' "Cause he bit my finger so." ' Maria laughed.

' "Which finger did he bite?" '

' "This little finger on the right," ' Maria ended, and pinched Edwina's little finger, which made her giggle deliciously.

'Let's go and let him out, then,' Edwina suggested. 'Are you going to mind me all day?'

'Looks like it, I'm afraid.'

'I'm not afraid. I'm really delighted.'

'Delighted?'

'That's what you say when you meet someone,' Edwina explained. 'Delighted to meet you, my dear Maria.'

'Delighted to meet you, Miss, Miss . . . What's your family name?'

'White,' Edwina replied. 'That's what we used to be called until my granddad died. Now we're called Bakewell.'

'Oh, I see. White?' Maria muttered. 'I know someone called Mark White,' she said.

'That's my uncle.' Edwina nodded, and peered at Maria. 'Do you really know him?'

'I think he's the same one.' Maria looked at Edwina. 'Does he live with you in that big house?'

'Yes, he does. Come on, we have to let my fishy out or he'll drown.' Edwina pulled at Maria. 'Come on,' she urged. 'We have to hurry.'

'OK,' Maria agreed, taking Edwina by the hand. 'But tell me more about Uncle Mark.'

'He's not really my uncle,' Edwina said, when they had successfully let the fish out. 'He's my daddy's cousin.' She looked into the water. 'Look, he's swimming away really fast. Maybe he's going back to his mummy and daddy? Maybe they were worried? I'm glad I didn't keep him.'

'You were right.'

'What will we do now?' Edwina looked at Maria expectantly. 'Do you want an ice cream? It's not too close to supper.'

'Why not? That would be really delicious.'

'It's getting a little late,' Maria said, looking at her watch. 'Where did you say your parents were?' They had been together for several hours and there was still no sign of Saskia.

'They went out on a big boat this morning,' Edwina replied. 'Are you going to take me home? You could stay the night if you want. Wouldn't that be fun?'

'I wonder where your nanny is.'

'She's not a real nanny. Only an au pair. She's from Amsterdam.'

'I see.'

Maria thought for a moment. It was nearly seven o'clock and the beach was beginning to look deserted. Where was that wretched girl? Maria hoped nothing had happened. And what was she going to do with Edwina?

'Let's go to my house,' Edwina suggested. 'I'm hungry. Maybe you could give me my supper?'

'OK.' Maria put on her shorts over her swimsuit and gathered up her things. She took the little girl by the hand. 'Let's get you home.'

And, hand in hand, they walked across the beach, around the rocks to the high fence that surrounded the property of Edwina's parents. A big sign told them in five languages that it was private property and the gate looked impossible to breach.

'How are we going to get in?' Maria asked. 'The gate seems to be locked.'

'Saskia hid the key behind this little rock here,' Edwina said, and pulled at a stone. 'She didn't have a pocket, you see.'

'No, she didn't,' Maria muttered, remembering Saskia's outfit.

'Here it is,' Edwina exclaimed triumphantly, and held up a key.

'You clever girl.'

They walked slowly across the private beach and up the path beside the immaculate lawn. Maria noticed that there were not one but two terraces, the lower of which contained the most beautiful pool she had ever seen. It was huge, shaped like an oval and surrounded by tiles of sandstone, wonderfully soft against her feet. They climbed the steps to the upper terrace, which was equally deserted. There were tables and chairs under big white umbrellas, and terracotta pots brimming with flowers. The tiles here were sandstone as well and the view of the bay was stunning.

'Where is everybody?' Maria asked, more to herself than to Edwina.

Except for the soft sound of the breeze and the interminable crickets, there was no noise and no one about, as if there had been some sort of disaster and all the occupants had left in a hurry.

'I think all the maids have taken the day off,' Edwina said. 'Because they probably had nothing to do.'

'But what are we going to do?' Maria asked.

'Why don't we go to the kitchen and raid the fridge?' Edwina suggested. 'That's what Uncle Mark likes to do.'

'OK. You show the way.'

They walked into a huge living room, which was exquisitely furnished in a Mediterranean version of impeccable English country chic. It looked at the same time beautiful and comfortable, the colours muted and warm, which went so well with the lovely

Provençal garden that could be seen through the tall windows. The room was wonderfully cool, with thick walls and high ceilings.

'What a lovely house,' Maria said, thinking that Eva would be green with envy if she could see this. Dieter's villa, although comfortable, suddenly seemed mediocre in comparison.

'It's called Villa Caramel,' Edwina said. 'Because my granddad made a lot of sweets.'

'But that's incredible!' Maria exclaimed. 'Imagine you being one of those Whites. Is your daddy going to run the factory now?'

'Yes, he is.' Edwina nodded. 'He's very busy.'

They walked into the kitchen.

'Wow,' Maria whispered as she looked around.

It was the kind of stone-flagged, granite-topped dream kitchen sometimes found in expensive interior design magazines. Two enormous stainless-steel fridges hummed in unison against one wall and the six-burner, state-of-the-art cooker was like something you'd see in the kitchen of a luxury restaurant.

'Let's get you something to eat,' Maria said, and opened one of the fridges. It was full of bottles of champagne. 'Let's try the other one. My goodness, what a lot of food.'

'I know,' Edwina giggled. 'They're always having parties.'

Maria took out eggs, butter and ham. 'How about an omelette? Would you like that?'

'OK,' Edwina nodded. 'And could I have toast with marmalade as well? I love that. And hot chocolate with marshmallows?'

'OK.'

Maria glanced at the big clock on the wall. Eight o'clock. Where was that silly au pair? And where was everybody else? What a very strange house, where they left small children on their own like this. Maria whisked the eggs, feeling both worried and angry. Should she call the coastguard? Or the police? Saskia had gone off with some guy, nearly naked. How well did she know him? Maria wondered.

'Where's your Uncle Mark?' she asked while she cut up some ham.

'Don't know.' Edwina shrugged. 'Maybe he's with his friends from that disco.'

'What friends?' Maria's heart beat a little faster.

'Those big boys he went to school with. They work all night at a disco. That's a dancing club,' Edwina explained.

'I see,' Maria mumbled. 'School friends, eh?' She poured the eggs into a hot pan.

'That smells lovely,' Edwina said. 'I'm so hungry I could eat an elephant!'

'It's nearly ready.' Maria gave a start as she heard footsteps. Someone was coming into the kitchen.

'Uncle Mark!' Edwina exclaimed. 'Look! We're having supper.'

But Mark didn't reply. He stared at Maria, alarmed. 'What the . . .' he stammered.

'Hi, Uncle Mark,' Maria laughed. 'Edwina has been telling me all about you.'

'Oh?' he said. 'About me?'

'Yes,' Maria said, smiling, 'and your little friends.'

CHAPTER 11

It's strange, when you try your best to avoid people, how you keep bumping into them, Eva thought as she was having a late-evening swim in the pool. She had gone to the open-air market in St Tropez that morning, not expecting to meet anyone.

The market was usually very enjoyable. Eva loved going from stall to stall, breathing in the heady smells, admiring the colours of the fruit and vegetables – melons, peaches, apricots, tomatoes as big as babies' heads, grown in the hot Provençal sun – bunches of lavender, spices, garlic and home-made olive oil, not to mention the cheeses, fresh fish, seafood, ham and sausages. Then there were stalls with local pottery in wonderful colours, fabrics in bright Provençal prints and other hand-crafted objects. Her basket became increasingly heavier as she succumbed to the temptations.

'Need some help?' a voice asked as she squeezed a melon.

She turned around, startled. 'Oh, hello,' she stammered, and nearly dropped the melon. 'No,

I'm fine, thanks.'

'Let me get this for you.' Yves laughed and turned to the stallkeeper. 'We'll have two of these, please.' He held the melons in front of him. 'Lovely, aren't they? Nearly as nice as . . .'

'Oh, grow up,' she snapped, taking the melons and putting them in her basket.

'I'm sorry, *chérie*,' he said, taking the basket from her. 'I'll try to be *really* grown up.'

'Go away.' She tried to take the basket back. 'I'm busy doing the shopping.'

'And you've succeeded remarkably well,' he said, looking at the items in the basket. 'Are you having a party?'

'That is none of your business.'

He took her arm. 'What's the matter, my darling?'

She wrenched free. 'Nothing's the matter. Please let me go.'

'But the other night you were a lot more friendly.'

'That was a mistake. I didn't mean it. Leave me alone. And give me my shopping.'

He shook his head and looked down at her flustered face. 'What an angry little *Hausfrau* you are today. All right. I will leave you to your chores.' He gave her back the basket and kissed her hand. '*A bientôt, mon amour*,' he murmured, and disappeared into the crowd.

On her way back to the villa, Eva felt a pang of regret at the abrupt ending to her short exchange with Yves. She looked in the rear-view mirror as she rounded the sharp hairpin bend. My God, there he was again, in his ridiculous little tin can of a car. He must have followed her. What was she going to do? Just ignore him, she thought. He might simply be driving home, in any case. She indicated to turn left as she reached the crossroads. He was doing the same. She drove up the narrow road that led to her house. There he was still. Well, what a nerve. She suddenly pulled into a lay-by just a few metres from the gate and slammed on the brakes. There was a screeching of tyres as the small Citroën 2CV came to a sudden halt behind her. Eva got out and marched up to the car. The driver rolled down the window.

'What the hell do you mean?' she demanded.

'*Pardon, madame?*' Officer Bernard asked. 'What can I do for you?'

'Oh.' Eva stared blankly at him. 'I'm sorry. I thought ...'

'Yes?' Bernard looked at her, a smile forming in his lovely brown eyes.

'Well, I ...' She didn't quite know what to say.

Officer Bernard got out of the car. Eva looked at him, surprised. Sitting behind the counter of the police station, he had looked, if not tall, of medium height. Standing here beside her, the top of his head only just reached her chin. 'Where is your uniform?' she asked irrationally.

'I'm off duty,' he replied. 'But please, call me Xavier.'

'Why should I?'

'Because it's my name. May I call you Eva?'

'No. Are you following me?'

'Of course not.'

'What are you doing here then?'

'Madame Connolly,' Officer Bernard chided, 'this is a public road. I have every right to –'

'To do what?'

'To drive here on my way to the golf course.'

'Oh,' Eva said, feeling stupid. 'I see. Right.'

'Yes.' He got into the car again.

She suddenly couldn't resist an opportunity to needle him. 'Have you caught the car thieves yet?' she asked.

He looked at her, annoyed. 'We're working on it,' he snapped.

'I'm sure you are. Have a nice day,' she chanted.

He didn't reply, but drove off in a cloud of dust.

'I think you have some explaining to do, Uncle Mark.'

'Stop calling him Uncle Mark,' Edwina giggled. 'Is my supper ready yet?'

'Oh, sorry.' Maria put the omelette on a plate and handed it to Edwina. 'There you are, darling. Sit down and eat. I'll get you something to drink.'

'But what are you doing here?' Mark insisted. 'Why are you looking after Edwina? And where's Saskia?'

'I'm here,' came a voice from the door. Saskia, still in her tiny bikini, but with a pink sarong around her waist, sauntered into the kitchen, looking as if she had merely been for a stroll in the garden.

'Where have you been all this time?' Maria demanded. 'I was out of my mind with worry. I was just about to call the coastguard. And the police,' she added.

'That's a bit over the top,' Saskia remarked, taking a peach from the fruit basket on the big table. 'I mean, I was only gone a little while.'

'You were gone the whole afternoon,' Maria protested. 'You left a six-year-old girl with a total stranger and just pissed off with that guy. What do you think Edwina's parents will say when they find out?'

'Could somebody please tell me what's going on?' Mark demanded.

'I'll tell you!' Maria exclaimed. 'That girl –' she pointed at Saskia – 'asked me to mind Edwina for "just a moment" while she left to scr–' she glanced at Edwina – 'socialise with her boyfriend in a rubber dinghy, and then she didn't come back until now. It's almost dark, for God's sake! Anything could have happened.'

'But it didn't,' Edwina piped in. 'Nothing happened. Can I have some more omelette, please?'

'Of course, darling,' Maria said, and took out more eggs from the fridge.

'So that's what happened,' Mark said. 'Well, with Saskia, that sort of thing was bound to happen.'

'I suppose,' Maria replied. 'But Edwina's starving, poor thing. Nobody seems to worry much about her around here.'

'I bet you're starving too,' Mark continued. 'And I'm a bit peckish myself. Make enough for two more, and then I'll get a bottle of wine from the cellar. You look as if you need a drink.'

'And I'll get some bread,' Saskia joined in. 'And maybe some cheese? There's a whole Brie in the larder. OK?'

'I don't think so, old girl,' Mark said, his voice as soft as silk. 'Maria and I need to talk. And you have partied enough for today.'

'But I . . .' Saskia protested.

'I think you should go and put on something a little less ... eh ... comfortable,' Mark suggested. 'And then put Edwina to bed.' His tone left no room for argument.

Saskia looked somewhat deflated. 'OK,' she mumbled, and walked slowly out of the kitchen. 'Come upstairs when you've finished eating, Edwina,' she said over her shoulder.

'So,' Maria said, when Edwina had disappeared to bed and they were having their improvised supper. 'What about that little chat, then? I have managed to use my tiny brain and figure out that it wasn't the way I looked that barred me from the disco the other night.'

'No, you looked marvellous.'

'So?'

'Well,' Mark started, looking embarrassed. 'Naughty of me, I know, but ...'

'Naughty?' Maria raised her eyebrows. 'That's not the word I would use actually. You bastard,' she muttered. 'How could you be such a shit? And you look like such a perfectly harmless little nerd. Old Etonians, eh? More like the bloody Mafia.' She shook her head in disbelief. 'I can't wait to tell Louise. She'll be so shocked. She actually *likes* you, God only knows why.'

'She does?' Mark asked, looking suddenly delighted.

'Yeah. I think she needs her head examined.' Maria sipped some wine. 'And I wonder what Paul will do to you when he hears? He was *really* pissed off, you know. I bet he's that silent type who goes berserk when he's annoyed. I can't wait to tell him.'

'Maria –' Mark put a hand on her arm – 'listen to me for a moment.'

'Yes?'

'You must know why I organised that little ...'

'Charade? You bastard,' she said again, only because it made her feel better.

'Well, OK.' Mark sighed. 'I'm really sorry. And I don't blame you for being seriously annoyed. But ...' He took a deep breath. 'I'm crazy about your sister. And I had to get her on her own just to find out if ...'

'If what?'

'If there was the slightest chance that she might feel the same.'

'And?' Maria stared at him, at his too-big short-sleeved shirt, his glasses halfway down his thin nose and his impossible haircut.

'Well, yes,' Mark smiled. 'I think there's a chance.'

'Jesus,' Maria muttered, 'you really are an optimist. And you do have some nerve.' She looked at him, disgusted. How could he? she thought. How could he move in on someone else's girlfriend like that? And I thought he and Paul were friends.

'All is fair,' Mark said, as if he could read her thoughts, 'in love and war.'

'But Paul is such a nice guy. He wants to marry Louise. Imagine what it would do to him if they broke up.'

Mark looked at her with interest. 'Mmm,' he said. 'Exactly. Just what I thought.' He leaned forward. 'Are you trying to tell me that you will cry your eyes out if those two split up?'

Maria looked down at her plate. 'I don't know what you mean. I just wouldn't like to see such a lovely guy hurt.'

'Then don't tell him about this.'

'What? You mean about how you fixed the disco thing? Or that you think Louise might be attracted to you?'

'Both.'

Maria stared at Mark with loathing. 'All right. I won't. But only because –'

'You're a saint?'

'Piss off.'

Eva was in her bedroom, waking up from her siesta, when the phone rang.

'Get that, darling,' she mumbled. But there was no answer. She opened her eyes. Dan was not there. The phone on her bedside table rang again. 'Oh, all right,' she muttered, lifting the receiver. 'Hello?'

'Frau Conolly?' said a woman's voice Eva did not recognise.

'*Ja?*'

'This is the Department of Justice in Berlin.'

'Yes?'

'I have the minister on the line for you.'

Eva sat bolt upright on the edge of her bed.

'*Guten Tag*, Frau Connolly.' The minister's deep voice was warm and apologetic. 'I'm so sorry to disturb you in the middle of your holiday.'

'Oh, that's no problem at all, Minister,' Eva gushed.

'You can probably guess why I'm calling.'

'Eh, yes, of course.'

'It's terrible that this sort of crisis should happen right in the middle of the holiday season.'

'I know.' What crisis? Eva thought, mystified. She racked her brain for a possible explanation. She hadn't kept in touch with the news, only half listening to Dan reading aloud from the morning paper. She had been too busy running the house, enjoying life in Provence and thinking about Yves. What was going on in the rest of the world seemed so distant somehow.

'I was half expecting a call from ... someone,' she said.

'Quite. Well, because of this crisis, the Austrians have called a meeting.'

'The Austrians?' What is going on? Eva thought. And what are the Austrians up to?

'Yes,' the minister continued. 'Their presidency of the EU has only just started and they have this to cope with straight away.'

'Indeed.'

'I'm glad you realise the seriousness of the situation, which is more than I can say for some of your colleagues. Most of them are unavailable and those available didn't seem to know what was going on.'

'That's a very irresponsible attitude,' Eva agreed.

'Absolutely. They do not seem to realise that a new Commission is being put together in the autumn.'

The minister paused. 'But, where was I? Oh, yes, the meeting. I assume that you're able to fly out at once?'

'Of course.' Despite her calm voice, Eva felt sheer panic rising in her throat. What had happened? And where was this meeting? And when?

'The other ministers are already gathering in Vienna, so I suggest you try to get yourself a hotel room straight away.'

Vienna, Eva thought, at least I know where I'm supposed to go. 'Yes, I will,' she agreed.

'The meeting starts the day after tomorrow.'

'I see. What about my boss? You know, Commissioner Fregene de Popolonia? He's in St Tropez as well. Do you want me to contact him?'

'I don't know.' The minister hesitated. 'Is his presence really necessary?'

You could say a lot of things about Guido, Eva thought, but 'necessary' wasn't one of them. 'Well, I think I should at least mention it to him,' she argued. 'But if I put it to him that the meeting will be long and tedious and that I can handle it on my own, I doubt he'll want to interrupt his holiday.'

'You're a very clever woman.'

'Why, thank you, Minister.'

'And I know that you have done some very good work in the cabinet. I've also heard that you're very knowledgeable about precisely this sort of problem. That's why we are very keen for you to attend.'

'Oh, really? That's very kind.'

'Not at all. I've read the paper you wrote about it. It was excellent.'

'Thank you,' Eva said again, feeling she was stuck

in some kind of nightmare. She hoped he wouldn't ask anything that would require an actual answer.

'Not at all. It's a pleasure to deal with someone who keeps in touch with events even on holiday.'

'I do my best.'

'Excellent. I'm looking forward to seeing you in Vienna, Frau Connolly. *Auf Wiedersehen.*'

Eva hung up, trying to get her mind in gear. I've got to find out what this all about, she thought. Then reserve a room in Vienna. Book flight. Pack. No, book flight, then pack, then room. No, that didn't sound right either. Clothes, she thought, I have to have the right sort of clothes. You can't attend a meeting about an international crisis in shorts and a T-shirt with 'I love the Côte d'Azur' on the front. How am I going to get together the sort of sombre wardrobe needed for this? I don't have time to go to Brussels first. She suddenly had an idea. Maria. She had arrived in a navy trouser suit and they were the same size. OK, that would be a good start. Feeling slightly more confident, Eva went downstairs to find Dan.

He was in the living room, watching a golf tournament on television.

'I have to go to Vienna,' she announced.

'I thought so.' He switched off the TV.

'You did?'

'Of course. There's a terrible crisis as a result of what happened in the Balkans. Weren't you listening when I read it out to you this morning?'

'No, not really.' Eva sank down beside Dan on the sofa. 'Tell me about it.'

'There have been awful riots in Albania and

refugees are pouring into Greece and Italy. I thought you would have been more interested, as immigration and refugee problems are your speciality.' He picked up the paper from the small table beside him. 'Here, read all about it yourself.'

Eva took the paper and scanned the first page. 'God, this is appalling. How come I didn't realise what was going on?'

'You've been a bit absent-minded lately.'

She put down the paper and looked at him thoughtfully. 'I know,' she said. 'I've been positively lethargic.'

'Is it the heat?' Dan wondered. 'Or are you not feeling well?'

'No, I'm fine. I have had a lot of things on my mind, that's all. And this place is so soporific somehow.'

'Maybe we sleep too much?' Dan suggested.

'The phone call from the minister woke me up, in any case.' Eva laughed. 'It was like a bucket of cold water in my face.'

'When do you have to go?'

'Tomorrow. Will you be able to hold the fort here until I come back?'

'Of course. But there's isn't much to worry about.'

'Just keep an eye on them.'

'Who? Paul and Louise? Or Maria?'

'All of them,' Eva stated.

'But they can look after themselves, surely,' Dan argued. 'I don't see why I have to play nursemaid to them.'

'You never know,' Eva said. 'Just keep an eye on them.'

The villa was very quiet all afternoon. Dan was driving Eva to the airport in Nice and Louise had gone with him to do some shopping in Cannes on the way home. The air was heavy with thunder and the heat oppressive. Paul was lying by the pool, trying to read but finding it impossible to concentrate. He put down his book and watched Maria as she stood on the diving board preparing to dive. He thought idly that she reminded him of the bronze statue of a young woman he had seen once in a museum in Rome: lithe and lovely, with small but perfect breasts, slim waist and only slightly rounded hips.

She stretched up her arms and dived, making just a tiny ripple as she hit the water. Paul did a slow handclap in appreciation as her head re-emerged.

'Oh,' she murmured. 'I didn't know you were there.'

'I don't know how you could have missed me. You're not going to the beach today?'

'It's too hot. And I have a little bit of reading to do as well. I just needed to cool off.'

'Reading?'

'For work. I had to bring some stuff with me and then I have to do a reader's report. It's for our list next spring.' Maria swam to the edge of the pool and got out.

'That's a bit tough, having to work in this heat.'

'Oh, I don't mind. I enjoy it.'

'Publishing must be very interesting.'

'I love it.' Maria dried her hair on a towel and sat down on one of the sun loungers.

'You seem very content these days,' Paul remarked. 'Does that Italian have something to do with it?'

'Maybe,' Maria replied airily.

'And is he the reason you take off to the beach every day?'

'Wouldn't you love to know?' Maria put the towel around her neck, slipped on her sandals and walked away. 'See you at dinner,' she said over her shoulder as she left.

The outline of her body seemed to shimmer in the heat as she walked up the path.

'I wonder where they are,' Paul said. 'It's getting late.'

'I'm sure they'll be here soon,' Maria replied, picking up the wine bottle. 'More wine?'

'Yes, please. That's a lovely rosé.' Paul held out his glass.

It was ten o'clock and Maria and Paul had just finished dinner on the terrace. Storm clouds were gathering over the hills and there was not the slightest breath of wind. There was a distant roll of thunder.

'It's coming closer,' Maria said.

'It's so still. Even the crickets are quiet tonight. It's as if they are bracing themselves.'

'The thunderstorms here are very violent, Mark told me.'

'Look, lightning.' Paul pointed to the east. 'Just over those hills.'

'Maybe the storm is over Cannes,' Maria said. She was interrupted by the sound of the phone in the living room and rose to answer.

'Hello?'

'Maria,' Louise shouted.

'Yes? What's that noise?'

'Rain. It's coming down in buckets here.'

'Where are you?'

'Just outside Cannes. The road is flooded and there has been a landslide, so we have decided to stay in a hotel until tomorrow.'

'But what about Eva?'

'She's gone. Her plane took off hours ago. She should be in Vienna by now.'

'Right.'

'So don't worry about us, we'll be home in the morning. Daddy said to close all the windows and stay indoors until it's over.'

'But the storm is very far away.'

'Daddy said it's heading your way. And it'll be right over you before you know it. So check everything at once and unplug the computer and the TV.'

'OK. We will. See you in the morning.' Maria hung up and went back out on the terrace.

'Who was that?' Paul asked

'Louise. The storm has just hit Cannes and the roads are flooded, so they're staying the night.'

'I see.'

Maria sat down again. There was a sudden clap of thunder and forked lightning lit up the hills. 'This is fantastic,' she exclaimed. 'Unbelievable.'

'You're not afraid?' Paul's eyes glittered as he looked at her excited face. Maria stared back at him. 'Afraid? No. Not of the thunder.'

CHAPTER 12

A fine drizzle fell from a grey sky and the air felt cold and damp. Vienna seemed like another planet, Eva thought, after the bright sun and blue skies of St Tropez. The trip from Nice had been endless, with the connecting flight from Geneva delayed by several hours. Then her bag had been lost and she had to wait an hour until it was finally found on the wrong carousel. Tired and bad-tempered, she had arrived at the Sacher Hotel very late. The professionalism and charm of the hotel staff cheered her up, however, as they did everything to make her feel welcome. A cheerful young porter helped her with her bags and showed her to a spacious, comfortable room on the top floor.

Finally, she could relax and get a night's sleep before the meetings started. She had always liked Vienna, the beautiful buildings and wide streets, the lovely parks and gardens, so well-kept and clean. And the Sacher Hotel was one of the most comfortable hotels in Europe, with its old-world charm and beautiful interiors. The rooms were spacious and beautifully furnished, with wonderful bathrooms. Eva felt as if she had walked straight into the 1930s when a liveried waiter wheeled in a table with a white tablecloth and covered silver dishes that contained her supper. Feeling very hungry, she sat down and lifted the lids. The smell of sautéed veal in Madeira sauce and new potatoes made her mouth water. She hadn't eaten since that morning and now it was nearly eleven o'clock. She poured herself a glass of red wine and switched on Sky News. Let's see what they say about the crisis in Albania, she thought.

She ate slowly as she watched the scenes of the refugees walking across the border into Greece. How horrible, she thought, having to leave your home that way. Hopefully, the ministers will be able to agree on some sort of aid package.

The phone rang beside her bed. Eva put down her fork and went to answer it.

'Hello?'

'*Guten Abend, meine liebe* Eva.'

'That's the worst accent I've ever heard.'

'I know.' Yves switched to French. 'German is not one of my strong points. And it's a terrible language to flirt in.'

'How can you talk of flirting now?'

'It's always on my mind,' he laughed.

'How did you know where to find me?'

'Where else would you be but in the best hotel?'

'When did you arrive?'

'I didn't. I'm still in Nice, trying to get on a flight. But there has been a storm which has cancelled everything, so I won't be able to be out there until tomorrow.'

'What has that got to do with me?' Eva demanded. Yves' voice both unnerved and irritated her. 'And why are you coming to Vienna? Isn't this more Jean-Claude Bonhomme's area?'

'They were unable to contact him. He had left his villa to go and visit a sick relative, it appears. Somebody who seems to be staying in the Carlton Hotel in Cannes. That's where I spotted him having dinner last night.' He laughed ironically.

'Is that why you called me? To tell me about that?'

'No, darling. I called to tell you I'm crazy about you. I'm really looking forward to spending a few days with you in that romantic city.'

'Vienna is not very romantic at the moment. It's wet and cold.'

'But there are so many things to do there. What about the opera? We could go and ...'

'It's closed for the summer.'

'The Spanish Riding School, then. I always thought those shows were so sexy, with the stallions prancing about and –'

'That's closed too.' Eva stood up straighter, trying not to be seduced by his voice, so warm and inviting, so soothing on this grey, lonely evening.

'What a pity. We'll have to think of something else to do together. But I have to go. Good night, *mon amour.*'

'Good night,' Eva said softly, and hung up.

'We'd better go around and close the windows,' Maria suggested, collecting their plates and glasses.

'OK,' Paul agreed. 'I'll go upstairs if you do the ones

down here. And close the shutters as well. We'll meet in the living room when we're finished.'

'And then go and hide in the cellar until it clears?' she mocked.

'If you want. It might be the best thing.'

There was a rumble as the thunder moved closer and then a loud crack as the lightning hit something close by.

'No way,' Maria said. 'I'm going to watch from here.'

'Well, whatever. Let's go. It's starting to rain.'

Paul ran upstairs and Maria could hear him closing the shutters on the landing. She closed the tall windows leading to the terrace and then proceeded to close every window on the ground floor. The sound of the rain increased, until the drumming on the roof and terrace was deafening. Lightning flashed again and again, and the rolls of thunder were ear-splitting. Maria could see the palm trees bending in the violent gusts of wind as lightning illuminated the garden with frightening regularity.

'Jesus,' Maria panted, as she came back to the living room. 'This is one hell of a storm.' She held up a bottle. 'Look. I found Daddy's favourite cognac in the kitchen. How about a glass each, just to settle our nerves?'

'Good idea. Where are the brandy glasses?'

'In that big thing over there.' Maria pointed to the tall oak cupboard at the far wall. But just as Paul started to walk in that direction, all the lights went out and the room was plunged into darkness. From time to time, a flash of lightning illuminated the room in a ghostly glow.

'It's like a Hollywood movie,' Maria laughed. 'Can you find them?'

'I think so,' Paul said from the other side of the room. 'I've got the door open, in any case. Yes. Got them.'

'Don't break them, for God's sake, they belong to Uncle Dieter. I think they are Baccarat. At least a hundred euro a glass.'

'Oh, God. I better be careful, then.'

'I'll come over with the bottle. Don't move.'

'Look, Maria,' Paul protested, 'let's forget about the . . .'

'Hi!' Maria said by his side. 'I'm right here.' There was a tinkle, then a crash of broken glass.

'Shit!' Paul exclaimed. 'I dropped them. Oh, God.'

'What will Uncle Dieter say?' Maria giggled.

'I think you've had enough to drink in any case. I seem to remember opening a second bottle of wine.'

'Yes, Uncle Paul.'

They looked at each other as lightning flashed again. But the thunder was suddenly less audible and the rain softer. 'It's going further away,' Maria remarked.

'So it seems. But you have no shoes on and here we are, in the dark, surrounded by broken glass.'

'We'll have to drink straight out of the bottle.' Maria pulled out the cork and put the neck of the bottle to her mouth.

'No, you don't.' Paul took the bottle out of her hand and put it down. 'Let's get out of here. I'll have to carry you or you'll cut your feet to ribbons.'

He picked her up as if she weighed nothing at all and started walking carefully in the direction of the sofa. Maria relaxed in his arms, closed her eyes and pressed her cheek against the soft fabric of his shirt. He smelled of some delicious aftershave and she could feel his heartbeat.

'Careful,' she whispered.

'I won't drop you.'

'That's not what I meant.' She put her arms around his neck. 'I had no idea you were so strong.'

'You don't weigh very much. Here's the sofa.'

'No. Take me out onto the terrace. I want to smell the air. And look, there are the stars.'

Paul opened the doors and carried Maria outside. He put her gently down on her feet and looked into her face. 'There. You're safe now.'

'Am I?'

The moon came out from behind the black clouds and shone on her upturned face. A soft breeze gently lifted a strand of her hair. She sighed and closed her eyes.

'Oh, God,' Paul whispered, and then his arms were around her again and his lips on hers.

They kissed for what seemed like an eternity. Maria didn't know how it happened, but suddenly they were on the sun loungers under the awning. She knew it was wrong, but it seemed to her the most natural thing in the world to kiss him and she thought she wanted to do it for hours, but then she found herself unbuttoning his shirt while he eased off her top. He slipped a hand behind her back, unhooked her bra and threw it aside in one easy movement.

'God, you're good,' Maria whispered.

Then she breathed in sharply as he caressed her breasts and she clung to him, the feel of his hot skin on hers making her dizzy with desire. The rest of their clothes dropped to the ground and their bodies seemed to find the right positions all by themselves.

They continued to murmur softly to each other, as they made love in the moonlight, with the thunder only a soft rumble in the far distance.

Maria woke up and looked around her with a feeling of confusion. She was in her bed, naked, with her clothes in a pile at the end of her bed. Was it a dream? she thought. Did I only imagine that we made love on the terrace? But no, she knew it was real. They had stayed there nearly all night, and, when the sun turned the clouds on the horizon a soft pink, she had left Paul sleeping in the sun loungers with a cotton throw from the living room over him. She hadn't known what else to do. She couldn't imagine what she would say to him when they faced each other in the bright light of the new day.

There was a gentle knock on the door.

'Yes?' Maria answered softly. Paul was coming to see her, to tell her he loved her.

But the door opened to admit Fatima with the morning tea. Maria clutched her bedclothes around her while she tried to smile at Fatima.

'Good morning, mademoiselle,' Fatima said, and put the little tray on the bedside table. 'There was a bad storm last night. I'm sorry I wasn't here to help you, but I was at my sister's in the village, and I was afraid to go outside.'

'That's all right.' Maria sat up in the bed. 'I understand. My father and sister were stuck in Cannes.'

'You were here all alone?' Fatima's eyes were concerned.

'No, Paul was here too. But we were all right.' Maria picked up her teacup.

'Oh? I'm glad. It wouldn't have been nice to be alone on such a night.'

'No, you're right.'

'The storm must have been terrible up here. There was even some broken glass in the living room.'

'Was there?' Maria said. 'I wonder how that happened?'

'The thunder must have shaken the house,' Fatima suggested. 'I will serve breakfast on the terrace in half an hour, if that's all right?'

'On the terrace?'

'Yes. It's not at all flooded. The awning is a little ripped though. I noticed when I opened the shutters.'

'Was ... there anyone there?'

'No, mademoiselle.' Fatima looked confused. 'Why?'

'Oh, no reason.' Maria smiled at Fatima. 'Thanks for the tea. I'll be down as soon as I'm ... eh ... dressed.'

'*Bien, mademoiselle.*' The door closed behind her.

Maria put down her cup. What have I done? she asked herself. She buried her face in her hands. Oh, God, what a bloody mess. What is Louise going to say? She'll never forgive me. How could I do this to her? I must be mad. How am I going to be able to face her after this? And how am I going to face Paul?

She closed her eyes as she thought of the night before. We shouldn't have, she said to herself. But, oh, it was magic. She knew she had never felt like this for anyone. Not ever. But why did it have to be him? She opened her eyes again. I have to talk to him before Louise gets here, she thought, and got out of bed.

There was no one on the terrace when she arrived down a few minutes later. The air was fresh and cool after the rain the night before, and there was the smell of earth drying rapidly in the sun. The sky was a deeper blue than before and the colours of the flowers and trees seemed more intense.

She had dressed demurely in a pair of white linen trousers and a long-sleeved top, and pulled back her hair in a severe knot. A breakfast for two had been laid out on the table. The coffee and fresh bread smelled lovely and Maria realised how hungry she was. She sat down and helped herself to coffee, orange juice, a large hunk of fresh bread and some strawberry jam. She was on her second helping when she heard footsteps coming through the living room and out onto the terrace. She looked up. It was Paul.

'Good morning,' she said, feeling suddenly shy.

'Lovely morning,' he remarked, and sat down beside her.

'Yes. Coffee?'

'No, I prefer tea.'

'Oh. Well, in that case . . .'

The sound of a car driving up to the steps below the terrace interrupted her. A car door slammed. Maria looked at Paul, her face white.

'They're back,' she whispered.

At the end of the second day of the emergency meeting, Eva thought she was going to faint with fatigue. The meeting had continued until four o'clock that morning and restarted at eleven o'clock. Everybody was stressed and bad-tempered, and Eva tried to keep her wits about her.

The German Minister for Justice had been charming, however, insisting she sit beside him during some of the negotiations and complimenting her on her work. Hans Mueller, the minister's very friendly personal assistant, was also very kind, and told her he had heard about the way she was practically running the cabinet in Brussels, and how impressed they all were in the ministry.

By five o'clock that afternoon, the member countries of the EU seemed to be a little closer to agreeing on how to divide responsibility for caring for the refugees and there was a much-needed break.

Eva headed to the ladies' to wash her hands and touch up her make-up. Sitting on the toilet cover in one of the cubicles, she closed her eyes. After a few moments, she got her hip flask out of her handbag. Just a few sips, to calm herself down after this hectic day. As she lifted the flask to her lips, she heard footsteps and voices. Two women speaking French. Eva sipped the vodka and only half listened to the conversation about hair and make-up and the annoyance of having one's holiday interrupted.

'God, this is a bit of a marathon,' one of the women said.

'You're telling me,' said the other. 'Where were you when you were hauled in?'

'La Baule.'

'I was in Biarritz.' The woman sighed. 'I was having a lovely holiday when they called from the Commission. I don't understand why they had to have so many interpreters. If some of them had bothered to learn at least one foreign language, things would be a lot easier. And I don't like the way they order you around.'

'The women are the worst, though. Did you see that Eva Connolly?'

Eva sat up straighter, almost dropping her flask.

'I know who you mean. She loves to shout orders at people.'

'Yeah, and she seems so ice cold,' her friend continued. 'But that's only an act. I saw her flirting in the corridor with that dishy man from the legal department. He was practically inside her dress.'

'You mean Yves Dutronc?'

'That's him. Lovely man. I worked for him for over a year.' She sighed. 'He was such a sweetheart to work for. But you should know, darling. Didn't you have a little fling with him last year?'

'Mmm, I did.' The other woman sounded wistful.

'Tell me all. What's he like in bed?'

'Let me put it this way –' her friend lowered her voice – 'I bet he was never teased in the shower when he went to school.'

The other woman laughed.

'But a bit of a sleaze, I'm afraid,' her friend continued. 'He was carrying on with someone else at the same time as me. The man's insatiable.'

'I wouldn't mind a bit of that,' the other woman giggled. 'I can't understand what he sees in that German tart, though.'

'She'd better be careful. That man's trouble. But she seems to be able to cope with any man. And she's sucking up to her own minister as well. That's probably how she operates to improve her career prospects.'

Eva could hear the door bang when the women left. Tears began to sting her eyes, but she brushed them away. She took a last slug from the flask. What awful little bitches, she thought. But they're just jealous. She pulled herself together, blew her nose, rose from the seat, pushed the cork back into her hip flask and shoved it in her bag.

'Isn't this fun?' Hans Mueller shouted to Eva over the din.

'Marvellous,' she shouted back.

They were in the Fuhrgassi-Huber, a *Heuriger*, one of the many little inns in the wine-growing hills surrounding the city where the Viennese went to have a casual meal and a glass of white wine. Hans had asked Eva to join him and his colleagues when the meeting was over, and, although she was very tired, she had agreed to go.

She smiled at Hans and tucked into the huge Wiener Schnitzel that a jolly waitress had just served. 'This is delicious.'

'And the wine?'

'Terrible.'

He laughed and lifted his glass. 'I know it's not exactly a vintage Chablis, but you can't have everything.' He put down his glass. 'You're looking at me in a strange way. Have I done something to offend you?'

'No, not at all. I just noticed someone I know.'

Hans turned to look at the door that had just opened to let in yet another customer. 'Oh, yes,' he said. 'Your French colleague had the same idea.'

Yves waved at her across the restaurant. 'Eva,' he called.

'Oh, no,' Eva mumbled.

'What's the matter?' Hans asked.

'I didn't want to meet him tonight.'

'Why don't we just ignore him?'

But it was too late. 'Here you are,' Yves said, looking at Eva with delight. 'I've been looking all over town for you.'

'I didn't think this kind of place was really your thing,' Eva replied.

'Not much of a choice when everything else is closed,' Yves remarked. 'Do you mind if I join you? Do you think there would be room for me if you all squash up a bit?'

'Of course.' Hans moved further in along the long table, ignoring Eva's look of annoyance. 'Do join us. The schnitzel is lovely but the wine is only just drinkable.'

'Great,' Yves said, and sat down beside Eva. He turned to Hans. 'Yves Dutronc is my name. I'm with the legal department in Brussels.'

'Hans Mueller, Department of Justice in Berlin.' He

shook Yves' hand. 'I saw you during the meetings.'

'How nice to meet you. And so kind of you to take care of Eva. But it was lucky I bumped into you like this, wasn't it? Now we can make an evening of it.'

'Well, we have planned to go on a bit of a *Heurigen* tour,' Hans said. 'I have a list of the best ones.'

'*Wunderbar.*'

'You're not too tired?' Hans asked Eva. 'The meeting was very long, but now it's over and we can relax.'

'I know,' she replied. 'It's such a relief.'

'And we can all go back to our holiday.' Hans beamed. 'I was walking in the Tyrolean mountains with my girlfriend when I was called. She's still there, keeping the tent warm, if you know what I mean.' He winked at Eva.

The evening became very lively. The bad wine flowed and everyone started to sing bawdy songs in German. Eva was really enjoying herself, laughing and singing in German. Amused, she watched Yves, who was looking at them with a mixture of anger and boredom on his face.

'We're going to another *Heuriger,*' Hans suddenly announced. 'It's called the Stippert.'

Eva turned to Yves. 'I don't suppose you'll want to come,' she said. 'You look as if you've had enough.'

'Not at all,' Yves said.

'Let's go, then.' Hans got unsteadily to his feet.

Before Eva had a chance to protest, she found herself in a taxi with Yves.

'How about going back to the hotel?' he suggested, putting an arm around her. 'Hans won't miss us.'

'No. You and I are not going anywhere. The Stippert, please,' she said to the driver

'Oh, no,' Yves moaned. 'I can't bear much more of it. I'm sorry darling, but...'

'I know, I know. The wine is like horse piddle and the songs are awful.'

'But I thought you liked it,' he argued. 'Isn't it the kind of thing you were brought up with?'

'I'm German,' Eva snapped, 'not bloody Austrian. But, unlike you, I have stamina.'

Yves leaned closer to Eva in the taxi. 'It's not a question of stamina. I just want to take you to bed.' He put his hand on her knee.

Eva looked at his handsome face, his eyes that were looking at her with such desire, and felt the warm hand slowly caressing her knee. Then she remembered the conversation she had overheard in the ladies' toilet and lifted his hand off her knee. 'Don't even think about it,' she said. 'If you can't hack it, why don't you go home?'

'And give you up to Hans Mueller? Never.'

What seemed like years later, Hans and Eva were slowly walking towards the Sacher Hotel with Yves in tow.

'Why is he following us?' Hans asked.

'He's staying in the same hotel.'

'I see.'

When they arrived at the hotel, Eva asked for her key, and Yves was making a superhuman effort to sound sober as he asked for his.

'How about a nightcap?' Hans suggested to Eva. 'I

have a lovely suite on the third floor. We could order up some more of that delicious wine. And I wanted to tell you about my student days in Heidelberg.'

'I think it's a little too late for that,' Eva replied.

'That's right,' Yves agreed, putting an arm around Eva. 'She's mine, you know. I'm going to take her to my room, and –'

'No, you're not.' Eva peeled his arm off her. 'Go to your room and sleep it off, Yves, there's a good boy.'

'But I have been good,' Yves argued, trying to put an elbow on the reception desk. 'All evening. I drank that awful wine, sang those silly songs and was very, *very* nice to Hans.'

'I think I'd better help you to your room,' Hans offered.

'No, thank you, I'm not really that attracted to you,' Yves said. 'Don't take it persh . . . press . . . Ah, you know what I mean.'

'It's all right,' Hans assured Eva, 'I'll take care of him.'

'Are you sure?'

'That's the least I can do after all you have done for us.'

'I don't know what you mean, but thank you.'

Hans smiled and propped Yves up. 'These Frenchmen are such wimps. Can't take a little bit of wine. But don't worry. He won't bother you tonight.'

'Thank goodness for that. You're very kind.'

Hans winked at her conspiratorially. 'We have to look after Germany's best asset in Brussels, you know.'

★

When Eva arrived home the next evening, only Maria was there to greet her. She was on the terrace, having a cup of tea, when Eva walked up the steps.

'How was your trip?' Maria asked.

'Awful.' Eva put down her suitcase on the terrace. 'Not the actual meeting, but the flight and the weather and ...'

'Good,' Maria said, staring out at the lights of St Tropez in the far distance.

'The meeting was very successful,' Eva continued. 'And Germany didn't have to take the biggest share of the responsibility. But it was such a marathon. I don't think I got more than three hours' sleep while it was going on. And the last evening we all went out to drink wine and I was so tired I could hardly move this morning.'

'Mmm. Sounds great,' Maria mumbled.

Eva looked at her. 'What's the matter with you? You look totally spaced out.' She felt Maria's forehead. 'Are you coming down with something?'

Maria jerked her head away. 'I'm fine.'

'Where's everybody?'

'Paul and Louise went to walk around St Tropez, and I think Daddy's gone to bed.'

'But it's only nine o'clock. Is he ill as well?'

'No one's ill,' Maria suddenly snapped. 'We're all perfectly fine.'

'What *is* the matter with you?' Eva demanded. 'You're acting very strange.' She turned around as Dan came out from the living room. 'Darling,' she sighed, putting her arms around him, 'I'm so glad to see you.' She suddenly realised it was true. Dan seemed so wonderfully comforting, so honest and good. What a lucky escape I had, she thought, thanks to Austrian wine and Hans Mueller.

He kissed her cheek. 'Lovely to have you back. Did everything go well?'

Eva sat down at the table. 'I'll tell you about it later. Could you get me a glass of wine? I'm a bit tired.'

'Here you are,' Dan said, and handed her a glass.

'Lovely. How were things here? I heard there was a storm. Did you get back from Cannes in time?'

'No, we didn't,' Dan replied. 'The roads were flooded, so we stayed in a hotel. Awful fleapit, I'm afraid, but we had no choice. We didn't get home until quite late the next morning. But Paul was here, so Maria wasn't alone.'

'Oh, good,' Eva said. 'Dear Paul. So reliable.'

CHAPTER 13

'Hi, sorry I'm late.' Eva's voice cut into Louise's thoughts as she sat waiting in the Porsche outside the hairdresser's in St Maxime.

Eva looked fantastic, Louise thought. Her skin glowed and her eyes were like polished emeralds. 'Where have you been all afternoon?' she enquired. 'Not that it's any of my business, of course.'

'I've been to the beauty salon.' Eva smiled and got into the passenger seat. 'I needed a lot done, so I had a full facial, a lash and brow tint and a body massage. I've been letting myself go during the holidays, so I really need to shape up.'

There was a determined tone in her voice, and Louise had a feeling she wasn't talking about her appearance.

'You look fantastic,' Louise said.

'Thanks. Your hair is nice. Maybe you don't want to take the top down?'

'Of course I do.' Louise touched the button and the roof soundlessly folded away. She put the car in first gear and started to pull away from the kerb.

'This is such a fantastic car,' Eva sighed and leaned back in the soft leather seat, 'It's much more sporty than mine.'

'Sporty?' Louise snorted, revving up the engine. 'Darling, a sports bra is "sporty", this is a PORSCHE!' she shouted as the car took off.

'Should you be going this fast?' Eva yelled, as she was pinned to her seat, her hair whipping around her face. 'The speed limit is fifty here.'

'Don't be such a bore,' Louise shouted back over the noise of the engine. 'Let's live a little.'

'But . . .' Eva tried, but the wind tore the words out of her mouth.

'Wait till you see what this car can do,' Louise yelled. 'It's better than sex.'

'Slow down,' Eva ordered a few minutes later, as they were on the open road.

'But there's no traffic. Not a soul around.' Louise pressed the accelerator a little harder. 'This car is so smooth.' The speed of the car and the wind in her hair made her reckless. She felt suddenly so free and careless. If Paul only knew. He would never let her drive his precious car like this. 'Isn't this great?' she shouted.

'You're right,' Eva agreed, closing her eyes as the car gathered force. 'This is amazing. Better than sex.'

'Sex?' Louise laughed. 'That was just foreplay. *This* is sex!'

She changed into fifth gear and pressed her foot down even harder. The car swept along the bay at high speed, making her feel as if she was flying. She only noticed the flashing lights of the motorcycle police behind them when Eva shouted at her to slow down.

'So mademoiselle,' the handsome policeman said, 'how fast do you think you were going?'

'Eh,' Louise stammered, 'I don't know really. Fifty?'

'Very funny.' He took out a notebook. 'You were doing a hundred and ninety.'

'Oh, really? I didn't notice.' Louise looked at him through her lashes. 'There was no one around, so I thought . . .'

'There was no one around, because we have closed this part of the road for tonight. Didn't you notice the roadblocks?'

'But why is the road closed?' Eva asked.

'The convention,' the policeman explained. 'They're all arriving tonight. May I have your licence, please, mademoiselle?'

'What convention?' Eva enquired.

But the policeman didn't reply, just wrote down Louise's name. 'Connolly?' he said. 'I think I've seen that name before. Have you already been booked?'

'No, she hasn't,' Eva snapped.

'Really? I could have sworn . . .'

'Are you from St Tropez?' Eva enquired.

'No, St Maxime. But this name . . .'

'What's that noise?' Eva suddenly asked, cocking her head. 'That droning sound?'

'That's the convention,' the policeman said, still looking at Louise's licence and writing out a ticket. 'You're Irish?' he asked. 'I didn't know Irish girls were blonde.'

'Some of us are,' Louise replied, with a little smile.

'But maybe you're not a real blonde?'

'Want me to prove it?'

Eva slid further down into her seat, as if trying to pretend she wasn't there.

'You'll still get a ticket, mademoiselle,' he replied sternly, but there was a smile in his eyes as he looked at Louise.

'You're very mean for such a good-looking man,' Louise simpered. Then she smiled again. 'When do you come off duty?'

'Louise, don't...' Eva started, touching her arm, but she shrugged it off.

The policeman lowered his Ray-Bans and looked at Louise over the rim. 'Ten o'clock.'

'Great,' Louise giggled. 'You know that bar called Le Vieux Port in St Tropez?'

'Yes,' the policeman replied, looking suddenly very happy, 'of course I do.'

'Be there at half-past ten, OK? And no ticket, of course.'

'Of course,' he agreed, and tore up the ticket. 'See you later, then, mademoiselle. And do try to stay within the speed limit in future.' He saluted and got back on his motorbike.

'Hold on a second,' Eva ordered, 'tell us about the ...' Her voice was drowned in the sound of engines as a huge number of motorbikes came into view.

The policeman kick-started his bike. 'It's the Harley-Davidson convention,' he shouted above the noise. 'Ten thousand motorbikes from all over

Europe. *Au revoir, mesdames.'* And he tore up the road in the direction of St Maxime.

'Why did you do that?' Eva demanded, as they drove sedately into St Tropez. 'Why did you agree to go on a date with that awful policeman?'

'I didn't.'

'But I heard you. You said you'd meet him at ...'

Louise laughed. 'Why didn't you listen? I told *him* to be there. I didn't say *I* would.'

'When I grow up,' Edwina said, 'I'm going to live in the country.'

'Really?' Maria asked. 'Why is that?' They were on the private beach of the Villa Caramel the following day, with Saskia and Mark.

'Because,' Edwina replied, 'it would be much better for the children. I'm going to have five. And a dog, no, two dogs.'

'Don't you have a dog?' Maria asked.

'No, because we live in town. In London. It's not a good place for animals. They suffer terribly. That's what Mummy said.' She sighed. 'I wish we could, though. I've seen dogs in the park and they didn't look as if they were suffering.'

'How is Louise?' Mark asked.

'Very well,' Maria replied.

'How are things between you and Paul?' Mark asked.

'Things? What things?' Maria felt herself blush.

Mark studied her face for a moment. 'Oh, nothing. You really have a lovely suntan.'

Maria got up. 'It's very hot. I'm going for a swim.'

She walked quickly to the water's edge, waded out and dived into the cool water. She swam hard and fast.

Paul had hardly spoken to her since the night of the thunderstorm. It was as if it had never happened. He was as attentive to Louise as always, although they seemed to argue a lot more than before. But it was nearly unbearable, Maria thought, to be in the same house and know he was sharing a bed with Louise. It was also difficult to see him every day, to look at his handsome face and hear his deep voice. And his smile ... But he didn't seem to smile much lately. She longed for his arms around her, his mouth on hers and his hands ... No, stop, she thought, don't make yourself miserable. Try to forget it. Put it behind you. She swam harder.

'Are you training for the Olympics?' Mark asked when she came back.

'Oh, shut up,' Maria said, and dried herself. She lay down on her towel and closed her eyes, still breathless. The sun and a humming noise in the distance were making her feel sleepy.

'Is there a wasp somewhere?' Edwina asked. 'I can hear it buzzing. I hate wasps. They're so mean.'

'It sounds like a whole swarm of them,' Mark said.

Maria sat up and looked around. 'I can't see anything, not even a fly.'

'It's becoming louder,' Saskia said.

'But what is it?' Mark enquired.

'It's a kind of droning noise,' Maria said. 'Like engines. It's coming from the direction of St Maxime.'

Mark listened. 'You're right,' he said. 'It sounds like

aeroplanes.' He looked up into the sky. 'But I can't see any.'

'Maybe they're too high up?' Edwina suggested. 'Sometimes aeroplanes go so high you can't see them.'

'Could be,' Maria said. She had finished drying herself and started putting on her shorts.

'Are you going home?' Edwina asked. 'It's not late.'

'I promised to walk the dogs today. Fernando is helping out at a dinner somewhere.'

'Dogs?' Edwina asked. 'You have dogs? Can I come and help too?'

'I don't see why not. Mark? What do you say?'

'I think that could be arranged,' Mark replied, sitting up. 'I could come with you. Is Louise . . .'

'She's gone to the hairdresser's in St Maxime to have her hair cut. Paul gave her his Porsche. God only knows why. He obviously doesn't know what she's like when she gets behind the wheel. She won't be back until at least seven o'clock.'

'Oh.' Mark lay down again.

'Where are your parents today?' Maria asked Edwina.

'They're gone to the airport to pick up Pickles and Bunty.'

'Who are they?' Maria asked. 'More dogs?'

'No, silly,' Edwina laughed. 'They're Daddy's friends from England.'

'Really?'

'That's right,' Mark mumbled, his eyes closed against the strong sunlight. 'Pickles went to school with my cousin Alistair.'

'Another Etonian?' Maria asked. 'How terribly jolly.'

'Ha, ha,' Mark muttered.

'Are we going, then?' Edwina asked, pulling at Maria's hand. 'Come on. I want to see those dogs.'

'But you have to change first,' Maria said. 'You have to put on something other than a swimsuit. And shoes. I'm going to walk in the woods.'

'Saskia,' Mark said. 'Go with them to the house and get some clothes for Edwina. Then you can have the rest of the afternoon off.'

'Great!' Saskia exclaimed, and sprang to her feet. 'Come on, then.'

'See you later,' Mark said as they walked off. 'And tell Louise I'll be in touch.'

The droning sound of engines was coming closer as they walked up the slope to the big house.

Paul sat on the edge of the pool wondering how his life had suddenly become such a mess. When he left college he had drawn up a plan for the rest of his life. It consisted of 1) start his own business, 2) make lots of money and 3) marry a beautiful girl. But instead, at this moment, his options seemed to be 1) tell Louise he had slept with Maria and watch her go ballistic, 2) pretend there was some sort of emergency at work and go back to Ireland or 3) drown himself in the pool.

What happened? he thought. My life was going so well, everything turning out exactly the way I planned.

When he met Louise, he had fallen for her pretty

face, her curvy figure and her bubbly personality within minutes of them looking at each other. She was very sexy, and so sweet and uncomplicated. She would marry him, he had been sure of that. He had been so pleased with himself.

Until he met Maria. She was not at all his type. Tall, dark girls with piercing blue eyes had never attracted him before. But here, in the south of France, he had watched her bloom, seen her grace and elegance close up. He loved watching her dive into the pool and swim in that athletic, graceful way.

Making love to Maria had been more exciting than he had ever imagined. There had been a tenderness and a depth of feeling he had never experienced with any other woman. But maybe he had only imagined it? She had been very distant with him afterwards, as if she was angry with both him and herself. She clearly didn't think much of the incident. I should really just leave, he thought. But he liked this family, he wanted to be a part of it. Bad move, mate, he said to himself. You should have left her alone.

Paul pinched the bridge of his nose and closed his eyes. All this thinking had given him a headache. There was a droning in his ears and the sun was hurting his eyes. He slipped into the cool, blue water.

Maria was in her room, changing out of her shorts and T-shirt, when Louise burst in without knocking.

'What happened to you?' Maria asked, staring at Louise's hair. 'I thought you were going to the hairdresser's.'

'I did. But then we decided to take the top down

on the car.'

'We?'

'Eva and I. She had some errands in St Maxime and I gave her a lift back. I thought I'd give her a thrill.'

'Knowing your driving, I'm sure she got more than that. Your hair looks like a crow's nest.'

'It was great fun, though. Paul's car is amazing. But I nearly got a speeding ticket.'

'God, not again. I thought you were going to be careful after that time on the Naas dual carriageway. How fast were you going?'

'I don't know –' Louise smiled mischievously – 'but I think my nose started to bleed.'

'You're completely mad, do you know that? What is Paul going to say? He treasures his car.'

'He is not going to say anything, because nobody is going to tell him. Eva promised and so will you, if you want to do me a favour.' Louise sat down on Maria's bed. 'What did you do today? Did something happen? You look a bit down.'

'I'm fine,' Maria snapped. 'I went to the beach for a bit and I've just walked the dogs with Edwina.'

'Who's Edwina?' Louise picked up a book from the bedside table and started to leaf through it idly.

'Mark's cousin. She's six years old and very sweet. We have become good friends.'

'How did you meet her?'

'It's a long story.'

'Have you seen Mark around lately?'

'I saw him today at the beach. Stop fiddling with my book.'

Louise looked at the title. 'Poetry? You seem in a

very romantic mood these days. Is it because of that Italian guy?'

'Yeah, maybe.' Maria snatched the book away. 'Did you want to talk to me about something? You have that brooding look.'

'Paul is acting very strange.' Louise started to twist the fringe of the bedspread between her fingers.

Maria's eyes were guarded as she looked at Louise. 'What do you mean?'

'He's a bit distant. And he hasn't laid a finger on me for days. I think he's angry with me for some reason. But when I asked him, he said he didn't know what I meant. And he bought me a lovely bracelet in St Tropez yesterday. Look.' Louise held out her arm to show a silver bracelet set with turquoises.

'Lovely,' Maria said, her voice expressionless. 'That's all right, then. I'm sure he's just tired or something. Where is he now?'

'Floating around in the pool, staring at the sky. He's been there for hours. He said something about considering his options. What do you think is wrong with him?'

'I have no idea.' Maria felt suddenly a little less bleak. 'I'm sure he'll snap out of it. Just leave him alone.'

'You look more cheerful now,' Louise remarked. 'Are you meeting your Italian boyfriend tonight? Is that it?'

'No, I'm not. I'm staying home.' Maria put on a white skirt and black top. 'I just wish that noise would stop. That awful droning from the road, I mean. There must be a lot of traffic tonight.'

'They're motorbikes. There's a Harley-Davidson convention this weekend, the policeman told us. Ten thousand motorbikes from all over Europe.'

'Ten thousand of them,' Eva moaned to Dan on the terrace. 'I don't know how we're going to get through the weekend.'

'The noise is rather hard to take,' he agreed.

'It's not the noise so much as those awful people. Have you seen them? Horrible greasy men with long hair and covered in tattoos. They're turning St Tropez into some kind of freak show. I don't know how it's allowed. I mean, they won't let you walk harmless little dogs on the beach, but they let these people go around freely wherever they –'

'But *they* wouldn't do what dogs do,' Dan argued.

'I wouldn't put it past them.'

Eva sighed as she looked at Dan. He had just come back from the golf course and had not changed out of his shorts and polo shirt. He looked relaxed but a bit tired. He didn't seem to have noticed the improvement in her appearance.

'Here's Paul now,' Dan said. 'That was a long swim.'

'I just felt like working out,' Paul replied, coming up the steps from the garden, dressed in swimming trunks, with a towel around his neck. Eva admired his suntanned chest and broad shoulders, thinking what a very lucky girl Louise was.

'It's nearly dinner time,' Dan said. 'I'd better go and put on a pair of trousers. Where are the girls?'

'We're here, Daddy,' Louise replied, coming out

from the living room with Maria in tow. 'Aren't you going to put on some clothes, Paul? Not that you don't look good like that.' She laughed, reaching up to give him a peck on the cheek. 'What do you think, Maria?'

'Oh, he's a babe,' Maria remarked. 'A fine specimen, I have to say.'

Eva darted a look at her. She had been very odd lately, even more sharp and sarcastic. Brittle, was the word that came to mind. Something was not quite right.

'There's a motorbike coming up the drive,' Louise announced. 'It's one of those Hell's Angels. I wonder what he wants.'

'Oh, no!' Eva exclaimed, as the noise became more and more deafening. 'Dan, do something. Don't let him ...'

The big machine stopped just below the steps and the rider took off his helmet and looked up at the terrace. His long blond hair was tied back in a ponytail and he was dressed in a black leather waistcoat, tight, studded leather jeans and cowboy boots. There was a tattoo of an eagle on one of his muscular upper arms and he looked very familiar. Eva suddenly knew who he was.

'Oh, my God,' she whispered. 'I don't believe it.'

'It's Uncle Dieter,' Louise squealed. 'He looks fantastic. You look fantastic, Uncle Dieter,' she shouted as he came up the steps.

'I didn't know old Uncle Dieter could look so sexy,' Maria said.

'What do you mean, old?' Dan asked. 'He's the same age as me.'

'Exactly,' Eva muttered. 'The age you'd expect a man to have a bit of sense.'

'*Meine liebe* Eva,' Dieter smiled, and enveloped Eva in a bear hug. 'How are you?'

Eva didn't quite know what to say to this man, so different from the correct businessman she knew her brother to be. He looked ten years younger and at least twenty pounds lighter than the last time she had seen him. And his eyes were so happy. It was as if he had been through a very thorough makeover, both mental and physical. 'So this was the convention you were talking about?' she finally said. 'Why didn't you tell me?'

'I wanted to give you a surprise.'

'You succeeded!' Dan laughed. 'I've never been so surprised in all my life.'

'But when did you start riding motorbikes?' Maria asked.

'Well,' Dieter explained, 'when I went to America two years ago to open a chain of shoe shops in California, I met some great guys. I've always been interested in motorbikes, and these guys showed me what a great time you can have driving around the States. I started working out on Venice Beach and then I bought a Harley-Davidson and joined them. And I brought it with me when I came home.'

'Is Gretchen here too?' Eva asked.

'Gretchen is still in LA,' Dieter replied, sounding oddly unconcerned. 'She didn't think it was worth it to come over for just a few days. So I'm here on my own. But don't worry, I won't be bothering you much.'

'I see,' Eva mumbled, still in a state of shock.

'It's so good to see you all,' Dieter beamed. He looked at Paul. 'But I don't think we've met. You must be Paul.'

'That's right,' Paul said, shaking hands. 'Nice to meet you.'

'And I was very happy to hear about Louise. You're a lucky guy, Paul. She's a *süsse Mädchen*, no?'

'Oh, yes,' Paul nodded. 'Very, eh, *süsse*.'

'And Maria? What about you? You look very well, I must say.'

'Good evening.' A voice interrupted them. Mark had just arrived. His eyes widened as he saw Dieter. 'I'm sorry. I didn't know you had guests.'

'Not a guest exactly,' Eva said. 'My brother, Dieter. Dieter Mebius.

'Oh?' Mark said, putting out his hand. 'I was wondering who that fantastic machine belonged to. I'm Mark White. Lovely to meet you, old chap.'

'Great to meet you,' Dieter replied, squeezing Mark's hand in a crushing handshake.

'What are you doing here?' Maria asked. 'I thought you said you had guests arriving.'

'Yes, we do . . . did,' Mark replied. 'I just came here to issue an invitation. Alistair, my cousin, is putting together a dinner at a restaurant in Gassin tomorrow night and he was wondering if you would like to join us.' He looked at Louise as he waited for an answer. 'You know Gassin, don't you? It's that village in the hills.'

'Oh, yes, of course,' Eva said. 'It's in the list of the most beautiful villages of France. An enchanting place. How lovely.'

'The restaurant is on the terrace. It's called Le Moulin à Vent,' Mark said.

'I know it,' Dan said. 'But did your cousin mean all of us?'

'Yes, of course,' Mark said. 'And Herr . . . eh . . .'

'Dieter,' Maria filled in.

'Dieter, of course. So will I tell Alistair you'll all come, then?' Mark asked.

'Oh, yes, do,' Louise agreed, without waiting for anyone else to reply.

'Great. See you tomorrow, then,' Mark said, and turned to leave. 'Eight o'clock. Casual dress.'

'Great,' Maria said. 'You can go the way you are, Uncle Dieter.'

'Casual chic,' Eva said, looking through her wardrobe the following evening, 'the most difficult thing to achieve. Elegant, yet careless, as if you threw something on that you just happened to find in your wardrobe.'

'I don't know why you're so worried,' Dan said from the bed, where he was reading the evening paper. 'I'm just going to wear *le look*.'

'No, you're not. You're going to wear your linen trousers and your light-blue shirt. I asked Fatima to iron them. They're hanging in your wardrobe.'

'Oh, all right. Can I at least wear the boat shoes?'

'Yes, if you promise not to tell anyone they're not the real thing.'

'What about Dieter?' Dan argued. 'You won't be able to tell him what to wear.'

'He can look after himself. And I have to admit he looks rather good like that. Very St Tropez.'

'He was very decent about the dogs,' Dan said. 'He didn't seem to be too annoyed at the way they were being kept.'

'They're more Gretchen's babies than his. Thank God she didn't come with him. She would have thrown us out.'

'Or that you had removed all his paintings and ornaments and covered his furniture in white fabric.'

'He's in such a good mood,' Eva replied. 'His business is doing so well. He thought it was a great idea to put the paintings away for safe keeping and to protect the sofas from stains.'

'Is that what you told him?' Dan laughed. 'Did he believe you?'

'He didn't seem to care one way or the other actually. I think that awful motorbike has rejuvenated him and made him more open to new ideas. He's thinking of going a bit more upmarket. He wants to start a designer line. Handmade shoes for the rich and famous. I hope he will. I hate having a brother who sells plastic clogs.'

She took out a pink silk blouse. 'Chanel? No, that's a bit passé.' She put it back in the wardrobe and pulled out a white sleeveless top with exquisite embroidery around the plunging neckline. 'Mmm. Maybe. Not designer, but ... Black trousers? Yes, I think I've got it. And just my pearls. Great. I think that will ...' She held the two items in front of her and turned around. 'Darling? What do you think?'

'Lovely,' he said, his eyes on the sports page.

'Might as well ask one of the dogs,' Eva muttered. 'No, I think I'll wear the beige trousers. Black and white is so hard to pull off. Makes you look like a waitress, if you're not careful.'

'Careful?' Dan said, looking up. 'Why do we have to be careful?'

'Never mind.'

Eva sighed and looked at him, sitting up on the bed with his back propped against the pillows. He looked all right, she thought, tanned and fit. Not a bit old or past it in any way. In fact, she realised, he was becoming very muscular. It was incredible how playing a lot of golf could give you this kind of body. Maybe she should try to play more seriously? Dan was certainly a great advertisement for the benefits of the game. But why did he seem not to take any interest in her any more? Last night she had gone to bed wearing her best black La Perla underwear and he had asked if she had forgotten to put on her nightie. What was wrong with him? She had ended up opening her briefcase and going through her notes from Vienna, while he watched a silly French sitcom on TV. The situation was beginning to seriously get on her nerves.

'I think I'll go naked,' she said, to see if that would wake him up.

'Mmm,' he muttered, studying the weather report. 'But won't you be a bit cold?'

CHAPTER 14

When Maria saw Lady Madeleine Bakewell, she knew this was class. Not Eva's contrived chic, but the real, *haute couture* kind. Lady Bakewell was six foot tall, thin to the point of being emaciated, and had the effortless elegance of the super rich. She appeared to be no more than thirty, with flawless pale skin and chin-length shiny black hair, cut in a sharp bob. She wore a grey linen skirt and a black top of such simplicity that Maria knew it had cost more than her own entire wardrobe, and no jewellery except for a platinum wedding ring.

'Oh, God,' Eva whispered behind her, 'I knew I was overdressed. Should I take off the pearls?'

'No,' Maria whispered back, 'you're fine.'

Their party moved forward to one of the long tables on the terrace of Le Moulin à Vent, which was on the edge of the small village of Gassin, perched high on a hill above the gulf of St Tropez, with stunning views of the mountains and the sea. It was the most beautiful spot on all of the Côte d'Azur, Maria thought, as she admired the old buildings basking in the rosy glow of the setting sun, the bays and inlets far below and the sea stretching out to meet the sky at the horizon. The daylight slowly faded, to be replaced by the light from the small lamps hanging from the umbrellas on the terrace.

Mark rose and smiled broadly as they reached the long table where he was sitting with his cousins and their friends. 'Hello,' he said. 'Let me introduce you. This is Madeleine, my cousin Alistair's wife. Maddy, this is Eva and Dan Connolly. And Maria, Edwina's special friend.' Lady Bakewell nodded with a uninterested look as Mark continued. 'Louise, Maria's sister, and her boyfriend, Paul, is that tall chap and this –' he stood back to let Dieter come through – 'is Dieter Mebius, Eva's brother, who is here for the convention, as you can probably guess, from his ...'

Lady Bakewell finally showed some interest. 'How marvellous,' she gushed, shaking Dieter's hand. 'A Harley-Davidson aficionado.' She put a hand on his arm. 'Please, you must sit beside me and tell me all about your machine.' She spoke with a clipped, barely noticeable American accent, reminding Maria of Katharine Hepburn.

'And this is Alistair,' Mark said as a tall, good-looking man with Edwina's blue eyes and straight nose and rather long fair hair stood up and shook hands with everyone. He was dressed in a worn navy Lacoste polo shirt and beige baggy trousers, looking nearly as unkempt as Mark, but infinitely more elegant. He smiled broadly and with such charm that Maria couldn't help liking him at once.

'Hello there, Maria,' he said. 'I'm so glad to meet

you. Edwina is always talking about you.'

'She is a lovely little girl,' Maria replied.

'I do agree,' Alistair smiled. 'But you haven't met my friends from England, Pickles and Bunty.'

Maria smiled and nodded at the couple who were sitting at the end of the table.

'Sit down here beside me,' Alistair suggested, and pulled out a chair for Maria. 'I've ordered for us all,' he said, 'just to make things a bit easier.'

Now that *is* class, Maria thought.

Eva toyed with her *tarte aux pommes avec sa sauce au calvados* and tried to look as if she was enjoying herself. The evening had not turned out to be as much fun as she had hoped. She isn't even pretty, Eva thought, looking at Madeleine, with that long nose and those strange, hooded eyes. Then Dieter had been the star of the evening, just because that woman turned out to be some kind of motorbike freak. Alistair Bakewell was nice enough, but he seemed more interested in talking to Maria. Louise and Mark had been giggling and sharing jokes the whole evening, making Paul look very glum. In fact, he had looked like that the past couple of days. What is the silly girl doing? Eva thought. If she isn't careful she'll lose that gorgeous man.

She felt uneasy and irritated and just wanted to go home. But there was more to come.

'Mr Connolly,' Mark said when there was a lull in the conversation. 'How is your new hobby turning out? Have you made a lot of progress?'

Eva looked at Dan in confusion. What was he

talking about? What new hobby? As far as she knew, Dan spent the afternoons at the golf course. She had seen him load the golf clubs into the car at about the same time every day.

'Dan?' she asked. 'What is Mark talking about?'

'Please, Mark,' Dan said, 'call me Dan. I'm not a hundred years old yet.'

'Not even close.' Mark laughed. 'I saw you at the beach yesterday. You're fitter than me.'

'Could someone please tell me what's going on?' Eva demanded, her voice sharper than she had intended. 'What has Dan been up to at the beach?'

'I don't know why you're so annoyed,' Dan said as they were undressing. 'You don't seem to care much what I do during the day, as long as I'm not under your feet.'

Eva took off her pearls. 'Why didn't you tell me?' she demanded. 'Why did I have to find out like that?' She was still very angry and also felt strangely betrayed. It was such a slap in the face to discover that he had been ... she could hardly bear to think about it. At his age as well. Ridiculous. She hung up her top and trousers in the wardrobe and turned to stare at him, standing there in his underpants, looking annoyed. 'Really, Dan,' she said. 'Can you not see that it is not appropriate to start that sort of thing at your age?'

'What do you mean? It's not as if I'd joined the Foreign Legion.'

'That would have been a lot less embarrassing,' she snapped. 'And what about that woman you were seen with? That brunette? Mark seemed to think that was really funny.'

'She's the instructor,' Dan protested. 'She was only teaching me the basics.'

'The basics of what?'

'Windsurfing, of course. I told you.'

'Windsurfing,' Eva repeated. 'What on earth possessed you to start something like that?'

'I don't know,' Dan sighed. 'It was just an idea at first. You see, Mercedes, that girl I met at the disco, is the instructor. I bumped into her at the beach one day and —'

'At the beach? You were supposed to be at the golf club. Which beach is it?' she demanded, as if that was an important issue.

'Tahiti beach,' he replied.

'Tahiti?' Eva shouted. 'You went to Tahiti beach?'

'That's right. And it's a beach, not a porn club. I wanted to swim,' he continued, a rebellious look creeping into his normally so kind and gentle blue eyes. 'That's not against the law. Do I have to ask your permission every time I want to do something other than play golf?'

'Of course not. It's just that you're always so . . .'

'Predictable? he asked. 'Predictable and boring? I thought you'd be pleased that I was doing something different for a change, something a little more exciting. I wanted to have a go, just to see if I could do it, if I could learn something new. Would you be surprised to learn that I'm actually quite good at it? That I'm a natural? That's what Mercedes said, in any case.'

'Mercedes?'

'My instructor. I told you. Aren't you listening? Anyway, I'm making huge progress. I've even been out on my own and didn't capsize more than a couple of times. She said she was proud of me.'

'Of course she did.' Eva's voice was full of irony. 'What else would she say, for God's sake!'

'You mean she was only being kind to an old man?' Dan demanded, sounding furious now. 'Well, thanks a lot.'

'No, darling,' Eva pleaded, this new Dan making her nervous. What's happening? she thought. We have never fought, not ever in all the years we have been together. 'That's not at all what I meant.'

She stepped forward to put her arms around him, but he turned away from her, took off his underpants, folded them neatly and put them on the chair. She watched as he took his pyjamas from under the pillow and started to put them on. He looked normal, just like the old Dan, neat, tidy, gentle and polite, except for the look in his eyes. It frightened her. She didn't know how to approach him.

He looked at her for a moment. 'I'm a man, you know,' he said finally, buttoning his pyjama top, 'still in my prime. I'm not some old fogey who you can forget about, just park in a corner and take out when you please.'

'Of course not.'

'I'm glad you agree.' Dan pulled back the covers and got into bed. 'Aren't you coming to bed?' he asked.

'Yes,' she replied, and lay down beside him. She was afraid to speak or move, uncertain how he would react.

'Good night.' Dan put out the light, leaving Eva lying there in the dark, wondering how things could have gone so horribly wrong. She reached out a hand and touched him, but he had already gone to sleep. But at least now she knew why he was so tired. I hope it's only the windsurfing that has taken all his energy, she thought.

Maria lay down on the bed in Louise's room, her hands behind her head. 'Wasn't it funny to see Dieter being the star of the evening last night?'

Louise laughed. 'It was hilarious. Eva looked as if she was eating a lemon.'

'She looked really sour.'

'That Maddy is an awful bitch,' Louise remarked.

'She's a Basset.'

'What?'

'She's one of the Bassets. You know, the dog-food empire in America.'

'Is she? Oh, my God. That's unbelievable.'

'And she has a passion for motorbikes. Alistair told me she can strip and assemble an engine in half an hour.'

'I bet men in tight jeans is one of her hobbies as well,' Louise remarked. 'She was looking at Dieter as if he was a particularly delicious dish. Strange people, the rich.'

'Their friends were really weird,' Maria said. 'Pickles and Bunty. Really horsy.'

'I know. That Bunty is a woman screaming for a makeover. Someone should tell her that Barbours are not really the thing in St Tropez.'

'And Pickles!' Maria giggled. 'He was unreal. I didn't think those kinds of people really existed.'

'Only in *Horse and Hound*.'

'That's probably the only thing they ever read,' Maria agreed. 'I tried to talk about books with him, but when I mentioned this really well-known French author, Pickles just asked if he ran in the Prix de l'Arc.'

'He thought you were talking about a horse? That's a scream.' Louise laughed.

'But I think they are more Alistair's friends. Maddy hardly spoke to them all evening. She seems so cold, somehow. Funny to think she's so wealthy.'

'It doesn't seem to make her happy.'

'Poor Edwina,' Maria sighed.

'And we complained about Eva,' Louise added. 'She seems positively cosy compared to Maddy.'

'It's incredible to think that she has such a lovely daughter.'

'And husband.'

'Yes, Alistair is a sweetie,' Maria agreed.

'Must be a family trait.'

'Oh, yeah?' Maria looked at Louise thoughtfully.

'It was a really enjoyable evening,' Louise said, changing the subject. 'But not for Eva, of course. She hated Maddy, I could tell.'

'And then she found out that Daddy had been misbehaving on the beach. It must have been an awful shock.'

'Yes, but don't you think he's fantastic?' Louise asked with pride in her voice. 'To learn how to windsurf at his age. He's amazing. I'm so proud of him.'

'Me too.' Maria closed her eyes with a little smile.

'Superdad,' Louise said.

Eva was practising on the tennis court after lunch with the machine that spat out balls at regular intervals. She hit a strong backhand and the ball flew into the fence, the force of the impact lodging it firmly into the steel mesh. Another ball. Eva hit a forehand so hard she felt a shudder all the way to her shoulder. She stopped for a moment to catch her breath and walked over to the fence to prise the balls out. She heard footsteps on the gravel path below the terrace and looked up. Dan was getting into the Saab. He was wearing a baseball cap, brightly coloured swimming trunks and boat shoes. He's going to the beach, Eva thought. Without thinking, she draped a towel behind her neck and ran to the small Renault parked behind the garage.

Dan had disappeared down the twisting road, but Eva knew the way. Fifteen minutes later, she pulled into the parking lot at Tahiti beach. The blue Saab was parked a few spaces away and Eva just caught a glimpse of Dan as he walked onto the beach. She locked the car and walked slowly behind him, ducking between the oleander bushes to stay out of sight.

Tahiti beach was a sea of blue-and-white-striped umbrellas over sunbeds hired out by the hour for exorbitant sums. Small makeshift boutiques and restaurants lined the dunes at the back of the beach. There were a lot of people finishing their lunch or having coffee, but Dan wasn't one of them. Eva finally spotted him walking towards the end of the beach, where a group of young people were taking out windsurfing boards. She inched closer, weaving between umbrellas and lowering her head in attempt not to be spotted. But Dan did not look around. He kept walking purposefully towards the group.

'Danny,' she heard a woman call, and a dark, deeply tanned, muscular girl wearing a red swimsuit dislodged herself from the group.

Eva sat down on the sand under an umbrella and hid behind someone's enormous beach bag. She was close enough to hear everything they said.

'*Bonjour,* Mercedes,' Dan replied, and kissed the girl on both cheeks.

Two more girls joined them. Eva stared in disbelief as Dan melted into the group, kissing girls and exchanging 'high fives' with the young men. With the baseball cap hiding his greying hair, his bright trunks and tanned, muscular body, he didn't seem at all out of place. He looked like an older brother to some of them. She watched as he accepted a can of beer and drank deeply, laughing at the girl called Mercedes, his teeth white against his tanned face. Mercedes leaned against him and put an arm around his waist. Eva fumed as the girl looked up at Dan with adoring eyes. So this is the new 'hobby', she thought, this is what he has been doing while I thought he was playing golf.

Eva sat on the sand and wrapped her arms around her knees, leaned her forehead against them and closed her eyes. This has to be a dream, she thought. I'll wake up any moment beside Dan in our bed. She lifted her head. No, it was real. The image of Dan now taking one of the surfboards and wading out into the sea was not a figment of her imagination. She saw Mercedes wade out behind him, shouting something. Dan walked out further and got up on the board. He lifted the sail and, caught by a strong gust, the surfboard at once swept out into the bay.

Eva would normally have thought it a lovely scene – the bright yellow sail, the surfboard and the tall figure expertly manoeuvring it through the waves. He was so good at it, she thought, truly a natural. But this was no anonymous windsurfer, it was Dan.

'Madame,' said an angry voice beside her, 'you're on my towel.'

She looked up. A very angry man was standing beside her, a dripping ice-cream cone in each hand.

'Oh, I'm sorry.' She got up.

'Where's my wife?' he demanded, as if Eva had somehow spirited her away.

'I have no idea.'

'But what am I going to do with –' He made a gesture with the ice cream.

Eva was going to suggest where he could put it, but a voice beside them interrupted her.

'Here I am,' a young, soaking-wet woman panted. 'I just went for a swim.' She looked at Eva questioningly.

'She was sitting on my towel,' the man complained, sounding like one of the three bears.

Eva looked at the man, his ice-cream cones and the young, wet woman and started to laugh. 'This is *really* ridiculous,' she said. The couple stared at her. Shrugging her shoulders with an apologetic smile, she walked away. Away from the people, the beach and

Dan sailing out to sea on his surfboard.

'Mummy wants you to come up to the pool,' Edwina said.

Maria turned around. She was on the beach, lying on her stomach reading a book.

'Oh, why?'

'She just wants you to.' Edwina shrugged. 'Maybe she's lonely? We were there all alone, and then she told me to go and see if you were here.' Edwina frowned. 'Don't you want to? Our pool is really big. I can do eight strokes without stopping. Don't you want to see it?'

'OK, sweetheart.' Maria got up and held out her hand. 'Come on, then.'

Edwina took her hand. 'Saskia is gone,' she volunteered.

'Gone? Why?'

'Because my real nanny came back from her holidays. She is called Nanny Walsh. She was my daddy's nanny too. She doesn't take any prisoners, Daddy says.' Edwina looked up at Maria as they walked. 'Where are those prisoners and why doesn't she take them?'

'It just means she's a bit strict,' Maria said, and wondered if anyone ever explained anything to this child. 'Do you like your nanny?'

'Yes, I do. She's really nice when we're alone. She reads me stories and tucks me in really tight at night. But she doesn't like Mummy.'

'I'm sure she does.'

'No, she doesn't,' Edwina argued. 'I heard her say,

"That woman doesn't give a tinker's curse about the child" to Cook once when I came downstairs for a glass of milk and they thought I was asleep. What's a tinker's curse?'

'Don't worry about that,' Maria soothed. 'Here's Mummy now.'

Maddy was reclining on a sun lounger under a big umbrella beside the pool. She was wearing a huge hat, a black swimsuit and a bland expression. Her hair was slicked back and she was applying sunblock to her long, pale legs. She looked up as Maria and Edwina approached.

'Hi,' she said in her throaty voice.

'Hello,' Maria said, feeling self-conscious and awkward. 'How are you?'

'Fine.' Maddy turned to her daughter. 'Darling, tell Nanny she can go but she has to be back at seven.'

'OK.' Edwina ran up the steps. 'Don't go away,' she ordered Maria. 'I'll be back in a second.'

'I won't go anywhere,' Maria promised. 'Where's everybody?' she asked, looking around the empty terrace.

'Alistair has taken his friends walking on the headland. They wanted to look at the view of the coast.'

'I see.'

'Sit down,' Maddy said. 'Make yourself comfortable.'

'Thanks,' Maria said, and sat down on the edge of one of the white loungers, wondering how Maddy managed to make people feel so *un*comfortable all the time. Was it something she was born with? Or had she practised all her life until it just came naturally?

Maddy continued to massage suntan lotion into her legs. 'Tell me,' she drawled, 'how long have you been here?'

'Here on the terrace?' Maria wondered. 'Or at the beach?'

'No, in St Tropez, of course.' Maddy looked at her as if she was slightly retarded.

'Oh, sorry.' Maria laughed nervously. 'Since the beginning of August.'

'You're in Dieter's villa?'

'That's right.'

'Isn't it amazing that he has been there, just minutes away, all these years and we have never met?'

'I suppose it is.'

'He's a very interesting man. Very clever.'

'Well, yes.'

'He told me about his shoe chain. What was it called again?'

'Tippy Toes.'

'Oh, yes, that's right. It's really taking off in America. They're starting a new line next year, he told me. I think it might be a great success.'

'I hope so.'

'Listen,' Maddy said, the sudden warm tone in her voice startling Maria. 'We're throwing a small party at the end of next week. A sort of last blast before the end of the holidays.'

'Yes?'

'And I was wondering if your uncle . . . and all of you too, of course, would like to come? Saturday week. Eight o'clock.' It sounded more like an order than an invitation.

'Well, thank you,' Maria murmured. 'I'm sure we would . . . I mean, I'll have to ask them.'

'Your uncle will still be here, then?'

'Yes, he will. He was supposed to go back to LA, but he has decided to stay until the end of August now.'

'Good.' Maddy seemed to think that the matter was settled. 'Does Dieter usually stay in his villa all summer?' she asked as an afterthought.

'He does, yes. Usually.'

'But this year he went to LA instead and you're staying in the house?'

'Yes, that's right. We're there because Eva promised to mind the poodles while Dieter was away with Gretchen, that's his wife, and we . . .' Maria stopped, knowing she sounded really stupid.

'Yes, go on.' Maddy lay down and closed her eyes.

'Well, that's it really.'

'Mmm, I see.'

There was a long silence.

Maria began to feel very hot. The sun burned her back and the heat bounced off the white tiles of the terrace. She wondered if it would be all right to slip into the pool, or if Maddy would think that was a huge faux pas. But Maddy looked as if she had fallen asleep. Maria padded silently to the edge of the pool, walked down the wide steps and sank gratefully into the cool blue water. She closed her eyes and swam down to the bottom of the pool. When she came up for air, she looked straight into Edwina's laughing eyes.

'You're such a good swimmer,' the little girl ex-claimed. 'Do you think you could teach me to do that?'

'Darling, you know you must practise your strokes,' Maddy's sleepy voice interrupted. 'Bruno will be back tomorrow to check on you.'

'Who's Bruno?' Maria asked.

'My swimming instructor,' Edwina replied. 'He comes every day to teach me. But he never does any-thing that's really fun like you do.'

'Come into the water, then, and we'll have some fun,' Maria said, and held out her arms. 'Jump in. I'll catch you.'

Edwina jumped into Maria's arms with a huge splash. She proudly did her eight strokes in the deep end. 'Look, Mummy,' she shouted, 'I'm really swim-ming!'

There was no answer from the sun lounger and Maria presumed Maddy had fallen asleep. She looked up. Maddy was gone.

'She has probably gone to have a drink with her friends,' Edwina suggested. 'She goes every day at six o'clock, but today she thought she might have to stay because nanny had to go to the dentist. But now you're here, it was OK for her to go. She broke a fill-ing chewing on a toffee, you see. Nanny, I mean.'

'I see.'

'And now we can play in the pool together until nanny comes back. Isn't that good?'

'Very good.'

'I think it worked out very well,' Edwina said with a satisfied air. 'Just the way Mummy planned.'

CHAPTER 15

It had been a strange day. Eva had come back from her spying mission at the beach in a filthy mood, but there had been no one at the villa to take it out on. The house had been eerily quiet and she had spent the rest of the afternoon working, trying to get Dan and his girlfriend out of her mind. Then Dan had appeared, behaving as if butter wouldn't melt in his mouth, followed by Dieter driving up the path, revving his motorbike until she wanted to scream. Louise and Paul had arrived separately to dinner, looking strained. And Maria. Eva shook her head as she thought of her. She had appeared at dinner still in her swimsuit, with a blank expression on her face, and then disappeared to her room saying she 'needed to think'. What was the matter with everyone? she thought. Why weren't they having the time of their lives? Why can't they just relax and enjoy themselves? Why can't I? She sat up straighter. I will, she thought.

'Tell me, darling, is it my job?' Eva asked that evening.

'Is what your job?' Dan asked, his eyes on the front page of *Le Figaro*. They were in the living room, having a brandy before going to bed. Everyone else was still out. Louise, Paul and Maria had gone to St Tropez with Mark, and Dieter had taken the poodles for a last walk before bed.

'You know, the windsurfing and that girl and ...'

Dan looked up. 'That has nothing to do with it. I have nothing against your job. I'm very proud of you and I hope you'll get a good position in the autumn. And what girl are you talking about?'

'Mercedes. The girl I saw you with at the beach.'

'She's a very sweet girl. But she's just my instructor and that's all. If you don't believe me, that's your problem. I don't want to discuss this any more.' He stood up. 'I'm going to bed.'

'But I want to talk about it,' Eva protested. 'I need to sort out this problem so we can –'

'There's nothing to sort out. Aren't you coming to bed? You look tired.'

'I'll be up in a minute.'

'All alone, *Liebling*?' Dieter walked into the room a few minutes later, a bottle of beer in his hand. 'You don't look very happy. What's the matter?'

'I don't know what you're talking about. I'm very happy.'

'No, you're not. You look *zum Tode betrübt*.'

'In the depths of despair? Don't be silly. I'm just tired.' Then she sighed, a sigh so deep and full of sadness, she surprised even herself.

Dieter sat down beside her and put his arm around

her. 'What makes you so sad, my darling little sister?'

His voice was so gentle and full of concern that it made Eva's eyes fill with tears. She leaned her head on his leather-clad shoulder and started to sob. Crying made her feel even sadder and she just couldn't stop. All her anger and frustration welled up from deep within, all the pent-up sadness that had been lodged inside like a lump of cement slowly dissolved and she found herself telling Dieter about Dan.

'Sweetheart,' he said when she came to the end of her tale, '*Liebling*, I had no idea. I thought you were blissfully happy with your Dan and his girls. I thought you had the life you always wanted.'

'That's what I thought,' Eva sobbed. 'When I met Dan I thought he would be the ideal husband for me. He was so good-looking and stylish. And so kind.'

'And so pliable. You just parked him in a suitable job so he would not get in the way of your drive and ambition.'

Eva looked up at him, her tear-stained face pale with shock. 'What did you say?' she whispered. 'How dare you tell me –'

'Shut up for a moment,' Dieter ordered. 'I think someone needs to tell you about men.'

'You don't need to tell me –'

'Shut up I said! Just listen to someone else for a change. You think you know everything. You think you can just organise your life and your family to suit you. I have watched this family over the years, ever since you and Dan married, and it's always you who comes first. I don't know how Dan stands it, to be honest. I would have walked out years ago.'

'What?' Eva stammered. 'What's come over you? Is it those jeans? Have they cut off the blood flow to your brain?'

But Dieter ignored her. He stood up and started to pace around the room. 'We men need freedom,' he declared. 'We need to be able to express ourselves freely without restrictions or rules. Women just want to cut off our balls and put us in a box.'

'What is this awful garbage?' Eva demanded, regaining some of her composure.

'It's not garbage, it's the truth,' Dieter declared. 'Dan and I are the same age. I understand what he's going through.'

'Which is?'

'He is wondering if he is still attractive to women of course.'

'But of course he is,' Eva said. 'We have a very good sex life, you know.'

'That's not the point. We need to find out if other women still find us attractive, younger women. Before it's too late.'

'Too late for what? You mean he needs to have an affair with another woman to feel happy? Is that what you're up to? How would Gretchen feel about that?'

'You're so stupid for someone who's supposed to be so clever,' Dieter sighed. 'Of course we don't want to go all the way and sleep with other women. Most of us anyway. We just need to know that we could if we wanted to. I mean that it would be available ...' He stopped. 'Oh, you know what I mean.'

'But I don't understand why Dan feels like that. He already has a younger woman. Me.'

'You still don't get it, do you? We need to feel that we could have *any* woman, even the really young and pretty ones, I mean. It's important for our self-confidence. You're his wife. That's different.'

'Is it?' Eva said, still staring at Dieter incredulously.

'You probably thought he was yours for ever, didn't you? You thought you wouldn't have to do anything to keep the pot boiling. You could go off and do your own thing, ignore him and then pick him up and dust him off when it suited you.'

'Please spare me the homespun psychology,' Eva protested, a growing feeling of guilt making her furious.

'Fine. Don't listen to me, then. Keep going like you are and don't come crying to me when it's all over.' Dieter sat down and picked up the paper, but Eva snatched it away from him.

'This is all your fault. You just waltzed in here on your bloody motorbike, looking so pleased with yourself. Dan must have thought he could do the same. Only it was windsurfing instead.'

'I refuse to listen to this,' Dieter said, getting up. 'It's very unfair to blame me for something that has been waiting to happen for years. And, in any case, he had taken up this new hobby before I even arrived. You only have yourself to blame, darling.'

'What should I do, then?' Eva asked sarcastically. 'Please tell me, as you seem to know all about it.'

Dieter folded his arms across his chest. 'Make Dan feel important,' he said. 'Make him feel he is first on your list of priorities. Look up to him. Adore him.'

'But I do,' Eva protested.

'Yeah, every evening between six and half–past eleven. Like clockwork, like some kind of household chore. Then you spend the rest of your time thinking about your job, your fitness routine and what to serve for dinner. You have to make Dan feel he is number one *all* the time. And also, I might add, it wouldn't hurt if he thought he was the boss occasionally.'

'But he is.'

'Bullshit. I've watched you. You're like a bloody sergeant major, shouting orders and not listening to anyone. A man needs to feel he is the master in his own house. Or, in this case, mine.'

Eva had had enough. 'Oh, shut up,' she snapped. 'I don't want to hear any more about what men need. Women have much bigger problems than you could ever imagine. And we need to feel attractive too, we need to be appreciated.'

'By other men?' Dieter asked, looking into Eva's eyes. 'Is that what you're up to?'

Eva felt her face redden and looked away. 'I don't know what you mean.'

'I know that look.'

'Go to hell.' Eva now felt really angry. How dare he?

'I'm going to bed,' Dieter announced. 'I just want to give you one piece of advice before I go. Will you listen?'

'Do I have a choice?'

'No.'

'Right. What is this amazing piece of wisdom?'

'Don't crap where you work.' Dieter slammed the door violently as he left.

★

'*Cara*,' Guido said, 'my darling Maria. I think I am falling in love with you.' He picked up her hand and kissed it. Then he held it to his cheek for a moment before he let it go.

They were in a pizzeria in the old harbour of St Tropez, sharing a huge pizza and a bottle of Italian wine.

'It's the wine,' Maria said. 'Italian wine makes me feel romantic too.'

'But I have a pain. Here, in my heart.' Guido put his hand on his chest.

'Indigestion. That was the biggest pizza I've ever seen, and there was enough cheese to make a dozen more, not to mention that hot olive oil you put on it.'

'You are not romantic, *amore mio*. Do you want to break my heart?'

'Your heart is in no danger,' Maria laughed. 'I've seen you with at least three different women since I came here. Did you tell them you were in love too?'

'But that was just, how you say ... *consolazione*?'

'Consolation?' Maria smiled, looking into his eyes. He was so cute.

'But I think you would be perfect for me. And your name. It's like the Madonna. My mamma would love you. You're so beautiful, so pure.'

Not that pure, Maria said to herself, and looked away.

Guido took her hand again. 'You blush,' he said. 'Does that mean you're thinking of him? Of that other man? Forget him. I will never hurt you.'

Maria looked at Guido with tenderness. He was a bit off-the-wall, but so kind and sweet. Wouldn't he be a lovely husband? Contessa Maria Fregene de Popolonia, she suddenly thought. What a mouthful. And wouldn't it make Eva as sick as a parrot? It's nearly worth it just for that. She shook her head and laughed. 'You're so nice, my darling Guido, the best friend I ever had.'

'Friend?' Guido protested. 'But I don't want to be—'

'It's late,' Maria interrupted, feeling suddenly very tired. 'I want to go home and try to get a night's sleep.' She hadn't slept very well lately, ever since Edwina had awakened something in her mind, a fragment of a memory that annoyed and worried at her, like a toothache. Toothache, she suddenly thought, what was that about a toothache? But no, nothing came to her. It was as if she had found a piece of a jigsaw but the rest of the puzzle was missing.

'All right. I'll drive you home.' Guido got up and gestured to the waiter. 'Let me just pay the bill.'

Ten minutes later, they pulled up in front of Les Cygales.

'*Buona notte*, Maria,' Guido said, and pulled her close. Before she knew what was happening, he kissed her passionately on the mouth, then let her go just as suddenly. 'Did you feel it?' he asked.

'Feel what?' she demanded, annoyed and a little shaken.

But Guido smiled sadly and shook his head. 'If you have to ask, it means you didn't.' He held up his hands. 'No more,' he promised, 'no more like that. We will be just friends, like you said. And I will go and jump off a bridge.'

'No, you won't,' Maria laughed. 'You'll find

another girl very soon.'

'I will always be alone,' Guido sighed.

'The way you kiss?' Maria said. 'Never.'

'It was good?' Guido asked, looking hopeful.

'Are you kidding? It was divine.'

'Did you have a nice time with Guido?' Louise asked as Maria came up to the terrace. She was sitting at the table, having a drink with Paul, and they looked curiously stiff.

'Lovely,' Maria replied. 'We went out for pizza.'

'Was it nice?'

'Mmm. Delicious.'

'Are you two getting serious?' Louise asked.

'Maybe. Contessa Maria Fregene de Popolonia,' Maria said. 'How does that sound?' She glanced at Paul.

'Who are you talking about?' Louise asked, looking perplexed.

'Me.' Maria sauntered across the terrace, into the living room and up the stairs to her room, where she lay down on her bed and stared up at the moon in the black sky.

'That ball was out!'

'It was on the line. Which means it was in.'

'It was miles outside. Are you blind?'

'Are you deaf? IT WAS OUT! Did you hear that, you twit?'

'Jesus, girls, will you stop arguing and play tennis,' Paul begged. 'Let's play the point again, if you can't agree.'

Maria glared across the court at him. Whose idea was this? she thought. To play tennis in the blistering heat of the midday sun at Villa Caramel? Paul and Louise versus Mark and Maria. 'I haven't played tennis since school,' she had protested when Mark had come up with the idea. 'And that is nearly fifteen years ago.'

'But then she played the knickers off everybody,' Louise said.

'Interesting school you went to,' Mark had said. 'I wish I'd been there. Knickers all over the place. Ah, please do, it will be fun. And we'll swim afterwards and have lunch on the terrace.'

The first few games had been awkward. Maria found herself stiff and nervous, the tennis racquet an alien object after so many years. She served badly at first, her service returns were worse and her backhand terrible. She felt sweaty and stupid in the tennis skirt she had borrowed from Eva. But at the end of the first set, Maria suddenly found her old form. She started to serve like she used to at school and her returns were, if not blistering, a lot better. She looked across the court at Paul, so beautiful in his tennis whites, like a film star in a 1930s movie, and felt a flash of hatred. Who does he think he is? she thought. Cary Grant? She threw the ball high against the hot blue sky and hit it with all the power she could muster.

He looked surprised as the ball bounced just inside the line and whizzed past his right ear. 'Ouch,' he cried. 'Lucky I missed it, or there would be a hole in my racquet.'

'At least there is no argument about that one,' Mark

said. 'It was way in.'

'Thirty–forty,' Louise announced.

'What?' Maria shouted. 'You mean forty–thirty, surely.'

'What's the matter with you?' Louise asked. 'Can't you count? You lost the last point. And don't call me Shirley.'

'For God's sake,' Paul pleaded, 'don't you remember, we agreed to play the point again.'

'Oh, yeah. Sorry,' Louise muttered.

'Isn't Maria pretty?' Edwina asked Alistair on the bench outside the tennis court, where they were watching the game.

'Oh, yes, very pretty,' Alistair agreed, admiring the way Louise's breasts were bouncing inside her tennis dress as she ran for the ball. 'I would go as far as to say she's gorgeous.'

'Isn't Alistair looking well?' Louise asked Maria as they were having a drink of iced tea between sets.

Maria looked at him, sitting with his arm around Edwina, wearing a pair of white shorts, his tanned feet encased in worn tennis shoes. He looked very well indeed, she thought, with his sun-bleached hair, bare tanned chest and broad shoulders.

'Time, ladies,' Mark called. 'Second set. Take your places.'

And the battle continued.

Louise and Paul had won the first set six–four, and Mark and Maria fought to gain the upper hand in the second. Maria's game improved steadily, and it would have been no problem to get into the lead, if Mark hadn't laughed so much.

'Can't you take this seriously?' Maria demanded, as he served a double fault, making the score three–all.

'It's only a game, for God's sake.'

'That's where you're wrong,' Maria retorted. 'It's a matter of life or death.'

'And we have to win?'

'You bet. But go up to the net, now, Louise is serving. That's one thing she never got the hang of.'

'You really are vicious,' Mark said. 'She is your sister, after all.'

'Exactly. That's the whole point. Don't you know anything about siblings?'

'I'm an only child.'

'I was wondering why you were such a wimp. Go on, go to the net.'

'All right.' Mark sighed and shuffled across the court.

'And use your racquet, wimp,' Maria laughed.

Louise served into the net and then just over the net, perfect for Mark to hit the ball into the far corner.

'Please,' Paul said, sighing, 'try to throw the ball a little higher next time.'

But Louise had lost all interest in the match and was idly waving her racquet about, missing shots and hitting balls into the net, smiling and chatting with Alistair.

'Six–four,' Mark announced at the end of the set. Alistair and Edwina applauded. 'One set all. Do you want to play a third and see who wins?'

'Yes,' Maria and Paul said in unison.

'Louise?'

'What?'

'Do you want to play another set?' Mark asked.

'In this heat? Are you mad?' Louise stared at him. 'I want to go for a swim.'

'Yea, swimming!' Edwina shouted, and jumped down from the bench.

'I think that wraps it up, folks,' Mark said, wiping his brow. 'No winners or losers, perfect.' He took a glass of iced tea from a waiter in a white jacket who had just appeared with a tray of drinks. 'Let's go on to the pool. How about a swimming race? Louise and Maria. We could place bets. I bet Maria wins.'

'Oh, shut up,' Maria said. 'I'm tired of competing. I'm dying to get into that water. Are you coming, Edwina?' She walked away from the court, with Edwina skipping happily beside her.

'You're very good at tennis,' Alistair said, smiling into Louise's eyes. 'I wouldn't mind a game with you sometime.'

'That would be great fun,' Louise replied. 'But Maria is much better than me.'

'I wouldn't say that.'

'What are you two muttering about?' Mark asked. 'Why don't we all go to the pool?'

'Absolutely,' Alistair agreed. 'Did you bring your swimsuits?'

'This is an amazing house,' Louise said to Alistair as the company sat down to lunch at the long table under the awning.

'It's quite nice,' Alistair replied. 'I'm very fond of it.'

'Fond?' Louise repeated. 'Is that all? I think it's heaven. She helped herself to some salad and smiled at a maid who poured her a glass of chilled white wine. 'Is the house yours or does it belong to your wife?'

'It belongs to my family,' Alistair replied. 'But you'd think it was Maddy's, the way she has restored it. She spent a fortune on it when we were married ten years ago. But it will never belong to her. It will remain in the family because it can't be sold. That was what my father's will stipulated. It has to go to the next generation and so on.'

'Do you want some potato salad, darling?' Maria asked Edwina.

'No, thank you. But could you help me cut up this piece of ham?'

'Of course.' Maria helped Edwina with the ham and poured her some orange juice.

'Why is he looking at us?' Edwina whispered in Maria's ear.

'Who?' Maria whispered back.

'That man over there beside Louise. Her boyfriend.'

'He's not looking at us.' Maria glanced at Paul, who was chewing on a piece of bread.

'He is,' Edwina hissed. 'He was staring at us when you were teaching me to swim and now he's doing it again.'

'I'll ask him.'

'No, don't,' Edwina begged. 'Then he might get cross.'

'He won't. Paul?' Maria said. 'Are you staring at Edwina?'

'Oh, no,' Edwina whimpered.

Paul looked at Edwina. 'Yes, I was. Very rude of me, I know, but I was just thinking what a very pretty young lady you are, Miss Bakewell.' He smiled at her. Edwina giggled. 'And I was also thinking that Maria takes very good care of you.'

'She does,' Edwina nodded. 'I like it when she looks after me.'

'I'm not surprised,' Paul replied.

'Where's Maddy?' Louise asked. 'And your friends, Biddy and Piccolo?'

'Bunty and Pickles,' Alistair smiled. 'Maddy's gone to Paris and will be back tomorrow and my friends have gone on a boat trip to see the islands. They will be back tonight.'

'And my nanny's having a sleep,' Edwina announced. 'She finds the heat a real killer. I think she'd cope a lot better if she didn't wear a vest or those tights. But she said that being on holiday doesn't mean you let your standards slip.'

'That's absolutely right, darling,' Maria agreed.

'Do you?' Edwina asked.

'What?'

'Let your standards slip when you're on holiday?'

Maria looked at Paul. 'Oh, no,' she declared. 'Never.'

'That's good. Can I have some more juice, please?' Edwina held out her glass and Maria filled it.

The lunch ended with coffee and petits fours served under an umbrella further out on the huge terrace, where there was a cool breeze from the sea.

'What a lovely day,' Louise sighed. 'Thank you so

much, Alistair. And Mark. I can't wait to tell Eva about this house.'

'You haven't seen much of it,' Alistair said. 'Would you like a tour before you go?'

'Love to,' Louise said, and rose.

'I'd like to see the house too,' Paul said, getting up from his deckchair. 'Maria? What about you?'

'No, I've seen most of it.'

'But you haven't seen my room,' Edwina protested. 'Come on, I'll show you. I have my own bathroom as well.'

'OK, darling. Show me your room.'

And, except for Mark, who stayed in his deckchair staring out to sea, they all wandered into the house.

CHAPTER 16

'It's the most amazing place,' Louise sighed. 'Wait till you see it, Eva, you won't believe it. There's a jacuzzi and a sauna in the basement and a fully equipped gym as well. And the bedrooms are divine. Every room has its own bathroom that is as big as our living room. But you'll see it all at the party, of course.'

'Would you mind concentrating on the beans? You've only snipped three in half an hour. I want them ready to cook in a minute. What party?'

'You know, the party next Saturday. Didn't Maria tell you? We're all invited, even Dieter. Or should I say especially Dieter? You *are* going, aren't you?'

'Yes, I think so. What about the beans?'

'OK. Don't be so impatient.' Louise snipped another bean.

'How many potatoes will you eat?'

'One, I think. It's so hot in this kitchen,' Louise complained. 'Why do we have to cook tonight? Where's Fernando?'

'He's helping out at another dinner somewhere

near Ramatuelle,' Eva said, and lowered the heat under the saucepan. 'But I don't mind cooking.'

'What are we having?'

'Grilled lamb with rosemary and roast potatoes. And those beans, if you could manage to finish them before tomorrow morning.'

'Lamb? In this heat?'

'It's Dan's favourite. And I thought we could do with a change from all that Mediterranean food.'

'But it isn't even his birthday.' Louise looked at Eva.

'What do you mean?'

'That's the only time you cook him his favourite food.'

'If you can't manage to do the beans, I'll do them myself. Go and lay the table instead.'

'All right, I will. This is so boring anyway.'

'And tell Maria there was a phone call for her while you were out. Some man called from Dublin. Said it was urgent.'

'A man?'

'That's right. I wrote his name and number down on the pad beside the phone in the study. Dominic something, I think he said.'

'Dominic? What a wimpy name. I've never heard her mention him.'

'She doesn't tell you about every man she meets, does she?'

'Oh, yes, she does. We tell each other everything.'

'Of course you do,' Eva said.

'So I would know if he was someone special,' Louise continued, ignoring Eva's sarcastic tone. 'Maybe you got it wrong?'

'No, I'm certain. He sounded very eager to talk to her.'

'Maybe he's an author?'

'I have a feeling he's a doctor,' Eva mused. 'Yes, that's what he said. Dr Dominic something.'

'There was a call for you while we were out,' Louise said to Maria as she came out on the terrace with cutlery and plates.

'Oh? Who was it?'

'Some doctor, Eva said. She wrote down his name on the pad beside the phone.'

'Doctor?' Maria stared at Louise. 'Why would a doctor call me here?'

'Maybe it's something to do with the hospital. Did you pay the bill?'

'Of course I did.'

'Dr Dominic something, Eva said.'

'But my doctor's name was Brian. Brian Murray.'

'Well, there's only one way to find out, isn't there?'

'Yeah, of course. I'll go and call straight away.' Maria looked at her watch. 'But it's seven o'clock in Ireland. No doctor would still be in the surgery at this hour.'

'Go and try the number,' Louise urged. 'And if there's no reply, try again tomorrow morning.'

'OK, you're right. I'll go and call from the extension in my room.' Maria walked into the study and found the piece of paper by the phone. *Dr Dominic McNally*, it said in Eva's strong handwriting. It was a Dublin number. Maria looked at the name and the beginning of a memory began to form in her mind. Puzzled, she went to her room and dialled the number.

'Hello?' a deep male voice said.

Maria froze. She knew that voice, she knew it so well. 'Oh, God,' she said. 'What do you want? And where did you get this number?'

'I rang your office and they told me you were on holiday. But that doesn't matter. Maria, I just wanted to talk to you, to explain . . .'

But Maria didn't want to hear any more. Her hand shaking, she replaced the receiver. She suddenly remembered everything.

Sometimes, Maria thought, as she sipped champagne in front of the blazing log fire in the cosy country inn, sometimes there are perfect moments in life. Not always, not even very often, and, in her case, extremely rarely, but from time to time these moments happened and you just had to thank the heavens for them.

It was a cold February night, with stars glinting in the black sky and a promise of frost in the air. But it was warm in the restaurant and the smell of burning timber mingled with the aroma of delicious food. Maria sighed contentedly and smiled at Dominic, who had just joined her on the comfortable sofa.

'This is fabulous,' she said.

'It should be,' he replied. 'It's the best champagne in the world.'

'No, I meant the whole thing. The hotel, the fire, you . . .'

'I know,' he said, and put his arm around her. 'I have been looking forward to this all week.'

She leaned her head on his shoulder, gazed at the fire and thought how lucky she was. Finally, she thought, finally I have found the love of my life.

After a series of disastrous relationships, she had given up hope of ever finding a man she could trust. But then she met Dominic. She had gone for a routine check-up to her dentist, but instead of old Dr Murphy, the usual dentist, there had been a new one, Dominic McNally, young, handsome and light on the drill. He had the best-shaped nostrils she had ever seen on a dentist and the loveliest brown eyes. He told her she had the most beautiful teeth and the healthiest gums of any woman he had ever seen, but that wasn't really why she had fallen in love with him. It was his kindness and understanding, and the way he made her feel special. She didn't tell Louise about him, knowing she would find it utterly ridiculous to fall for your dentist. And keeping their dates secret was exciting too. They had been going out for six months and she was beginning to believe that this time it would work out.

Their dates were always so special, mainly because they usually left Dublin and went to these lovely places in the country. It was so good for both of them, she thought, so relaxing. Dominic had a very busy practice and needed to take a break, he had explained. 'I want us to be completely separate from work and stress,' he said. 'Our time together is so precious to me.' And she had agreed with all her heart.

'I'm starving,' she said a little later, as they were handed the menus at their table. 'I'm going to have everything.'

'Absolutely,' Dominic agreed. 'And we don't have to go back tonight. I've booked our usual room.'

'Great idea,' she smiled. 'That big corner room? With the huge double bed and . . .'

'The big bath,' he filled in. 'Don't forget the bath . . .'

'How could I?' Maria smiled back at him and winked, then turned her attention to the menu. 'I'm going to have the pâté and the lamb with garlic potatoes,' she said. 'Very fattening, I know, but what the hell. And I can smell that lamb all the way in here. What about you?' She glanced across the table at Dominic, but his face was hidden by the big menu. He didn't reply.

'Dominic?' She laughed. 'Yoo-hoo? Are you there?'

'Just a minute,' he muttered.

'They have pheasant, I see,' she announced. 'That's your favourite. Why don't you have that?'

'Mmmm. Maybe.'

'What's the matter? Having an attack of indecision? I thought you were hungry.'

'Hello, Dominic,' a voice interrupted.

They both looked up at the man standing in front of them.

'I thought it was you,' he smiled. 'You're a long way from home.'

'Oh, hello, Robert,' Dominic stuttered.

'Haven't seen you for such a long time,' the man continued. 'Not since your daughter's christening. And now I hear you've had a second one. Daughter, I mean. Congratulations. And how is Brenda?'

Maria suddenly felt ice cold. This is not happening,

she thought. I'm having one of those nightmares. But the awful exchange of words continued.

'She's fine,' Dominic snapped.

'Great,' Robert replied. 'But I was interrupting you. And I haven't introduced myself.' The man held out his hand to Maria, who, with a face set like a stone, shook it automatically. 'I'm Robert Murphy. An old friend of Dominic's. Are you one of his colleagues?'

'That's right,' Dominic replied, before Maria had time to say a word. 'Miss Connolly is here on business. We're having a working dinner. We're discussing a possible partnership.'

'Oh, I see. Better let you get on, then,' Murphy said. 'Let's get together soon, Dominic. Give my love to Brenda. Bye for now. Nice to meet you, Miss Connolly.'

But neither Dominic nor Maria replied. They stared at each other across the table as Dominic's friend walked away.

He cleared his throat. 'Well,' he said. 'That was a little unfortunate.'

Maria looked at Dominic and suddenly his face was not handsome any more, his voice not deep and warm, or his smile dazzling. Now he just looked small and pathetic. She didn't know what to say or do, she only knew that she didn't want to spend another second with him. She rose from her chair and gathered up her things.

'Maria? Darling? Will you just let me . . .'

She didn't reply, just held up a hand to silence him. 'Don't,' she had said. 'Just don't say a word. I don't want to hear anything from you.' Violently angry and deeply wounded, she marched out of the restaurant, got into her car and drove at speed through the hotel gates.

'Everything's ready,' Eva announced from the kitchen door. 'I'll be serving dinner straight away.'

'OK,' Dan said, and switched off the television. 'Louise? Paul?'

'We're here, Daddy,' Louise said from the terrace.

'Where's Maria?' Dan asked as he sat down at the table. 'Eva's grilled lamb can't wait, you know that.'

'Here it is,' Eva chanted, coming out on the terrace with a huge dish.

'That smells wonderful, darling,' Dan said, and rubbed his hands together. 'I'm really looking forward to this.'

Eva smiled back. It was the first time he had called her 'darling' for over a week. 'But where is Maria?' she asked, handing the dish to Dan.

'In her room having a flashback,' Louise replied with a little laugh.

'A what?'

'A flashback. It was that phone call,' Louise explained. 'It made her very upset. I think she remembered something about the accident. I asked her if she was OK, but she shouted at me to get out.'

'But we're having lamb for dinner,' Dan said.

'I told her. I went up again a minute ago, to see if she had calmed down, but when I told her what was for dinner, she put her hands over her ears and shouted, "Not lamb, oh, please not that!"'

'How very strange,' Eva said, and sat down. Then

she got up again. 'Maybe I should go and ...'

'No, give her a little time,' Dan suggested, helping himself to a big piece of lamb. 'Sit down and have your dinner.'

'Yes, maybe you're right,' Eva agreed, sitting down. 'And maybe it should be you or Louise. She may not want to tell me about it.'

'This is absolutely delicious, darling,' Dan said. 'How marvellous of you to go to all that trouble. It can't have been easy in this heat.'

'I'm so glad you like it, sweetheart,' Eva smiled.

'You're very quiet, Paul,' Dan suddenly remarked.

'He's tired after all that tennis,' Louise laughed. 'He wore himself out trying to beat Mark and Maria.'

'Lovely meal, Eva,' Paul said, 'really delicious. You have a way with lamb.'

'Thank you,' Eva replied automatically. She wasn't really listening to the conversation, she was too worried about Maria. She had looked very strained lately. What was troubling her?

'I'm going to see if there's anything I can do for Maria.'

'I don't think she'll want to talk to anyone, the mood she's in,' Louise said.

'Well, I just want her to know we're worried about her. There's an apple tart in the kitchen, Louise. Will you serve that when you've finished?'

Eva left the terrace and went up to Maria's room and knocked on the door. There was no answer. Eva gently opened the door. 'Maria?' she whispered. 'Can I do anything?'

'No,' Maria mumbled from the bed. 'Go away.'

'I'm not your mother, Maria, but I do want to help, if I can. As a friend.'

'Friend?' Maria said bitterly. 'Oh, God, when this comes out, I won't have any friends.'

'What are you talking about? When what comes out? Surely it can't be that bad?'

'You have no idea.'

'But what could be so terrible?' Eva sank down on the bed.

'I don't want to talk about it.'

'Maria,' Eva said sternly. 'How can I help you if –'

'I don't want your help.'

'Oh, God,' Eva sighed. 'I know I haven't exactly been the most understanding person in the world, but ... I ... I do care about you.'

'Oh, yeah?'

'It's true.'

'I don't believe you.'

'I don't care what you believe,' Eva said, exasperated. This was going nowhere. 'I don't know why you hate me so much. But maybe you don't know that yourself?'

'Oh, yes, I do. You ruined my life.'

Something suddenly snapped in Eva. 'That is outrageous!' she exclaimed angrily. She grabbed Maria and made her sit up and face her. 'Don't blame me for what has happened to you,' Eva exclaimed. 'Don't you dare say I ruined your life. It wasn't my fault your mother died. I tried my best to help you, but you were always so hostile. I thought it would be a good idea for you to go to school in Ireland, and I still think so. You did very well there. But I'm not responsible for the fact that your love life is a mess. And it isn't my fault that you're going through some sort of trauma right now. It's probably your own doing. You have never been taught to manage on your own. You have been emotionally breastfed by your father all your life. It's time you grew up and faced your own music. And I just want to tell you, in case you were wondering, that your father and I still love each other after fifteen years, that's more than a lot of couples can say.'

'Is that why he's taken up windsurfing?' Maria's voice was nasty.

'That's just a diversion. He's looking for a new experience. We're as close as ever.' Eva rose from the bed. 'I came in here to see if I could help. I thought you might want to talk to someone who wouldn't judge you, someone who would just listen. But I suppose that is out of the question now.' She was about to walk out, when she heard Maria whisper something.

'What?' Eva demanded. 'What did you say?'

'Don't go.'

'Men are such shits,' Eva said when Maria had finished her tale.

'Yes, they really are,' Maria agreed, squeezing her handkerchief into a ball. 'Except Daddy, of course.'

'Him too,' Eva said, sounding angry. 'They're all the same. Always going on about their needs.'

'I know.'

'What was the worse thing? Was it that he was a married man with two children, or that he lied to you?'

'Neither,' Maria sighed. 'It was just that I felt such

an eejit. And of course it was really ridiculous to fall for my dentist, especially with a name like Dominic.'

'I once had a huge crush on a Dutch aerobics instructor called Henk,' Eva confessed.

'Really? You're not saying that to make me feel better?'

'Do you think I'd make that up?'

Maria laughed. 'No, I suppose you wouldn't.'

'Isn't it a little strange that you had this affair for six months and didn't remember a thing about it? I mean, forgetting the accident was understandable, but . . .'

'If you met him you'd understand,' Maria said. 'It was probably some sort of denial. And that man was infinitely forgettable, believe me. But Eva —' she sighed — 'what will people say when this comes out? What will Daddy say? And Paul? Louise will laugh herself sick, I just know it.'

'They won't say anything, because you're not going to tell them. You're going to try and forget the whole thing and carry on.'

'As if nothing happened?'

'Exactly. Everyone has secrets, you know. And we don't go around telling them to the whole world.'

'I suppose you're right,' Maria agreed. 'But there's more, you know. I've —'

'Shh,' Eva murmured, 'let it alone. You don't have to tell me more. Just forget about it.'

'OK. Maybe you're right.'

'You have always been such a complicated girl. I never knew how to handle you really. Louise was always a lot easier.'

'Oh, Louise.' Maria sighed. 'She was always the

pretty girl. Still is. All eyes are on her when she walks down the street. Nobody ever looks at me, except if I do something stupid, like tucking my skirt into my knickers or –'

'But you're a very good-looking girl,' Eva interrupted. 'Very stylish.'

'Yeah, right.'

'Guido is very taken with you, you know.'

'That's another problem.' Maria sighed again. 'He's getting really serious. And I don't feel the same for him. I like him a lot, he's so nice, but ...'

'You could do a lot worse,' Eva stated.

'But I couldn't marry a man I don't love.'

'You might learn to love him. He's not the brainiest man in the world, but he's very sweet. And he has a title and lots of money.'

'What does that matter if I don't love him?'

'Maybe you will one day.'

'Maybe.'

They were silent for a moment.

'I feel very grateful to that dentist,' Eva said. 'If it wasn't for him, we wouldn't be here talking like this.' She gave Maria's hand a little squeeze. 'I'm so glad we're friends at last.'

'Yes, so am I.'

'Good friends, very good friends.'

'Of course.' Maria squeezed Eva's hand back. 'I'm so sorry I was such a little bitch when I was younger. It can't have been easy.'

'It was probably my own fault. I shouldn't have tried to replace your mother. But I thought, as I had no luck having a baby, that you and Louise would be a kind of substitute.'

'Oh,' Maria said, feeling really guilty. 'I thought you didn't want to have children. I thought your career was more important.'

'Oh, God, no. But when I had no luck getting pregnant, my job helped me to cope with my disappointment.'

'I see. Lucky you had your job.'

'And your father. He would have loved to have had more children, maybe a little boy. But when it didn't happen, he was very good about it. He said he was so happy with me and his little girls, he didn't need anything else. But that was then, of course.'

'I'm sorry I said what I did about Daddy and the windsurfing.'

'That's all right.'

'Are you worried about it?'

'Yes . . . No.' Eva shrugged. 'I think it's just a guy-thing. Dieter explained it all. It's about getting older and being attractive to women. I think I can handle it.'

'Good. But what are we going to say to the others about me?' Maria asked. 'They will want to know what this drama was all about.'

'We'll just say what I usually do when I don't want men to ask me any questions.'

'What's that?'

'PMT,' Eva said. 'Works every time.'

Eva is looking so well, Dan thought. There is a calm about her, something soft and lovely. He had just come back from the beach and was thinking of having a drink on the terrace.

'Darling?'

Eva looked up.

'Would you like a drink?' Dan asked. 'Or a cup of tea? Or something else?'

'No, thanks. I'll just finish this and then I'm going to have a swim in the pool. Then it's nearly time for dinner. Did you have a nice time at the beach today?'

'Lovely, thanks.'

Dan looked at her, surprised. There was no anger in her voice, no disapproval. Was she beginning to accept his new lifestyle? Or was she planning something? It wasn't like her to be so gentle and accepting of something she didn't agree with. And she and Maria were getting on really well these days, which was another thing that made him nervous.

'How is Mercedes?' she asked.

'Fine. Very well.' What was she up to?

'Good.' Eva turned back to her laptop.

'How's everything going? Finished your report about Vienna?'

'Yes, that's nearly all done.'

'And they were pleased in Berlin?'

'Very.'

'That's good.'

'Dan?' Eva said a few minutes later as she walked up to him and put her arm through his. 'What are you thinking about?'

'Nothing, really. Just wondering if the wind will pick up again tomorrow.'

'Oh.' She put her head against his shoulder. 'Why don't we go upstairs? I've changed my mind about that swim.'

'But I haven't. I need to keep fit for the competition next week. I'm going to do a few laps before dinner.'

'What competition?'

'There's a windsurfing championship,' Dan replied. 'Just a local thing, really. But Mercedes said she thought I would be up to it.' Not that he wanted to do it, he thought, it seemed a little too ambitious for him.

'Did she now?'

'Yes, she did.' Dan bristled. 'What's wrong with that?'

'Nothing, darling. I hope you do very well.' Eva walked to the door. 'I'm going upstairs now. See you at dinner.'

Maria couldn't sleep. She had woken in the middle of the night bathed in perspiration. It must be the hottest night of the summer, she thought, as she twisted and turned in the bed. She flipped the pillow over, hoping the other side would be cooler. She opened the window wide in an attempt to catch any little breeze. But the night was still, without the slightest breath of wind, and she watched as the dawn made the sky a light grey with just a strip of pink at the horizon. I have to get up, she thought, I can't breathe. She got out of bed, threw her cotton kimono over her nightgown, stuck her feet in a pair of leather thong sandals and silently padded down the stairs, across the terrace and down the path towards the pool. She would just have a quick dip to cool off, then go back to bed. She carefully made her way down the winding path, trying her best not to bump into trees and bushes, as there was barely enough light to see by. There was complete silence, not even the slightest breeze, birdsong or the usual chirping from the crickets. The whole world was asleep and Maria felt all alone. But suddenly, as she was about to step onto the tiled area around the pool, she bumped into a tall ghostly figure. Maria screamed.

A hand covered her mouth. 'Shut up!' a voice hissed. 'You're going to wake the whole house.'

'Mmm wwwau ...' Maria tried to wrench the hand away.

'Do you promise not to scream again?'

Maria nodded. Paul took his hand away.

'What on earth are you doing here?' Maria whispered.

'The same as you, I suspect. I'm going for a dip in the pool to cool off.'

'And Louise?' Maria peered into the gloom behind him.

'Fast asleep.'

'Oh.'

Maria felt the heat of his body. He was so close, dressed in only a pair of pyjama pants. She tried to look at his face, but could barely see it. He put his hands on her shoulders, but she stepped back.

'What's the matter?' he asked.

'No ... I don't know ... I ...' Oh, God, she thought, why does he make me feel like this?

Paul cleared his throat. 'I realise that you must be angry ever since ... But I should have apologised for what happened that night. It was my fault. I was drunk and ...'

Maria was suddenly furious. 'Oh, I see. It was all a mistake, then? A horrible drunken little mistake?' She laughed bitterly. 'Of course. It would have meant nothing to you.'

'Well, you didn't seem to care much.'

'What do you mean?'

'You seemed totally cool afterwards.'

'What did you expect? What was I supposed to do? How do you think I felt? I had just slept with my sister's boyfriend, the man she's going to marry. I didn't know what to think, or what to do. Then you acted as if nothing had happened, so I realised it was just a small glitch to you, a little mishap to be forgotten about. And I tried to do the same.'

'And you did?'

Maria stuck out her chin. 'Yes, I did. I forgot all about it.'

'That's what I thought. Then you took up with that ageing gigolo. I suppose he is a fantastic lover?'

'Yes, he is, actually. Really fantastic.'

Paul put his hands on her shoulders again and tried to look into her eyes through the gloom. 'Better than me?'

Maria nearly stopped breathing. His bare chest almost touched hers, his hands were warm on her shoulders and his breath hot on her face. 'Oh, yes,' she whispered, 'a lot better.' She wrenched herself free and turned on her heel. She could hear a splash as she hurried back to the house.

'I did it.'

'Did what?' Eva looked up from the evening paper

and stared at Maria.

'Got engaged to Guido.'

'I don't believe it!' Eva threw her newspaper on the terrace and went over to hug Maria. 'Congratulations, darling. But where is he?'

'He's gone to phone his mother. He wasn't too sure how she'd take it.'

'I thought you said she was dying for Guido to get married at last.'

'Well, yes, in theory. But he is the eldest son and she absolutely dotes on him. And I'm a foreigner and . . .'

'What do you mean, foreigner?' Eva demanded. '*She's* the foreigner, surely. I mean, she *is* Italian.'

'Are you feeling all right?' Maria laughed. 'Just listen to yourself.'

'Oh, God, you're right. That was a bit weird.' Eva shook her head. 'But now we have to get some champagne for tonight. We'll have a celebration. Is Guido coming over later?'

'No, he's not. We have decided not to tell anyone about it for the moment, so not a word.'

'But why?'

'Well, Guido wants his mother to get used to the idea. And we haven't decided on a date for the wedding yet. When we have, we'll announce the whole thing.'

'Oh? But have you no idea at all when?'

'As soon as possible,' Maria said with a little smile, 'or he'll go crazy.'

'What do you mean? Why will he go crazy?'

'Because we can't go to bed until we're married. It's the Italian way.'

'What happened to "I can't marry a man I don't love"?' Eva enquired.

'To hell with love. I prefer like. Much better. And in any case, he loves me. It's so wonderful to have found a man who wants to look after me for the rest of my life.'

She smiled to herself as she remembered how Guido had finally persuaded her while they were in the park, admiring the sunset over the mountains.

'Maria? *Amore mio?*' he had said. 'Do you not think you might change your mind?'

'Oh, Guido, you're so persistent. This is the fourth time you've asked me.'

Guido put his arm around her. 'I wouldn't do it if I didn't feel there was a chance. And the way we kissed just now ...'

Maria put her head on his shoulder. 'I know. It was lovely.' Not in the same league as Paul, Maria thought, but then pushed him out of her mind.

Guido studied her. 'You haven't replied yet,' he said.

Maria looked up at his handsome face. 'Maybe I will,' she mumbled.

'Maybe you will what? Reply? Or marry me?'

'Marry you. Maybe I ...'

'Oh, Maria!' Guido exclaimed, wrapping his arms around her. 'You make me so happy. My beautiful, lovely Maria.'

'But I was just kind of thinking about it,' Maria protested, feeling a little frightened by his sudden fervour. 'I'm not sure if I —' But her words were interrupted as his mouth met hers and he kissed her again in that wonderful, expert way. Oh, God, she thought, as his soft lips caressed hers, there's no going back now. But what the hell, I'll marry him, then. I'll put up with his good looks, title, money and that gorgeous castle in Tuscany he showed me a picture of. OK, she said to herself as his hands squeezed her waist, the flat in Rome is not bad either. 'All right,' she said, when they came up for air, 'I will marry you, my dearest Guido.'

'I'll call my mother straight away.'

'I'm going shopping in St Tropez,' Louise announced at breakfast. 'Just to cheer myself up.' She glared at Paul. 'It has been so boring around here lately. And I have to get something nice for the do at Villa Caramel tomorrow. What about you, Maria?'

'I don't need to buy anything. I'm just going to raid Eva's wardrobe. She brought enough clothes for a whole year.'

'Yes, she belongs to the "just in case" school of packing,' Dan joked.

'You're so lucky to be able to fit into Eva's clothes,' Louise said, sighing, as she spread jam on a croissant.

'If you cut down on the croissants, you'd have a better chance,' Paul remarked.

'What?' Louise demanded. 'Are you insinuating that I'm fat?'

'Of course not,' Paul replied, looking annoyed. 'I wouldn't dream of saying a thing like that.'

'But you did think it?' Louise asked, her eyes narrowing. 'You think I'm fat, don't you?'

'No, I certainly do not,' Paul insisted. 'You're

lovely the way you are.' He looked across the table at Dan for help, but he just smiled and shook his head.

'I'm not getting into that minefield,' he laughed. 'I'm surprised you fell into the trap, Paul.'

'I'm not on the ball this early,' Paul replied.

'What are you wearing?' Louise asked Eva as she came out on the terrace with more bread. 'To the party, I mean.'

'I don't know. By the way, has anyone seen Dieter?'

'No,' Dan said. 'I don't think he's up yet.'

'I don't think he's even been to bed,' Louise contradicted him. 'Because here he is, coming up the drive on his machine.'

The sound of Dieter's motorbike filled the air as he swept up the drive and stopped in a shower of gravel just below the steps.

'Good morning,' Dieter said, sauntering onto the terrace. He looked a little tired and he had obviously not shaved for several days, but his eyes were bright. 'What a lovely day.'

'Is it?' Louise muttered. 'I hadn't noticed.'

Dieter looked around at the assembled company. 'What's the matter with everyone? Why do you all look so glum?'

'Where have you been?' Eva demanded. 'You look as if you slept in your clothes. This is the second time you have been out all night.'

'Just having a bit of fun, my darling sister,' Dieter said, pouring himself a cup of coffee. 'I had no idea a motorbike was such a sex symbol. The women go mad for it.'

'For what?' Dan asked. 'Sex or the bike?'

'Wouldn't you love to know?' Dieter smiled.

'I'm sure Gretchen would,' Eva muttered under her breath.

'What's biting you?' Dieter demanded. 'Is this bad mood affecting everyone today? Have you forgotten how to have fun?'

'Some of us, yes,' Louise muttered, giving Paul another sour look.

'But we're all going to the party tomorrow,' Maria said. 'That should be very enjoyable. I'm looking forward to it in any case.'

'Talking about the party,' Eva said. 'I was thinking about that little girl.'

'Edwina?' Maria said.

'Yes. I was wondering what she'll be doing during the party. I don't think she'll be attending it, will she?'

'God, no,' Maria snorted. 'Maddy wouldn't want to have a child there to ruin her image.'

'In that case,' Eva continued, 'do you think she might like to spend the evening here? With her nanny of course. It would be a lot quieter than her own house, and she could watch a video and play with the dogs. Fatima loves children, so I'm sure she would be happy to give Edwina dinner.'

'That's a wonderful idea,' Maria said, putting her napkin on the table. 'How kind of you to think of it. I'll go and ring Maddy at once.'

It took nearly half an hour to locate Maddy. Maria spoke to innumerable servants, who kept switching her to different extensions all over the house. Then they finally located her in the gym and Maddy's bored voice came on the line.

'Ya?'

'Maddy, hello.'

'Who is this?'

'It's Maria Connolly.' They have only told you twelve times who it is, Maria thought.

'Connolly ... Eh ... Oh, yes, of course. How are you?'

'Very well, thank you.' As if you care, Maria said under her breath. 'And you?'

'Very well.' There was a pause.

'Well, eh, I'm calling you because I wanted to ask about Edwina ...'

'Yes?'

'I was wondering ... we were wondering if she, Edwina, I mean, would like to ...' Shit, Maria thought, why does she make me feel so nervous? 'Would Edwina,' she started again, 'like to come here and spend the night? Tomorrow, the night of the party?'

'Why?'

'Well, because I thought it might be nicer for her to be here, rather than upstairs in her room with all the noise and so on ...'

'How very kind. Lovely suggestion. But it won't be necessary.'

'Oh? Why?'

'She's not here. She left this morning.'

Maria slowly opened the letter Mark had brought.

Dear Mareea
I am going awy tomorow and I just wanted to rite

you a letter to say goodby. I now that my spelling is
aful and nanny usully chex it but I dont want an-
nyune to reed it, so Im just goin to giv it to Mark
and he can giv it to you. I hav to go to Landun to
get my skool uniform and then Im going to my grany
in Long Iland for a week and then Im going bak to
Landun to start skool. I hop you hav a nice time at
the party. Mummy is having a red dres sent from
Paris and shes goin to wer her dimond nekless. It
was so much fun to play with you in the pol. Tell
Mark to giv you my adres and then we can rite to
ich other. You ar such a nice gurl and I relly lik u
very much. I hope I will see you next yer. I hav to
go now. by by,
    lots of luv,
    EDWINA

'Oh, God,' Maria laughed, tears stinging her eyes. 'She really needs to improve her spelling.'

'I know,' Mark said. 'But she didn't want anybody to help her with this.'

'Will she be all right?'

'Of course. She's as tough as an old boot. Even nanny is scared of her.'

'I'm really going to miss her. Thank you for bringing me the letter.'

'No problem.' Mark looked around the terrace. 'Is Louise here?

'No. She's gone into St Tropez to buy a dress for that party at your place tomorrow.'

'OK. Well, in that case, see you then.' Mark bounced down the steps whistling a little tune, while

Maria read her letter once more.

'I have to go to Italy,' Guido said that evening. 'My mother is a little sick.'

'Oh, no, darling, I'm so sorry,' Maria said. 'I hope it's not serious.'

'I can't understand it. She was so well, and then, when I was talking about you and our wedding, she suddenly ... I don't know, she just said she was feeling very bad.'

Guido shook his head, looking worried. They were having a drink in the bar of the Byblos, and Maria had been looking forward to having dinner there later on. But now Guido had to go to Italy and was leaving nearly straight away.

'She was always so healthy,' he said, 'and so brave since my father died. But now ... all of a sudden, she is not well.'

'Are you sure it's not because you're getting married? Maybe she wanted you to marry an Italian girl? Or maybe she doesn't want you to marry at all?'

'No, no, I'm sure it's not that. I told her what a beautiful, lovely girl you are and how much I love you and that we would be married very soon and live there with her in Toscana, and she said she was very happy for me.'

'But maybe she wanted you to continue as Commissioner in Brussels? You told me she was so proud of you when you were appointed.'

'No,' Guido argued, 'she knows my work there is finished. I only took the post for *la famiglia*.'

'For your family?'

'That's right. And now all my nephews have jobs in the Commission, so I can go home and look after my own interests. I have done my duty.' Guido took Maria's hand. 'Don't worry, *amore mio*, I will return very soon. And I will bring back the family ring and we can be officially engaged. And plan the wedding.' He kissed her hand. 'Does that make you happy?'

'Of course, darling,' Maria smiled.

'It's a very old ring. A big ruby and some diamonds. Very beautiful. It is given to the bride of the eldest son on their engagement.'

'Who's wearing it now?'

'My mother. But she knows she will have to give it up. And she will have to move out of the master bedroom in the castle, of course.'

'I see,' Maria said. 'But that might be what she's upset about. Maybe that is why she felt ill.'

'No.' Guido shook his head. 'Of course not. I told her she would be very fond of you and that she would make a wonderful grandmother to our children. I told her also that you are so beautiful and young and that you will make such a wonderful *contessa*.'

'How old is your mother?' Maria suddenly asked.

'My mother? How old is she?' Guido thought for a moment. 'She is sixty-one. But she looks a lot younger than that. I think I have a photo of her in my wallet. Let's see.' Guido took out his wallet and searched among the bits of paper. 'Here. It was taken last year.'

Maria looked at the picture of a stunningly beautiful woman with shiny brown hair and dark flashing eyes. 'She looks more like your sister.'

'I know. She looks very young. She was only

eighteen when she married my father.'

'And you're the only son?'

'Yes. I have four sisters, who are all younger than me.'

'Are any of them married?'

'No. None of them have been able to find a man that my mother likes.'

'I see.'

Guido rose. 'But now I have to say goodbye. The taxi is waiting to take me to the airport.' He took Maria's hands, pulled her up and put his arms around her. '*Cara mia,*' he said, and looked deeply into her eyes, 'I will hurry back as soon as my mother is better.' And, after having kissed her hard on the mouth, he picked up his bag and ran down the stairs to the waiting taxi.

Maria looked at his departing elegant figure with mixed feelings of elation and doom.

'What's going on here? Has there been an accident?'

Maria looked around Eva and Dan's bedroom, where what seemed like Eva's entire wardrobe was spread all over the bed, the chairs, the floor and also draped over the doors.

'I'm just doing a kind of inventory of my clothes.'

'You're trying to put together an outfit for tomorrow night, you mean?'

'Well, yes, something like that. But I haven't a clue what I'm going to wear.'

'Shouldn't be too difficult. There seem to be enough clothes here to dress a dozen women for a dozen parties. But it depends.'

'Depends on what?'

'On what kind of effect you're after. Do you want to knock their eyes out or are you going to settle for quietly elegant?'

'I just want to look right,' Eva sighed. 'You know, like someone who understands how to dress. And of course, I realise that whatever I put on, that woman will be so subtly elegant, so ultra chic, that we'll all look like overdressed waitresses beside her. I bet she'll be wearing some sort of little black number that cost the earth.'

'No, she won't.' Maria smiled conspiratorially. 'I happen to know exactly what she'll be wearing.'

'You do?' Eva stared at Maria incredulously. 'Where did you find that out?'

'Straight from the horse's mouth. Or maybe I should say the filly's mouth.' Maria thought about Edwina and suddenly felt a dart of sadness. She sank down on the bed.

'What's the matter?' Eva asked. 'You look so upset.'

'Edwina has left,' Maria said bleakly. 'She's been sent away to London with her nanny. Something to do with her school uniform.'

'Oh, no. I'm so sorry.' Eva sat down beside Maria. 'You're going to miss her so.'

'Yes.' Maria blinked away the tears that were threatening to well up in her eyes. 'Yes, I will.'

'But going to the party will cheer you up.'

'I'm not going.'

'Not going? But why? I thought you were looking forward to it. Guido was so pleased you had both been invited. He was going to tell everybody about your engagement then, he said.'

'That's all over too. All over bar the shouting, as the saying goes.' Maria let out a bitter little sigh. 'Why do I always end up such a loser?'

'What's the matter with you?' Eva demanded. 'Are you feeling sorry for yourself again?'

'Yes, I am. I am feeling very sorry for myself. That's the only pleasure I have left. And I'm going to wallow in it.'

Eva got up from the bed. 'What's wrong with you now, for God's sake? I understand that you're upset about having to say goodbye to Edwina, but you must have known that was coming sooner or later. Everything else was going so well. You were so happy a few days ago. What's happened between you and Guido? Have you broken up with him?'

'His mother has suddenly thrown a wobbly and he's had to rush to Italy to calm her down. He thinks she has come down with some sort of strange disease, the fool. I know what's bothering her, even if he can't see it.'

'What are you talking about?'

'I'm talking about a ring with rubies and diamonds, the master bedroom in that castle in Tuscany and a doting son, none of which a certain Italian beauty will give up without a fight.' Maria sighed, feeling tired. 'And I don't feel like taking her on. I'm fed up. I just want to go home, to be honest.'

'You mean you're giving up? You're going to let that lovely man get away? And you're going to let me go to that party on my own?' Eva looked at Maria angrily. 'I need your support, you know. You're not the only one with problems. I have a certain little Mercedes to deal with. Not to mention what's going to happen to my job.'

'Mercedes?' Maria asked. 'Are you buying a new car?'

'No, but I wouldn't mind giving that particular one a few dents.' Eva sighed. 'I'll just have to manage on my own, I suppose. Unlike you, I never give up.'

'Fernando?'

'Yes, Mr Connolly?'

'Could you get me a gin and tonic?'

'Yes, sir.'

Fernando stopped watering the geraniums, put down the watering can and went to the drinks trolley in the living room. 'Ice and lemon?'

'Yes, please.'

Dan sank down into the sofa with a tired sigh. He had spent practically all day at the beach, practising for the competition the next day. He knew Eva and the girls were fussing about the party, and all they could think of at the moment were clothes and make-up. He hadn't reminded Eva about the competition, knowing she would have a fit if she knew he was doing something so exhausting the day of the party. He would just slip away, he thought, when they were all having their siesta. And then he would surprise them with the cup when he came back. Wouldn't that put them in a party mood?

'Here you are, sir.' Fernando handed him a tall glass.

'Thank you, Fernando. You make the best gin and tonic in Europe. Probably the world, actually.'

'Thank you, sir.'

Dan sipped the drink. 'Delicious. So,' he continued, in the mood for a chat, 'how are you? We haven't seen much of you lately.'

'I'm fine, sir. I have been very busy. There have been a lot of parties in the area. And some of my colleagues from Brussels are also here.'

'And you have been working with them?'

'Yes, sir.'

'Who are these, eh, colleagues? Other Filipinos?'

'Yes, some of them. But there are also some Poles and some Spanish waiters. And French too.'

'Oh, really? French? From here, you mean?'

'No,' Fernando said. 'They work in Brussels in the winter. They usually do the entertaining at the French embassy there.'

'Oh, yes, I remember them. I saw them at the French national day.' Dan laughed. 'I told my wife they looked like thugs, but she told me they were the latest in French chic.'

'Yes, sir,' Fernando said, and slipped out of the room.

CHAPTER 17

'Monsieur Connolly?' Officer Bernard looked at Dan questioningly. 'How nice to see you again. We haven't had any member of your family here for quite some time. What can I do for you?'

'It's about that man,' Dan said, pointing at the opposite wall. 'The man on the poster over there.'

'Yes?'

Dan walked over to the poster and studied the picture. 'That's him. Why didn't I realise it before? It has to be the same one. The spitting image.'

'Does your wife know you're here?'

'What does that have to do with it? I have come to tell you that I have seen this man before. This ... this criminal here.'

'Really?' Officer Bernard's voice was slightly patronising.

'Why don't you listen to me?' Dan snapped. 'No wonder you're having no luck solving crime around here.'

'I beg your pardon?'

'Well, as far as I know, cars are still being stolen

every week. I read it in *Nice Matin* yesterday.'

'We're very close to cracking the case.'

'This might bring you even closer.'

'Really? Well, go on. Tell me, then. But don't hang around. I come off duty in ten minutes and then I'm going home to have my dinner.'

'OK, I will. This man here –' Dan pointed at the picture – 'was in Brussels in July. At the French embassy, as a matter of fact. It was 14 July.'

'At the French embassy,' Officer Bernard repeated. 'You are trying to make me believe that the French ambassador invited a wanted criminal to his house? On 14 July?'

'No, of course not. He wasn't a guest. He was one of the waiters. He served me a damned good gin and tonic, as a matter of fact. That's why I noticed him. French waiters normally don't know how to make a decent one. Now Fernando –'

'Never mind. Let's get to the point. You say that this man was working as a waiter at the French embassy in Brussels?'

'That's right.'

'I find that impossible to believe. That man is dangerous. He has been convicted of two armed robberies and escaped from prison six months ago. He has been spotted in several different parts of France and he was last seen in Marseilles.'

'Why didn't you catch him, then? Why was he just spotted?'

'He got away.' Officer Bernard picked up the phone. 'I'm going to phone one of my superiors to tell him what you said. And then I have to ask you to sign a statement.'

'Of course.'

'Do you think you'd recognise him if you saw him again?'

'I'm sure I would. Especially if he made me a gin and tonic.'

Officer Bernard shook his head while he dialled. 'The French embassy,' he muttered. 'Is nothing sacred?'

'Where have you been now?' Eva asked, looking at Dan with a feeling of irritation when he arrived back. 'We have already eaten. I couldn't hold dinner for more than half an hour. I told you to be here at nine o'clock, and then, when we were all ready to eat, you had gone. Maria looked for you all over the house.'

'I had to go down to the police station.'

'What? Don't tell me you've been in some kind of trouble as well? Haven't we had enough problems with Fernando and Maria without you getting –'

'No!' Dan snapped. 'Will you listen to me for once! I had made this amazing discovery. I suddenly remembered where I had seen that man before.'

'What man? Officer Bernard?'

'No, don't be silly. The man on the poster. That wanted criminal.'

'And? Don't tell me that he's lurking around here somewhere. I find that hard to believe.'

'OK. I won't tell you, then.' Dan walked away across the terrace. 'What's the point if you don't believe me?'

Eva ran and grabbed him by the arm. 'No. I want

to know. Where did you think you saw him?'

'Let's drop the whole thing.'

'All right. If that's what you want.'

'It is. But now I'm feeling really hungry. Is there anything left from dinner?'

'There's chicken and some ratatouille. Fatima put it in the oven.'

'Will you join me? Have a glass of wine while I eat?'

'I'm going to bed. I want to be fresh for the party tomorrow.'

'Oh, yes, the party,' Dan sighed.

'You don't seem very happy about it.'

'It's just that I have that competition beforehand. The windsurfing competition.'

'Oh, that.' Eva shrugged.

She was really fed up with Dan and this silly new hobby. She knew she should be more interested, more supportive, but it was very difficult. And that girl was far too pretty to be considered harmless.

'Yes, that,' Dan snapped. 'I'm going to take part, whatever you think. I'll be back in plenty of time for the party, so don't worry. I'll be there like the trained monkey I've always been.'

'What do you mean?' Eva stammered.

'You know perfectly well.' Dan strode across the terrace and disappeared through the door.

'Name?'

Maria looked at the tall young man and recognised him as one of the bouncers from the disco. He was standing just inside the front door of Villa Caramel, looking through a long list of names.

'Brigitte Bardot.'

He barely glanced at her. 'Sorry. No one by that name here. I don't think she was invited to this particular knees-up.'

Maria glared at him and lowered her voice. 'My name is Maria Connolly and if you don't let me in I'll give you a knees-up you'll never forget.'

The bouncer looked up. There was a glimpse of recognition in his eyes. 'Oh, I see,' he drawled, 'the girl with attitude. You have sharpened up your act, darling.'

'And you're even more pathetic than before.'

'Maria,' Louise hissed behind her, 'stop bitching. I want to go inside.'

'Don't we all?' Maria snapped. 'Now, be a good boy and step aside. We don't want to stand here all night. What would Lord Bakewell say?'

'I didn't know he liked the butch type,' the bouncer said.

'And I didn't know he employed poofs,' Maria retorted, and sailed in through the door.

'Wow,' Louise whispered as they walked across the marble floor. 'Did you see? They had valet-parking. I just hope my dress is all right.'

'You look stunning,' Maria said, and looked at the image of herself, Eva and Louise reflected in the huge hall mirror. 'We all do.'

Louise was looking elegantly sexy in a sleeveless black dress with a softly flared skirt, demure in the front, but plunging to her waist at the back, bought for a small fortune the day before in St Tropez.

Maria was quite pleased with her own choice from Eva's extensive wardrobe: a short, floral-print dress of thin silk which whispered softly over her body, showing off her slim tanned arms and legs. Her dark curly hair shone in the light of the candles and her eyes sparkled.

But Eva was the loveliest of them all, in a cream silk dress, showing just a little shoulder and a lot of leg, wearing dangerously high heels and long drop-pearl and diamond earrings.

'Let's go and say hello to our host,' Eva suggested. 'If we can get through the crowd that is. The whole town must be here.'

'Good evening, ladies.' Mark was standing before them, looking unusually tidy in navy trousers and a white open-necked shirt. 'You all look terribly smart.'

'So do you,' Louise smiled.

'Maddy made me dress up.'

'And I just saw Alistair in a white tux,' Maria said.

'I know. Very Noël Coward, don't you think? It belonged to his father. He always wears it to the end-of-the-hols party. But where's Mr Connolly? Dan, I mean?'

'He'll be along later,' Eva snapped. 'If you'll excuse me ...' She turned abruptly and swept through the throng towards the terrace and Alistair.

'What did I say?' Mark asked. 'She seemed suddenly a little annoyed.'

'It's Daddy,' Louise whispered. 'He went off to the beach earlier. Said it was the last day. There was some sort of competition and an end-of-season party there, I think. But Eva didn't want him to go and, when he didn't appear this evening in time to get ready, she decided we should all go ahead. He'll be along soon, I'm sure.'

'I see. And where's Paul?'

'Here,' Paul replied, walking into the hall.

'Oh, nice to see you, old chap.'

'And you.' Paul nodded and offered his arm to Louise. 'Let's go out and meet everyone.'

'Shall we?' Mark asked, and offered his arm to Maria. 'You look fantastic tonight, I have to say.'

'Thank you.'

Maria took his arm and they made their way to the French windows which led onto the terrace.

Maria looked around her, mesmerised. They had stepped straight into a Hollywood fairy tale. If this was 'just an informal party', as Maddy had described it, she wondered what a really formal one was like. The terrace was lit by hundreds of candles that flickered in the light breeze. Waiters in white jackets were weaving through the crowd, serving champagne and canapés. Long tables covered with starched white tablecloths lined the end of the terrace, and there was even an ice sculpture of a swan. Soft music could be heard from a chamber orchestra in the conservatory.

'There's going to be a nine-piece salsa band later,' Mark said. 'We'll be dancing till dawn.'

'This is just amazing!' Louise exclaimed. 'What a fantastic party.'

'I'm glad you're enjoying it,' Alistair said, kissing her on the cheek. 'Lovely to see you.' He greeted Maria the same way. 'You all look fabulous.'

Maria spotted Eva at the far side of the terrace, talking to an distinguished-looking gentleman.

'That's Jean-Claude Bonhomme,' Mark whispered in her ear. 'One of the top people at the Commission.'

'Oh? I didn't know Alistair and Maddy knew anyone in Brussels.'

'Oh, yes, they do. Alistair is very pro-Europe, you know. Very interested in the European Union.'

'I didn't even know he spoke French.'

'Oh, well, he doesn't go *that* far,' Mark laughed.

'Where the hell has Louise disappeared to?' Paul said, scanning the crowd. 'She was here a minute ago and then she just –'

'I'm going to make sure she's all right,' Mark said, disappearing just as fast.

'So,' Maria said, looking up at Paul. 'Nice weather we're having.'

'Oh, shut up. I'm going to get a drink.' And then he was gone as well.

Maria suddenly found herself alone. 'Oh, so what?' she muttered to herself, and grabbed a glass of champagne from a passing waiter. 'Might as well drown my sorrows.'

Eva looked around to see if Dan had arrived. The party was in full swing, the band had already started to play, people were dancing at the far side of the terrace and the waiters were beginning to prepare the buffet. Where was he? Why did he have to do this to her tonight of all nights? Was it some sort of revenge? Or were Mercedes' charms proving irresistible? Everyone was asking her where he was, even Maddy, who had made a dramatic entrance half an hour earlier on Dieter's arm. She looked amazing, of course, in a long deep-red dress that plunged nearly to her navel. She wore her hair piled on top of her head, a diamond choker around her long, thin neck and her eyes were heavily made up with black kohl.

'Wow,' Eva heard a man behind her whisper, 'she really looks dangerous tonight.'

'The dress was made especially for her by Delacroix,' his lady companion replied, 'and Marcel came from London to do her hair and make-up.'

'But who is that brute beside her?' another woman asked. 'I've never seen him before.'

'One of her tame motorcycle boys,' the man laughed. 'You know how she likes to slum it.'

Eva turned around. 'That is Count Dieter Mebius,' she snapped. 'Of one of the oldest families in Germany.'

'You could have fooled me,' the man said.

Eva glared at him, but decided not to start an argument. She sipped her third glass of champagne and watched as the waiters prepared an elaborate buffet.

'Holy shit.' Louise was suddenly standing beside Eva. 'What a spread.'

'You seem a little tipsy,' Eva remarked.

'A little? You must be joking.' Louise laughed and drained her champagne glass. 'I'm *very* tipsy. What a party, eh? Have you noticed, the ice cubes all have grapes frozen in them. How did they do that?'

'I have no idea.'

Louise sighed happily. 'I have danced with loads of men. And everyone's so *nice*. Someone just gave me a hundred–dollar bill for coke. I didn't know Coca-Cola had become so expensive.'

'I don't think he meant that kind of coke, darling,' Eva said. 'And that bill was not for spending, it was for ... Never mind.' She took Louise's arm. 'Let's go and sit down for a moment.'

'Oh, OK.'

Eva led Louise inside and sat her down on one of the sofas in the living room.

'Where's Paul? Why isn't he looking after you?'

'He was having a huge whisky when I saw him last. I think he got into a bit of a snot because that nice Frenchman was flirting with me.'

'What Frenchman?'

'Your friend. Yves something. Very sexy. But I think he's kind of stuck on you actually. That was all he could talk about, in any case.' Louise drew breath. 'I'm not that bad really. You don't have to worry. I won't embarrass you in any way. I just need to eat something. But here's Paul now. Hi, darling,' Louise beamed. 'Are you having a lovely time?'

'Wonderful,' he replied flatly. He held out a plate. 'I got you some food.'

'Oh, thank you, darling,' Louise said. 'Just what I need.'

'Have you seen Maria?' Eva asked, sounding worried.

'No, not for a while,' Paul replied.

'I'm sure she's having a lovely time too,' Louise said. 'But why isn't her Italian boyfriend here tonight? And she looks so lovely and everything.'

'He's gone to Italy to tell his mother about their

engagement,' Eva said, without thinking. She clapped her hand to her mouth. 'Oh, God, I shouldn't have said that. It's supposed to be a secret.'

'What?' Louise squealed. 'They're engaged? I don't believe it! Why did no one tell me? How fantastic! My sister a *contessa*!'

'Shhh,' Eva whispered. 'Not a word to anyone. Not until Guido comes back.'

'OK, I promise,' Louise whispered back, and tucked into the food. She looked up. 'But where's Paul?'

Maria was at the beach. She had taken off her shoes and was enjoying the cool water lapping up against her hot and sore feet. It had been a great party, she thought, really great. And she had done her best to enjoy it. She had danced with both Alistair and Mark, and a nice Frenchman who had told her he was a very good friend of Eva's. She had sat down beside an elderly gentleman at supper and he had entertained her with funny stories from his youth in the 1940s. She had drunk champagne and eaten some delicious dessert. She had danced some more, laughed and chatted and even smoked a cigarette. But it was no good. She had not been able to get into the swing of it and now she had had enough. She was feeling tired and lonely. She looked up at the stars in the black sky and wondered what Guido was doing at that moment.

'Maria?'

She looked around. 'Paul? What do you want?'

'I came to talk to you. I believe congratulations are in order.'

'No, they're not. Nothing's in order here. Every-thing is *out* of order actually.'

'What do you mean? Eva just told me . . .' His face looked oddly white in the floodlighting from the house.

'I don't want to talk about it right now.'

'I see. All right.' Paul cleared his throat. 'Can I get you anything? A drink, or . . .'

'A pint of Guinness,' Maria sighed. 'That's what I would really like. And could you blow some smoke in my face as well? That would make me feel really at home. It's that cosy pub atmosphere that's missing here.'

'What's the matter? Are you feeling a little home-sick? I thought you loved the south of France.'

'I hate the bloody place,' Maria snapped. 'I'm sick of it. I'm sick of the sunshine and the blue sky. I'm sick of the heat, the rosé, the olive oil and the lovely little tomatoes grown in the sun and . . . and . . . You know, those tiny deep-fried fish that are so delicious?'

'Eh, yes?'

'I'm sick of those too. And those rich people on their yachts, do you know what I think of them?'

'No, what?' Paul asked, with an amused smile.

'They can take their bloody yachts and stick them up their bottoms.'

'Good idea.'

'And,' Maria ranted on, 'I'm sick of always being too warm. I want to feel the rain on my face, I want to feel the damp and the cold, to cuddle up in front of a fire and smell that lovely turf smoke. And I could kill for a plate of sausage and chips. And the chips should be soggy. Do you think you could conjure that up?'

'No. I'm afraid that would be a little bit difficult.'

'I knew it. You're hopeless.'

'Why are you mad at me?' Paul demanded. 'What have I done?'

'Nothing,' Maria replied. 'That's the trouble. You have done absolutely nothing!'

Eva was feeling increasingly restless and she was not enjoying the party. Dan had really overdone it this time. No matter what he felt about her, he could have had the decency not to embarrass her like this.

'Eva.' Jean-Claude Bonhomme was walking towards her with two plates of food. 'You haven't eaten anything. I brought you a few things.'

'Oh, thank you. That is so kind.'

'Why don't we sit down and eat? There are tables in the conservatory that aren't too crowded.'

'Good idea.'

'So,' Jean-Claude said, tucking into his *saumon en croûte*, 'have you enjoyed your holiday?'

'Very much. But that sudden trip to Vienna was a bit annoying, to say the least.'

'I know. Not really the kind of thing you need when you're trying to relax,' Jean-Claude agreed. 'But you seem a little down for someone who has done so remarkably well in her career.'

'Oh, I don't know. It's not a big deal really.'

Jean-Claude's eyebrows rose. 'Not a big deal? You're very modest, I have to say, which is admirable.

If it was me, in the same position . . .' He shrugged and smiled.

What does he mean? Eva thought, and smiled back at him. Is he a bit drunk? Why would he want to be deputy *chef*? 'I'm aiming a bit higher than that actually,' she said.

'Really? Even higher? I must say, you are the most ambitious woman I have ever met.'

'You don't seem to have a very high regard of women,' Eva remarked, feeling annoyed. Why didn't he think a woman could be *chef de cabinet*?

'But I do,' he protested. 'I really do. Especially women as capable as you. I have always been very impressed with your work, and now, of course, even more so.'

'Good, because I'm going to show you a thing or two in the autumn.'

'Of course you are. I can't wait. It is going to be so very exciting to see what you are going to do next.'

'Really?' Is he on drugs as well as drunk? Eva thought.

'Oh, yes. I'm very excited about it.'

'Madame Connolly?' Someone tapped Eva on the shoulder.

'Yes?'

Eva turned around and recognised Mercedes, Dan's windsurfing instructor. Her wild black hair was damp, she was dressed in only her red Speedo swimsuit and a pair of ragged shorts, and she looked very upset.

'Madame Connolly –' Mercedes wrung her hands – 'I have come to tell you that your husband is . . .'

Eva rose. 'What? My husband is what?'

'Missing, madame. He's missing at sea,' Mercedes sobbed.

'You dance very well,' Alistair muttered into Louise's ear.

They were dancing on the lower terrace. Very close. Body to body, cheek to cheek. She closed her eyes and just enjoyed the music and being held by this gorgeous man.

'It's you,' she whispered back. 'Dancing with you is so easy.'

He stepped back and smiled into her eyes. 'We could have a lot of fun, you know, if it wasn't for the fact that you're engaged to be married.'

'I'm not really,' she replied. 'Not at all, actually.'

'Oh? Good.' He held her close again and they continued dancing, until someone tapped Louise on the shoulder.

'Guido!' Louise exclaimed. 'What on earth are you doing here? I thought you were in Italy with your mother.'

'I was,' Guido said. 'But I came back nearly straight away. I need to talk to Maria. Where is she?'

'Oh, I don't know,' Louise laughed and grabbed him by the waist. 'I haven't seen her for ages. But dance with me instead. I have never danced with a real Italian count before.'

'Oh, but I really need to talk to Maria,' Guido protested.

'Plenty of time,' Louise smiled. 'Let's just dance one dance, and then we'll go find her. You don't mind, Alistair?'

'Of course not.'

Alistair stepped away and Louise started to move to the music, holding on to a worried-looking Guido.

'She told us, you know. Maria. She told us about the two of you. I mean, she told Eva and Eva told us.'

'Oh?' Guido looked down at Louise.

'It's really very exciting actually. My sister a *contessa*.' Louise smiled to herself and closed her eyes. Then she opened them again and peered at Guido. 'But when is the wedding?'

'Well, that is the problem,' Guido said. 'It won't be for a while. My mother is more sick than I thought. That's what I came to tell Maria.'

'Oh? I see. But that doesn't matter, does it? *We* can still be friends?'

'*Certo*,' Guido replied, looking at Louise with a little smile. 'I never noticed what a very pretty girl you are. It is nice to have a beautiful sister-in-law, no?'

'Of course,' Louise agreed. 'Very nice.'

All the blood had drained out of Eva's face and her knees suddenly buckled. She sank down on her chair again. 'What do you mean?' she whispered.

'It happened late this afternoon. We were having a competition. Dan was so excited about it. And he was doing really well, and then –'

'Then?' Eva said, not noticing the hush in the conservatory or the glass of brandy someone was holding to her lips.

'Then there was a squall and he was swept out. We

thought he would come back, but we saw him disappear out to sea ...'

'But what have you done since then? Have you called the coastguard? The fire brigade? The police?'

'Well, no. Not until just now actually. We thought he might still come back.'

'You stupid girl,' Eva snapped, waving away the brandy. 'How can you be so ... so bloody careless? My husband is swept out to sea and you do nothing?'

'Well, I ...'

'Oh, God,' Eva sobbed, 'what am I going to do?'

'Why are you suddenly so hostile?' Paul demanded.

'Hostile? I'm not hostile. I'm just making an observation. When in doubt, do nothing. That's your motto, isn't it?'

'That's a bit unfair.'

'Unfair?' Maria laughed ironically. 'That's rich, coming from you. You're such a creep, do you know that? First, you ask – no, you *beg* Louise to marry you. Then, when her back is turned, you have sex with her sister. Me, that is. And then you go straight back to her and act as if nothing happened. And you say that *I'm* unfair!'

'Well, it wasn't exactly rape, was it? And you lost no time at all consoling yourself. I have to admit you did it in style. I'm full of admiration.'

'You're full of shit.'

'Oh, God, you are the most infuriating woman I've ever met!' Paul exclaimed. 'In fact, you are the only woman I have ever wanted to hit.'

Maria stared at him, angry tears welling up in her

eyes. 'Oh, how I hate you, Paul Ryan,' she sobbed. 'I really, really hate you.'

'Eva, try to calm down,' Alistair said. 'I've spoken to the coastguard and they said they are still looking. And when the helicopters go out in the morning, they're sure to find him. The weather is good. There is practically no wind. You'll see. It will be all right.'

'Oh, I hope so,' Eva said distractedly. Will I ever see him again? she thought. Why did I have to be so cold and sour the last time we spoke? This is all my fault. 'Where are the girls?' she asked. 'Should we tell them?'

'No. Leave it for the moment,' Alistair suggested. 'No need to upset them just yet. I have called the officer in charge at the *gendarmerie* as well. He's in touch with the coastguard every hour. He said he would be over as soon as he could to give you the latest news.'

'Oh, that's good.' Eva glared at Mercedes, who was sitting on a chair at the other side of the table with her head in her hands. I'll never forgive her, she thought bitterly.

'But you are also engaged to be married,' Guido said to Louise as he expertly guided her around the improvised dance floor.

'Sort of,' Louise said. 'But not really.'

'I don't understand.'

'*He* thinks we are and I . . .' Louise shook her head. 'I just don't want to think about it right now. It's making me dizzy. Oh. Here's Mark.'

Mark touched Guido's shoulder. 'I hope you don't

mind, old chap. But I would really like to dance with Louise now.'

'Of course,' Guido said. 'I have to go and look for Maria, in any case.'

'She's on the beach with Paul,' Mark said. 'And I would go down there straight away if I were you, old man.'

'Thank you,' Guido said, and let go of Louise so fast that she nearly fell.

'Maria,' Paul said, and put his hand on her shoulder, 'Maria, I –'

'Let her go,' a voice shouted. 'Let her go at once!'

'Guido!' Maria exclaimed. 'Oh, Guido, you came back.'

'Oh, yes, my darling Maria,' Guido said, and put his arm around her.

'Leave her alone,' Paul ordered. 'She doesn't want you really, you know. She doesn't want to live in Italy.'

'What do you mean?' Guido glared at Paul.

'Of course I do,' Maria sobbed, putting her arms around Guido.

'No, you don't,' Paul protested. 'You want . . .'

'I know what *you* want,' Guido snapped, and let go of Maria. He took a step towards Paul, his fists clenched.

Suddenly there was a strange noise, a whooshing sound and then a splash. Maria turned away from Paul and Guido and looked out across the dark sea. 'What was that?' she asked. But nobody heard her.

'You need a punch in the face,' Guido declared.

'And I am going to give it to you right now.'

'Madame Connolly,' Officer Bernard said, 'I came as soon as I could.'

'Have you found him?' Eva asked.

'Not yet, but they're doing everything they can, believe me.'

'Oh, God,' Eva groaned. 'I feel so helpless. Here I am at a party and my husband is somewhere out there, lost, maybe drowned. And all around us people are enjoying themselves.'

'Try to stay calm, madame.'

'That's easy for you to say.' Eva rubbed her eyes tiredly. When would this nightmare be over? 'I should really tell the girls,' she muttered. 'They'll have to know sooner or later.'

'There's something going on at the beach,' someone suddenly shouted. 'Someone is . . .'

'Eva.' Mark, who had just run up the steps, was trying to catch his breath. 'You have to come down to the beach right now.'

CHAPTER 18

'Oh, my God,' Maria gasped, looking at the figure that had just emerged from the sea. 'It's Daddy.'

She ran towards Dan, who was wading onto the shore, dragging the windsurfing board, looking exhausted.

'Where am I?' he asked.

'You're here, Daddy, with me. Look, Paul. It's my father. He windsurfed to the party. What a surprise!'

'Party?' Dan asked. 'I thought it was Nice. I saw the lights and heard the music. I was sure it was Nice.'

Suddenly the beach was full of people. Eva carefully took off her shoes and ran across the sand to Dan's side. 'Darling,' she sobbed. 'Oh, my darling. I was so worried. I thought you were dead!' She wrapped her arms around his wet and naked torso and hugged him tight.

Dan looked down at her. 'Why did you think that? I just went a little further than I had planned, that's all. And then it got dark and I lost my bearings a little.'

'Never mind,' Eva laughed. 'You're here now.

And you're all right.'

'Of course I am,' Dan replied. 'Why wouldn't I be?
But just tell me one thing.'

'What darling?'

'Did I win?'

'Isn't he amazing?' Maria said to Paul, watching the
group a little further away.

'He sure is.'

'Where's Guido?'

'I don't know,' Paul replied. 'I think he went to get
a blanket for your father. Maybe he believed me when
I said I was the school boxing champion?'

'You were?'

'No. We didn't do boxing at school.'

'I'm going to find him,' Maria said, and turned
away.

'Just a second.' Paul grabbed her arm. 'I'm not finished with you yet.'

'I'm bloody well finished with you. And I really
don't want to make a scene here in front of everybody.'

'Nobody is watching. Look, they are all going up
to the house.'

'I'll go with them.'

'No, you won't. You're going to hear this first.'

'Let me go!' Maria tried to kick him. 'I can't imagine there is anything you can say that I would want
to hear.'

'You're going to hear this.' Paul's eyes bored into
Maria's. 'I love you, you silly bitch. I don't care what
you say.'

Maria stared at him, feeling as if she had been hit by lightning. 'Oh, God,' she whispered. 'Don't you see? I love you too, you stupid bastard.'

'Well this is nice,' Dan said, sitting in the library of Villa Caramel half an hour later, dressed in a pair of jeans and a shirt borrowed from Alistair. 'Together at last, eh, darling?' He put his arm around Eva, who smiled happily and put her head on his shoulder. 'Sorry about the little upset, Alistair. I hope it didn't break up the party.'

'Not at all, old chap,' Alistair assured him. 'Most people thought it was part of the entertainment. But don't you want something? A drink? Or something to eat?'

'A gin and tonic would be nice. And then maybe some food.'

'Right.' Alistair turned to one of the waiters. 'A gin and tonic for Mr Connolly.'

'*Oui, monsieur.*' The waiter nodded and left the room.

'Well, I think that's all, then,' Officer Bernard said, and closed his notepad. 'I've contacted the coastguard and called off the search.'

'Good,' Dan replied. 'I'm very sorry to have caused such an uproar.'

'Don't worry. It wasn't your fault.'

'You're very understanding.' Dan sipped the gin and tonic the waiter had just handed him. 'Mmm, lovely.' He suddenly sat bolt upright. 'Jesus Christ, I don't believe it!'

'What?' Eva asked, staring at him in alarm. 'What's

wrong. Is it the drink?'

'It's delicious. But that's the whole point.' Dan pointed a finger at the waiter, who was just leaving the room. 'It's him!' he shouted. 'Arrest that man!'

'There's some kind of commotion at the house,' Maria said, as they made their way back from the beach. 'And there's a police car at the front door. I wonder what's going on?'

'Looks like someone's just been arrested,' Paul said. 'One of the waiters is being led away.'

'What's up?' Paul asked one of the guests as they reached the top terrace.

'I don't know,' he replied. 'I just heard someone shouting, and then this guy was taken away in hand-cuffs.'

'Paul,' Louise called, coming out from the conservatory. 'I want to talk to you.'

'There you are,' Dan said. 'You missed all the excitement.'

'What happened?' Maria asked.

'Your father just exposed one of the biggest criminals in France,' Eva beamed. 'And only because he has such a fantastic memory for faces.' She looked at Maria. 'Where have you been all this time?'

'Well, eh . . . it's a long story,' Maria replied, taking Paul's hand. 'And we have something to . . .'

'Me first,' Louise cut in. 'This can't wait. Paul, I just have to tell you . . . I can't marry you, I just can't.'

'What?' Paul exclaimed. 'But I just . . . Why not?'

'Because I just can't.'

'Sorry about that, old chap,' Mark smiled, putting

an arm around Louise.

'Oh, I see,' Paul said. 'You prefer the nerdy type, do you? You're going to marry a ...'

'No!' Louise shouted. 'You're so stupid. You don't understand.'

'I don't believe this!' Eva exclaimed. 'Louise, don't tell me you're thinking of marrying Mark?'

'You're all stupid,' Louise said. 'Don't you see? I'M NOT GOING TO MARRY ANYONE!'

'What's going on?' Dan asked. 'Why is Louise shouting? And why are you cuddling Maria, Paul?'

'Because we are in love,' Maria replied.

'When did this happen?' Dan demanded. 'Why does nobody tell me anything?'

'But where's Guido?' Maria asked. 'I have to talk to him.'

'Over there. At the end of the terrace,' Eva replied. 'Talking to Dieter. They seem to have a lot to say to each other.'

'Oh, God, I don't know how I'm going to tell him this,' Maria mumbled.

'Do you want me to go with you?' Paul asked.

'No. I have to do this on my own.'

'Excuse me,' Officer Bernard interrupted, pushing his way through the crowd. 'But I just need Monsieur Connolly for a moment. I need you to sign a statement.'

'Of course,' Dan nodded.

'We're very grateful to you, of course,' Officer Bernard said. 'That man was the missing link in the car-theft case. We knew that the gang was connected to the catering trade. All these waiters had a network going and were communicating with each other while they were serving at big parties.'

'Very clever,' Dan remarked.

'Oh, yes, very. But now we can break up the whole operation because we have the leader of the gang.'

'The case is closed, then?' Eva asked.

'Not quite,' Officer Bernard replied. 'There are a lot of loose ends still. But I can say that, in any case, you, madame, are no longer under suspicion.'

Eva stared at him. 'What do you mean, under suspicion? How dare you?'

'You and your family have been under surveillance for the past few weeks.'

'But that's outrageous!'

'It's not my fault. You were behaving very suspiciously. All of you.'

'What?' Dan said. 'In what way?'

'In every way,' Officer Bernard replied.

'Guido.'

'Not now, Maria.'

'But there is something I must tell you.'

'Can't you see that we are having a very important conversation?'

'Yes,' Dieter said. 'Come back later. We are in the middle of a business meeting.'

'But why can't you just hear what I have to say. Can't you take a break?'

'No.' Guido was still looking at Dieter. 'What was that about ankle straps?'

'I'm going to say it anyway,' Maria insisted. 'I don't care. I have to get it off my chest.'

'Of course,' Guido said. 'How high do you think the heels should be for this particular range?'

'I can't marry you,' Maria said. 'I'm sorry, but I can't.'

'OK.' Guido waved his hand in the air. 'Fine.'

'I don't really know,' Dieter said. 'I have to check with my stylist.'

'Did you hear?' Maria exclaimed. 'Did you hear what I said?'

'I like them high,' Guido stated. 'Really high. What was that, Maria?'

'It's off,' she replied. 'Our engagement, I mean.'

'Stilettos,' Guido nodded. 'That's what really sells. What, Maria? Off, did you say? What is?'

'The ankle strap,' Maria said, and walked away.

Maddy was standing in the door of the library, staring at the scene. She still looked amazing. Despite the hours she had spent dancing, eating and drinking, her dress didn't have a wrinkle and there wasn't a hair out of place, although there was a strange glitter in her eyes and her pupils were dilated.

'What is going on?' she asked. 'Why are the police here?'

'It's a long story,' Alistair said. 'But I'll explain it all, if you like.'

'Don't bother,' Maddy drawled. 'I hate long stories.' And she wandered off, out through the door and across the terrace, magnificent, like a yacht in full sail.

Eva looked at her departing figure, then turned back to Officer Bernard. 'Did you hear what I said? I want an apology now, or –'

'I don't see that I have anything to apologise for,' Bernard protested. 'I am just stating a fact. You were behaving in a suspicious way and –'

'*Attention!*' Jean-Claude stepped forward, pointing a finger at Officer Bernard.

A very angry conversation followed in French, so rapid that even Eva had difficulty in keeping up. 'Demotion', she heard, 'transfer to the *gendarmerie* in le Havre', 'insubordination' and, finally, 'insulting a future Commissioner'.

'Oh, my God,' Eva murmured when there was a break in the tirade. 'They have made you Commissioner, Jean-Claude. How wonderful. Congratulations.' She nearly curtsied as she stepped forward, feeling deeply honoured to be there at that moment. He would be one of those Commissioners who became a legend, she thought, and maybe he'll ask me to be his deputy *chef* . . .

Jean-Claude stared at her as if she had lost her reason. 'But Eva,' he said. 'Didn't you know? *I'm* not the new Commissioner.'

'Oh? But who is? I just heard you say to Officer Bernard . . .' She looked around the room. 'Where is the new Commissioner?'

'Right here,' Jean-Claude said, and kissed her hand.

'What?'

'It's you.' Jean-Claude beamed. 'You're the next German Commissioner, *ma chère* Eva.'

'I still can't believe it,' Eva said, when the excitement had died down and she was sipping a brandy with Jean-Claude Bonhomme.

'I was sure you knew. That's why our conversation earlier was a little bit strange.'

'I thought you were drunk,' Eva laughed.

'And I thought you were impossibly arrogant. I find it hard to believe that you didn't know. Has your government not been in touch with you?'

'I have had a few messages from the Ministry of Justice to call them, but I've been so busy and so pre-occupied with personal problems, I never had the time to return their calls. Isn't it strange that they told you and didn't make more of an effort to contact me?'

Jean-Claude smiled. 'Well, you know your own countrymen. It wouldn't have been quite correct to tell you until it was all official. And the portfolios haven't been decided yet, of course. There's going to be an awful lot of wheeling and dealing about those, as usual.'

'I know. I hope I get a good one.'

'Well, that is something we have to discuss straight away actually. I know it's late, and I'm sure you are tired and want to go home, but ...'

'Yes?'

'Well,' Jean-Claude continued. 'I'm sure it won't come as a surprise to you that Germany is hoping that you will get Justice and Home Affairs. That is why they have appointed you, of course.'

'I know.'

'And they have told me that they would like to appoint a man called Hans Mueller as your *chef*.'

'Of course,' Eva nodded. 'Hans would be a very good choice.'

'But the deputy will have to be French. Paris would

insist on that.'

'That's no problem.' Eva smiled.

'And it has to be an *enarque*. A graduate from ENA, I mean.'

'The French National School of Administration. Your very own alma mater. Of course.'

'I already know the perfect candidate,' Jean-Claude said. 'You don't mind if I suggest this appointment? You wouldn't have any objection?'

'Of course not. I would trust your judgement completely. I suppose they have agreed in Paris already?'

'You're very sharp. And so kind not to disagree.'

Eva laughed. 'Well, as Henri IV said, "Paris is worth a Mass."' She held up her glass in a toast. 'Here's to my deputy.'

'There's nobody here,' Eva said, looking up at the dark and silent house as Dan switched off the engine of the car. 'It's so late. Or early actually,' she added, consulting her watch. 'It's four o'clock in the morning. Where are they all?'

'I don't care,' Dan said, putting his arms around her. 'For once I couldn't give a hoot. They can all go to hell.'

'But Louise seemed so hysterical. Maybe she's upset about breaking up with Paul?'

'Serve her right,' Dan said, kissing Eva's neck.

'And Maria,' Eva mumbled, 'she had to go and break her engagement ... I wonder how Guido took that?'

'Who cares?' Dan said, and started to undo the tiny buttons at the back of Eva's dress. 'You smell divine, my darling. Is that a new perfume?'

'Please, Dan, not in the car,' Eva protested, and tried to stop him from sliding the dress off her shoulders.

'Can't think of a better place.'

'Aren't you worried about the girls?'

'No, not a bit. Time they took care of themselves. How does this clasp open?'

'And Dieter ... I hope that woman doesn't get her claws into him.'

'He should be so lucky.' Dan finally managed to get the clasp of the bra to come undone. 'You have the most beautiful skin, my love, like silk.'

'But Dan, we have to ... ooh ... Oh, no not here, right in front of the house.'

'Why not? There's no one here.'

'But what if ... Oh, God, do that again ...'

'You mean this?'

'Yes ... ooh ...'

'You know,' Dan mumbled, 'I have never made love to a Commissioner before. Especially in a Saab.'

'I thought you preferred a Mercedes.'

'Oh, no. A little too heavy in the rear. This one is much smoother.' Dan continued to kiss her neck.

Eva pushed him away and sat up, trying to pull herself together. 'No, this is not a good idea. What if someone comes?'

'Someone will, very soon,' Dan smiled and slid his hands up Eva's thighs.

'Dan, I'm serious. This is not right. I'm worried about the girls and ...'

Suddenly Eva's seat snapped back and she found

herself lying down. 'What?' she exclaimed. 'What happened?'

'I've always wanted to do that,' Dan laughed. 'Ever since you bought this car.'

Eva looked up at him, helpless. 'Let me out of here,' she protested. 'This is really silly. You can't . . .'

Dan leaned over her. 'Oh, yes, I can,' he whispered.

EPILOGUE

The snow fell softly outside the office window. It settled on the roofs across the street from the Commission building, on the cars parked in the street below, on the pavements, garbage bins and park benches, on the bushes and trees.

Eva looked up from her computer and stared at the white world outside. It's winter, she thought, winter already. What had happened to the time? What had happened to the rest of the summer and the autumn? It was nearly Christmas and she had only just settled into her new job as Commissioner for Justice and Home Affairs.

The summer and all that had happened in the south of France seemed so far away. It was as if it had all happened many years ago. But they are all settled now, she thought, settled and happy in their new lives.

Maria and Paul were married and already expecting their first baby. They had moved out of Dublin and were living in a lovely house in Kildare. Maria had left her job and was working from home as a freelance editor. She had just been on the phone and told Eva that the baby would be a little bit premature, but it was nothing to worry about. 'You don't mind becoming a grandmother?' Maria had asked. But Eva had reassured her that she would be delighted.

Louise had surprised them all. She had become a successful game-show hostess on television. 'I don't know how it happened,' she had said. 'I was dating this guy, and, before I knew it, he had offered me a job on TV.' She was born to be on television, Eva thought, she was so bubbly and cute. Louise didn't mind at all about Paul and Maria. 'I'm so glad you're staying in the family,' she had said to Paul, 'and I'm so happy I didn't have to marry you in order to achieve it.'

Dan had settled back to his office and his golf. At least, that's what Eva thought he was doing. God only knew what he was up to in the afternoons. But she didn't care if he was skydiving. He seemed happy and their relationship had fallen back into its old, comfortable rhythm. Except in the bedroom. There, it was as if they had just met, and Eva discovered a different Dan, younger, stronger and even more loving.

Things were running smoothly on the home front and the new Filipino was settling in very well. Fernando had gone back to the Philippines. Eva had driven him to the airport, where he was joined by his very pretty niece, who was going back home on the same flight. They were, to Eva's surprise, flying first class, because, as Fernando explained, he could afford it. All the extra catering he had done over the summer had proved very lucrative. 'Very good tipping,' he had said, beaming. 'My employers were so generous.' They must have been, Eva thought, as she watched his brand-new Louis Vuitton luggage disappear past her on the conveyor belt.

She looked down at her shoes. Yes. They were really lovely. A pair of Guido Fregene shoes was the latest must-have for the fashionable woman and she owned three pairs.

She turned back to her computer. She was preparing for the weekly meeting of the Commission. The door to her office opened and Hans Mueller came in.

'Everything under control?' he asked.

'Except for the agenda.'

'That's the job of the deputy,' Hans replied. 'And neither he nor the agenda is available as usual. I don't know why you keep that man, Eva. He is never around when you need him.'

'I know. But the French insisted. And we're stuck with him, I'm afraid.'

'He was supposed to be so brilliant. The only thing he's any good at is chasing women. I saw him having lunch with the Swedish Commissioner yesterday.'

'It was a working lunch.'

'They seemed a bit too cosy for work. I bet he continued examining her briefs at his flat.'

'I'm not interested in gossip, Hans. He does a good job most of the time. I'm sure he will be here soon. But I'll try him again.' Eva pressed the intercom. 'See if the deputy is in his office, Elsa.'

'He's here, Commissioner. In my office.'

'Tell him to come in.'

The door to the office opened. Eva looked up as her deputy entered. 'You're late, as usual,' she said.

'I'm sorry, Commissioner,' Yves replied.

Also available from
beeline

SUSANNE O'LEARY

Diplomatic Incidents

Anna O'Connor is a beautiful, if slightly overweight, ex-ballerina. As the wife of a successful Irish diplomat, she moves to Paris, city of her dreams. But the dream starts to turn into a bizarre nightmare when Mícheal, a drunken, womanising Irish journalist comes to stay.

Her unattractive house guest and workaholic husband are driving her to distraction when she meets Juan, a sexy, sophisticated and definitely attractive Spanish diplomat. More than a little smitten, she agrees to deliver a secret letter to a top Irish politician – an act that will cause a scandal, threatening her marriage and her husband's career.

'A flirty, witty, romantic tale . . . The behind-the-scenes scandal and the glamorous back corridors of diplomacy produce a riveting outcome.'

Irish Echo

'glamour, political intrigue and betrayal . . . compulsive reading'

Image Magazine

ISBN 0-85640-719-4
£5.99

Available now at all good bookshops

Also available from
beeline

ANNIE McCARTNEY
Desire Lines

London-based actress, Clare Murphy, has decided to
return home to Belfast to take stock of her life.
Unable to find any acting jobs, she agrees to help a
local drama group led by the rather gorgeous
Father Lorcan O'Carroll. The immediate attraction
she feels for the priest is not only strongly sexual,
but it appears, disturbingly mutual.

'a page-turner of a book ... an impressive debut'
Irish Independent

ISBN 0-85640-720-8
£5.99

Available now at all good bookshops